HOUSE OF IMPERIAL

SECRET KEEPERS SERIES #2

JAYMIN EVE

Jaymin Eve
House of Imperial: Secret Keepers Series #2

Eve, Jaymin
House of Imperial: Secret Keepers series #2

Editing: Lee from Oceans Edge Editing
Proofed: Jamie from HolmesEdits

ISBN-978-1-925876-04-8

STAY IN TOUCH

Stay in touch with Jaymin:
www.facebook.com/JayminEve.Author
Website & Mailing list: www.jaymineve.com

To Heather.
Thank you for being a wonderful friend. Your enthusiasm for my
books means everything to me.
I appreciate you so much.

p.s His death is still your fault.

NOTE FROM AUTHOR

I had to change some locations, schools, and landmarks of the town/s used in this book. To fit with my world building. I did thoroughly enjoy my research of New Orleans, though, and hope to visit one day. :)

1

———

The French Quarter was a place I wanted to tell my children about – not that kids or family were an actual possibility in my life – but this city ... it was a world worthy to be passed on, to be spoken about in stories and song. There was something special here. I had felt it the first moment we arrived.

As I strolled along the colorful street that led into Jackson Square, I wondered what my life would have been like if I'd been born here. I mean, not right here on this somewhat grimy pavement, but in New Orleans. Maybe I would be reading tarot cards like the woman on my right, set up at her small white table, long dark curls spilling out from under the jeweled headpiece adorning her forehead, purple nails flashing as she placed cards down for an eager tourist.

Or maybe I'd paint. That always looked like a fun way to tell a story. Street artists were everywhere, expressing their creativity in a way that I couldn't imagine doing. I'd never held a paintbrush, not even as a child. Circumstances from before my birth dictated that my life would never be my own.

Something I'd grown numb to over the years.

As if to prove me wrong, a haunting saxophone tune started up from a jazz musician leaning close to the wall of a café; the low reverberations hit me deep in my soul, in the place that had been cold and dormant for a long time. I basked in that feeling for a moment, closing my eyes and letting the music take me away.

I probably looked like a crazy person, standing in the middle of the Quarter, face lifted to the sky, shoulder-length ash-blond hair sticking out in a million directions. Okay, so it was NOLA, I no doubt fit in perfectly, but for someone who had always tried to blend, being in public like this was making me uneasy. It was just that for the first time in a long time I felt alive. I wasn't sure if letting myself feel things was a good idea, but I couldn't seem to stay away. I kept coming back here, to experience this world filled with life and vibrancy, watching the tourists as they took their spooky tours and filled their bags with fancy masks, religious trinkets, and hot sauce. I envied their laughter, and ability to afford copious amounts of beignets. Those puffy balls of magic were everything. I'd had one my first day and since then I must have thought about their deliciousness at least seven times a week. I was addicted ... and totally okay with it.

Mostly, I envied them their happy moments and families. That existence was not for me, but at least by being here I got to experience a small sliver of *that* life. Glancing at my watch, I stifled my groan: 3:50 P.M. I'd already been gone for two hours, wandering the streets.

It was Wednesday. I was supposed to be at the farmers market on Peters Street. My mom allowed me to make this once-a-week trip from our tiny condo in the Marginy to gather some groceries. I'd be punished for taking my time today. We had strict rules in my family – my mom and me – and one of the most important was that I never put us at risk of exposure. We were to always stick to the shadows and live like ghosts.

Most days I felt about as substantial as a ghost, so she had achieved one of her goals.

With reluctance, I turned away from the square and started my trek back toward the market area. It was only a few blocks, but in this million-percent humidity it would feel longer. Heat didn't usually bother me, but I hadn't quite understood the true scope of "sweating like a pig" until we moved here.

As I walked, I let my eyes roam across the streets, waiting for the next new and crazy sight. One literally never knew what was going to happen here. We'd only lived in New Orleans for a few months. To the locals I'd always be a tourist, but I was okay with that. I would take that title in exchange for getting to experience this world. I was fascinated with it all. This city was hard to truly describe, a place like no other, and considering I'd moved two to three times a year since I was born, that was really saying something. Its French influences, not only in architecture but food and culture ... I loved them all.

I'd started hoping each night, before I went to sleep, that nothing would spook my mom into running again. We should still have at least another two months here, if she kept to her normal timeline.

I was not giving up one second of NOLA – not without a fight.

Far too quickly I arrived at the market, hurrying about to finish my shopping before it closed. The walk back to our condo would take forty minutes, but I'd brought some bags with cold packs for anything that could spoil in this hot weather. As I left the market, a group of kids pushed past me. They'd probably just finished school for the day, coming straight here with their parents.

I'd been homeschooled. Sort of. I wasn't sure there was an actual name for what my mom did, which was teach me the basics, lecture me incessantly about the dangers in our lives, and fill my young mind with the sort of scary stories that not even adults should hear. I was probably one of the few kids who had wished to go to school, instead of being stuck inside a small house ninety percent of my life.

My mom literally never left our home; never worked. She told me that neither of us could leave a paper trail, which included social security numbers and tax declarations. We lived off a large settlement payout from my father's death. He was killed when my mom was pregnant with me. It had been a big deal, something to do with a workplace accident. Whatever the cause, I lost a parent, one who might have actually loved me, and in exchange, we got enough money to live like nomads.

The money was almost gone now. Eighteen years of being on the run was pretty expensive, even if we did live in rundown, no-names-asked rentals.

"Callie!"

The shout had me spinning on the spot, heavy bags swinging against my legs. There were only two people in this town who knew my name. One was my mom, the other was a pain in my butt.

Turning away again, I yelled over my shoulder. "Not in the mood, Michaels. I have to get home."

Jason Michaels was a persistent bastard, I'd give him that, but even after he'd challenged me and I'd kicked his ass in the gym, he still hadn't given up. What his endgame was, I had no idea. He never asked me out, or even implied that he wanted to go on a date. He just ... asked too many questions and was always around. If my mom got any hint of his consistent presence in my life, my one other piece of freedom would be yanked away from me.

Along with New Orleans.

I was not letting this tenacious bastard take this place from me.

"Are you training this afternoon?" he asked, falling into step beside me.

"No," I replied shortly.

He just laughed. "You always say no, and yet you're always there."

Spinning on my heels, I swung back in his direction, startling him enough that he blinked wide eyes at me. Michaels was a good-looking guy, tall, broad shouldered, bleach-blond tousled hair, the same as I'd seen from surfers when we lived in California – but in manners and speech, he was all Southern.

"What exactly do I need to do to make you go away?"

He just shrugged, flashing me that slow smile. "You like me, I know it." He turned to walk away, calling over his shoulder. "See you this afternoon, *cher*."

I glared at his retreating back, before shaking my head and hurrying along again. After powerwalking for a block, I turned back once to make sure Michaels wasn't following me. Leading him home would be the best way to kick Mom into flight mode. The street was empty of all tall blonds, so I felt safe in continuing – navigating the path to get me home quickest, while also being somewhat safe. We didn't live in the best neighborhood, but during daylight hours, I hadn't had too many issues. So far.

When I finally reached the stairs to the condo, I paused and took a deep breath. I had to prepare myself. My mom was about to lose her shit at me. Some days I was just tired of this life, of my existence.

You're eighteen now...

The stupid voice in my head had been reminding me of this for the last few months. My birthday had been in June, not that anyone remembered or mentioned it. But I knew, because it marked the moment I no longer had to follow my mom around. I could leave, get a job – paper trail be damned – rent my own shitty apartment and live an actual, normal life. But the same part of me that continued to hold people at a distance, the part that believed her stories, wouldn't let me make the final break.

With one more deep breath for courage, I started up the two flights, mentally bracing for the fight which was to come. As I put my key in the lock, the door pushed inwards, which didn't surprise me. Mom was no doubt waiting right on the other side for me. But as the empty living area and kitchenette came into view, I ground to a halt.

What in the...?

Stepping forward again, my senses were firing as I catalogued everything, searching for something out of place to explain what was going on. I left the bags of food near the front door, wanting both hands free. I wished my hair wasn't hanging loose; I didn't like to fight with it in my face. I had at least just cut it back to my shoulders, so it shouldn't be too much of a problem. As if to prove me wrong, strands of ashy blond fell in front of my face; a flick of my head put them back into place. The ceiling was low in here, and since I was five foot eleven, I ducked under the arched accents in the hallway. The last thing I needed was to smash my head and alert whomever was inside that I was here.

My Converse were quiet as I crossed the threadbare carpet heading toward the first small bedroom, just off the hall. The bedrooms were across from each other, the bathroom at the back. That was all there was to this place. Nowhere really to hide.

It was deathly quiet, a bad omen, because my mom played Mozart and Bach constantly. She said it helped ease the turmoil of worry that plagued her mind. I wasn't sure how I felt about classical music – I was starting to think I was a jazz girl at heart – but I sure as hell missed it now.

Because something was wrong.

Using my foot, I nudged my door open to reveal the twin bed, white dresser, open closet – or locker as they called it here – with my few clothes spilling out onto the floor, but nothing amiss. Ducking my head inside, I looked around to double-check, but as far as I could tell, the room was empty.

I sucked in some fortifying air and crossed the hall to my mom's room. In normal circumstances, I would never enter her domain. She was fiercely private, totally crazy, and prone to smacking me with wooden spoons. But this was no normal day. Her door was firmly shut. I twisted the handle, wincing at the telltale creak of the lever lifting. Stepping back, I swung the door wide open and waited a second for something to jump out at me. When nothing did, I peeked around the edge.

Her bed was twice the size of mine, neatly made with a faded green duvet. Her closet was closed, not a single item out of place, not even a shirt on the floor. I let my eyes run over everything, even dropping down to glance under the bed.

What was happening? Where was she?

Just as I was straightening, a creak from the living area sent a shot of adrenalin through me. I froze and unfroze almost in the same instant, crossing back to the door. I took two deep breaths, ducking my head out to look along the hall.

Holy fuck...

A man filled the doorway to the condo. I mean *filled* to the point where there was no space around him and he had to almost bend himself in half to fit inside. I was tall, but he had to be at least six inches taller than me. Our eyes locked across the room. Since my first step into the condo, everything had felt like it was going in fast forward. But right then, I couldn't move.

He stepped inside, untangling himself from the doorframe, only to find that the ceiling in the rest of the place wasn't much higher. With a scowl, his body hunched forward and he took another step toward me.

"You need to come with me. You're in danger."

His accented demand was low and husky. For an instant I craved to hear some sort of music or song from him, because he had a voice like an instrument, deep and rich, vibrating right through my body.

"Did you hear me?" The snap of his question knocked me out of my stupor and, managing this time to ignore the way his voice made me feel, I sent a scowl right back at him.

He took another step toward me and I straightened, shifting into a fighter stance. "Who the hell are you? Where is my mom?"

Those intense eyes remained on my face. I couldn't even tell what color they were; the lighting was shit in here, but they looked dark and ... somehow also light at the same time. I wasn't sure I'd ever seen a man like him before. He looked to be a few years older than me. A shaved head. A crap-ton of ink

– from what I could see. Very well-toned biceps and chest muscles. This dude was ripped, and yet, despite his bulk and height, he moved smoothly, which was the most worrying thing so far. Every now and then, there'd be a fighter like him in the gym. They were lethal: strong, athletic, able to kick ass without breaking a sweat.

I needed to get out of here.

We were only a few feet apart now and I remained outwardly calm, hoping to distract him enough that he would be unprepared for my sudden breakaway. "Where is my mom?" I repeated, mostly to keep him talking. I did not expect an honest answer. He clearly hadn't been in the apartment when I first entered – no way could I miss him – but he might have already taken my mom and was back now for me.

"I have no idea. I got here just after you did."

My stomach clenched at that voice again. On top of that he had the sort of raw masculine beauty that I generally thought existed only in Hollywood. Why was it always the physically-perfect men who were deranged psychopaths?

"You need to leave. Now!" I was slowly edging to the right, aiming for a clear path to the door. "Or I'm going to call the police."

I would never call them, of course. We didn't trust police. They were corrupt, blah, blah, blah. Even when my mom wasn't here, her voice was still in my head.

Tall, dark, and deadly paused, tilting his head to the side. "You're caught up in a world you have no idea of. The police can't help you, Human. I'm your only hope. Right now, I don't have time to enlighten you, so you're just going to have to trust me."

Panic like nothing I'd ever felt before hit me, so hard that my knees went weak and I almost dropped to the ground.

A world I have no idea about...

Oh, he was wrong. So very wrong. I reacted then without another thought.

Dive-rolling forward, I popped up right before him. As I rose, I slammed my fist into his groin and he let out an angry rumble. I continued rising, smashing my fist into his gut with a power hit, and then finally into the side of his head. I was fast; it was my greatest asset, and I knew exactly what angle to use and how hard to hit for maximum impact.

He let out a low groan, dropping to his knees, eyes wide as he cupped himself, blinking at me. The shock on his face was almost laughable; he had definitely not seen that coming.

Never underestimate a woman. You'll end up on your knees holding your balls.

His eyes, only inches from mine now, locked on to my face and it felt like I'd been the one punched. They were even more beautiful than he was, and that was saying something. The color was an unusual light brown, cinnamon dusted with gold. These gilded circles cut through the deep amber color. They were also framed by ridiculously dark and thick lashes.

Focus, Callie...

I called on my years of training – this was what Mom had been preparing me for. The only reason she allowed me to fight and train was because one day I would have to deal with this other world. One day the Daelighters would come for me.

Looked like today was that day.

And no stunning-eyed musical-voiced angel face was going to stop me from escaping.

I made it past him with ease, sprinting for the door he had left open. I had only the clothes on my back; my cash was still in the bottom of the grocery bags. I'd just have to figure it all out later. For now the immediate danger was far worse than having no money.

Rushing down the stairs, I jumped the final few, landing softly and taking off. I decided that heading back to Jackson Square was my best chance. There were always people there, crowds to lose him in. More than likely he wouldn't attack in public, which was a double advantage. These *Daelighters* liked to stay under the radar, or so my mom had told me. I was going to have to recall everything she'd ever said in her lectures. I wished I'd paid better attention. Most of the time I'd been internally rolling my eyes and counting dust bunnies. It all seemed so crazy and farfetched. Nothing had happened in the first eighteen years of my life.

But she had been telling me the truth. They really did exist.

My breathing grew harsh, and even though I was fit from all the Muay Thai cardio – I was trained in multiple martial arts disciplines – I was going to tire out quickly. Running in New Orleans' weather was not advisable, especially with the huge storm brewing on the horizon – those thick, dark clouds were definitely adding the right sort of ominous feel to my afternoon.

After a few minutes, I glanced back and there were no immediate signs of a scary, sex-on-legs guy behind me. Turning back, my breaths coming out in harsh puffs, I berated myself for not guessing immediately that he was one of these aliens. What human dude looked like that? My mom could have added dangerously attractive to her list of things to look out for. All she had told me was that they were taller than average, with a scary aura ... but she had missed so much else.

Mom...

What the hell happened to her? In most cities we had a

contingency plan. If one of us went missing or was hurt, we generally had a clear course of action to follow. But for some reason neither of us had worked out a strategy for New Orleans. We'd grown complacent. Stupid. So freaking stupid. I'd just have to lie low for a few days, then double back to the condo to see if she had returned. Or maybe left me a note. I hadn't had a chance to check for anything like that, mostly because I'd been looking for a rapist with a gun, not a note stuck to the fridge.

I almost sobbed as a large group of rowdy people came into sight dressed in full Halloween getup, even though it was still a week until the 31st of October. No doubt they were heading for a witchy tour, maybe toward Lafayette Cemetery. Wherever they were going, they looked excited as they loudly chatted.

"Saw a ghost in my hotel room. It was hovering in the corner..."

"Less than ten bucks to buy a voodoo doll – she swore it would work on my ex."

Their conversations went on and on, loud even when I was well past their group. The closer I got to Jackson Square, the more I was forced to slow down, weaving in and out of the people that filled the area. I remained on high alert, scanning the early evening crowd, and realized that while I was going to be able to hide in the throng filling the square, he would be hidden, too. I'd have to remain doubly alert.

Café Du Monde came into sight, famous for its chicory coffee – which I'd never tried – and beignets – which I'd had just that one time. It was always open, always full, and way too obvious a place for me to hide in. Not to mention, I didn't even have a dollar on me. My eyes fell to the line of homeless I could see just outside the square, like they'd been swept to the side in an attempt to keep them out of sight. Would I end up there with them? Right now my situation was looking pretty grim. All of my money and possessions were back at the condo.

Joining the homeless would be better than the alternative. I didn't fancy being an experiment or play-thing for some supernatural race of beings who secretly controlled Earth.

Damn that stupid Daelighter. What did he want with me? All I knew was that my dad was part of some special sector of humans who knew about these beings. He had made a deal with them long ago, before I was born, and it had affected us for the rest of our lives.

Moving cautiously, I let the street music calm me, still jazz, but unlike earlier today it was mostly upbeat numbers, more swing and less blues. A few couples nearby started to dance, and I edged in close to the crowd, watching them, hiding myself in the masses. The scary dude would be a foot taller than most of this crowd, which would help in spotting him. Since he'd also have a height advantage to spot me, I crouched down. Usually, I liked being tall; the extra reach was very useful with fighting. But right now I'd give anything to be five foot nothing.

Pushing my way forward, I decided to head toward St. Louis Cathedral, which was next to Jackson Square, facing the river. It would be closed at this time of night, but I felt like there were quite a few places for me to hide out in its grounds. I hated this feeling of being out in the open, like prey waiting for the eagle to dive from the sky and snatch me up.

Ducking my head even lower, I stepped away from the main group I'd been hiding in, but before I made it more than a few feet, someone grabbed my arm. The gasp slipped out first, then my instincts took over. I yanked myself free, almost overbalancing and smashing into a nearby light pole.

"Callie?"

The low voice shook me from my panic and I focused enough to see Jason standing before me for the second time that day. With him were four or five guys, all similar in build and clothing. They were clearly heading out for dinner or something like that, dressed nicely.

"Are you okay?" he asked, stepping closer, concern creasing his features. "You don't look so well."

I swallowed roughly, ragged breaths escaping my lips. *Pull it together*, I silently berated myself, because even though this was the first time in my life I'd had to face the truth of my mom's warnings, I should be handling it better than I was. Panic attacks and scattered focus was not going to get me out of this situation.

"Totally fine," I said as casually as I could manage. "Just got a little spooked. You know how it is, always someone in costume jumping out at you here."

He crossed his arms, staring me down. Maybe it was that my mom's suspicions had been confirmed, and I was now suspecting everyone, that I had to ask him: "Why am I always running into you, Michaels?"

Seriously, I ran into him multiple times a week, and considering I almost never left my house, it was ... odd. I hadn't stopped to think about it until now, but everything was different today. Today, I had all but confirmed the fact that supernatural beings existed side by side with me.

When he remained silent, I took a step back, letting my gaze run from his feet up to his surfer locks. "You're one of them, aren't you?" My whisper was tinged with anger and worry. It wasn't as immediately obvious as with the inked guy

– who was just so far beyond human – but the more I stared, the clearer it was to see the special touches that Michaels had.

His expression grew serious. He flicked a look toward his friends. Without a word, they started to close in on me, moving as a unit.

Shit. Dammit, I was in trouble. I knew his interest in me had been abnormal. From the moment he introduced himself a month ago I'd had a feeling about him. Not good or bad, more cautious. I should have paid better attention.

Backpedaling, I tried to keep all of them in sight. Which grew steadily harder as they fanned out to surround me. "You don't have to run, Callie," Michaels said. "I'm not going to hurt you. We're the good guys in this situation."

I snorted but didn't stop backing away. "I don't believe a single word which comes out of your lying mouth. You've been playing me this entire time. What the hell were you waiting for...?" I broke off before a hard laugh escaped. "Of course, you were waiting for the inked Adonis from my condo."

No one denied it and I congratulated myself on finally putting the pieces together. Five minutes too late, as always.

"We're here to keep you safe," Michaels tried again, but I was done listening.

Spinning on my heels, I took off zipping between stalls and groups of tourists, ducking in and out wherever I could. There wasn't much outside of white noise in my head, my body struggling to deal with the shock. I took a sharp right, but because I wasn't paying close enough attention, I missed the horse and cart turning at the same time. Pain shot through my face as I plowed headfirst into the side of the white carriage, bouncing back and landing on the street. Stars burst before my eyes as my head slammed onto the pavement; the world went dark around the edges as my mouth filled with the metallic taste of blood.

Everything after that was pretty blurry, the pain pounding incessantly in my head, random thoughts and voices confusing me over and over until I was finally released into blessed darkness.

2

Waking up to a pounding head was not something I was used to. I never drank or indulged in anything that would impair my senses; that was one of my mom's rules I absolutely agreed with. I liked to stay in control.

So why was I about to ... I rolled across the bed and dry heaved over the side, thankful there was nothing in my stomach to come out. The pain in my head became even worse as I gagged and spluttered, eventually just hanging half off the bed. I wiped my mouth, desperate for some water, but unable to pull myself up to crawl to our tiny bathroom.

Laying my head against the super soft throw, I tried to remember what had happened. The pounding didn't ease, but as my head started to clear, I realized that the light wasn't coming from the normal direction it did in my room. In fact ... nothing was as it should be, including the fact I was in a massive king-size bed.

I jerked myself upright, fighting the disorientation and

nausea. *Shit.* The last hours before I blacked out came back to me in jerky mental scenes.

Hot Daelighter … Michaels … on the run.

As I scanned the bedroom I was in, which was at least the size of my entire condo, I paused at a pair of long legs stretched out in front of a chair in the corner. The owner of those legs appeared to be asleep – judging by the soft snores – his face back in the shadows, making it difficult for me to see who it was.

I eased myself off the bed. I was still dressed in my clothes from earlier; only my shoes were missing. *Thank God.* Hopefully "human" wasn't the right type to get these aliens going – sexually that was. It would be nice not to have to fear rape at their hands.

As I took the first step toward the window, my feet sank into the carpet. It was soft and thick, cushioning my soles as I crept forward. Adrenalin pumped hard within me and I had to fight the urge to just flat-out sprint. I forced myself to take a moment to figure out my escape. The window was the older kind that had a latch which twisted to open it, and then the bottom half slid up. I would easily be able to fit out through the opening, and there looked to be a small landing on the other side, which was helpful, because I was on the second floor of wherever I was.

It was dark outside, but the well-lit street below was familiar, one of the rich areas in the French Quarter. I was pretty sure it was Esplanade Avenue. I recognized one or two landmarks from my first days exploring here.

The latch twisted without a sound and I moved the glass frame up slowly, letting in the billowing heat. I hadn't noticed until that hot blast hit me how pleasantly cool it was inside. The heat increased my headache, but I shoved the pain to the side. I'd deal with it later. I needed to hurry, before the humid air woke whomever owned the legs in the corner.

When the frame was eighty percent open, I swung my leg out, resting my weight on the ledge below. Just as I ducked my head and shifted to bring my other leg across, a voice from below had me freezing. Deep, accented, and sexy as hell, it was immediately recognizable as the tatted hot-alien.

I stopped breathing as I waited to see if I'd been sprung.

"We're currently at Jason's place near the Quarter." Pause. "Her mom was gone by the time I got there..." There was another pause before he continued. "I'd say that Laous has her. He's clearly going to try the same thing he did with Emma ... using this girl's family as a bargaining chip."

Air whooshed out of me when I realized he was on the phone, talking about my mom and this Laous asshole he thought had taken her. My heart was pounding rapidly, caught between fear and anger. I didn't always like my mom – most days I fantasized about running away and never dealing with her shit again – but part of me loved her. She was all I had.

I had to get her back. But how the hell was I going to do that on my own? As I sat there, one leg in and one out of the building, I realized that I needed to find out exactly what the deal was with these Daelighters who had kidnapped me. Michaels said he was protecting me, and I had to take into account the fact that he hadn't attacked me in all the weeks he'd been around.

Truth was, I needed more information. At the moment I only had half the story, and it wasn't adding up. Maybe it was worth sticking around a little longer, finding out exactly what they had to say. Besides, I couldn't exactly escape out this window with that guy below anyway.

I was just about to slide myself back inside when he said: "I don't know anything about her..." Pause. "No way. Fuck. She punched me in the dick. There's no way I'm hanging around any longer than I have to."

I grinned at that. He shouldn't have entered my place acting like a creepy shit. Creeps get punched in the dick.

"I'll tell her the deal, convince her to get her ass back to Astoria, and then we can go from there."

It sounded like he was about to hang up, but the person on the other end of the phone must have said something more, because the Daelighter was all of a sudden very serious.

"The council cannot expect me to hang around here waiting for Laous to reappear," he bit out the words. "I might not be ready to be overlo ... completely in charge right now, but I have to at least check in. I mean, how long do they think I can be away?" More pauses. "I'll let you know tomorrow."

I'd heard enough, so I eased myself back through the window into the bedroom. When I stood and turned, I sucked back a scream at the sight of cinnamon eyes ringed with golden circles staring down at me. Breathing rapidly, my eyes darted between the outside garden he'd just been standing in and the spot he now occupied. In the bedroom. Right by the window.

"You better get your skinny ass back in this room," he growled, clearly not a happy alien.

From this angle, I had a really good view of the dark maroon tattoos on the side of his head. They were symbols, swirling and arching in thick lines, slightly tribal in design, and I'd bet all the money I did not have right now that they were words.

He cleared his throat and my gaze returned to his eyes. Eyes which were so at odds with the rest of his bad boy look. I tried to ignore the sparks of intrigue that shot through me. I didn't care that those cinnamon irises were depthless, seeming to hold the weight of the world within them. And I definitely didn't care that he could actually be the most beautiful male that had ever walked this world.

Falling back on my false bravado, I drawled, "Clearly I was coming back inside, so let's save the macho display for another time. Okay? Okay..."

I crossed my arms, letting my attitude shine brightly from me. For most of my life I'd been referred to as "difficult" by my mom. She'd even tried to beat it out of me. But I'd never changed. This was who I was, and he would have to deal with it.

"Look ... Human..." He shook his head. "I'm not your enemy. I'm not here to fight with you."

"What do you actually want? And how did you get from that garden into the room so fast?"

His gaze slammed into mine and I choked on my next words. Not only could he move as fast as a superhero, he could also apparently hypnotize me with one look. And don't even get me started on that voice of his. It was a weapon.

I was seriously at a disadvantage.

Before I hyperventilated, he released me by turning toward the window, resting both hands against the frame as he stared out. His next words had less anger in them, that low drawl wrapping around me: "I'm here because my uncle is an evil bastard. He's searching for the location of an object here on Earth, and unfortunately, your family is one of the secret keepers who know the location."

"My mom," I gasped, my right hand clutching at my throat. "Is that why he took my mom?"

My thoughts were in turmoil, trying to reconcile everything I thought I knew with this new information coming to light. Was this about my father and his involvement in that group?

Footsteps distracted me as Michaels hurried over, his eyes drowsy, his hands shifting through his surfer locks. "Daniel ... sorry, man, I must have crashed."

He noticed me standing there then, his eyes flicking across to the open window.

"She almost escaped, didn't she?" he said drily.

I crossed my arms. "She's standing right here, Michaels."

I got a sheepish look in return. "I was up half the night making sure you didn't die from your concussion. Which you gave yourself because you never listen to me."

It was dark outside, but we must be near morning. Which meant I'd been unconscious for hours, damn them.

Dropping my arms, I took a step forward and Michaels had the intelligence to hold his hands up and take a step back. "Whoa, killer, I've been on the receiving end of your right hook before. No need for violence."

Shaking my head at the pure stupidity of this guy, I turned back to the scary one. Daniel, apparently.

"Why did Laous take my mom? What the hell is a secret keeper?"

Daniel wore a look which was part amused, part exasperated. "He took her *because* you're a secret keeper. Which, as the title suggests, is a person who keeps a secret."

I was going to punch him. Again.

"He needs you," Daniel continued before my plans of violence could go any further. "Your blood will lead him to the next secret keeper, who will lead him to the last, and then he will find this object he is searching for."

My head kind of felt like it was going to explode. The headache, on top of this information, was a little too much. "I don't understand," I finally admitted, not at all happy about my continued confusion.

"It's a long, complicated story." His voice was softer now, and so soothing I almost closed my eyes. "All you need to know now is that Laous wants you, he has taken your mom as a way to force your compliance, and he is going to try and lure you out again."

"Why didn't he just wait at the condo for me? He must have known I'd be back soon."

Daniel and Michaels exchanged a look. "He probably sensed Daniel in the area," Michaels finally said. "I couldn't believe it when Dan showed up telling me about a secret keeper down here in New Orleans that he needed to find. Who would have thought it'd be the same chick I like to rile up at the gym?"

I was surprised to hear that he hadn't been watching me the entire time for the Daelighters, that his interest might have actually been genuine. Not that I cared. Michaels was not my type. Even if he hadn't been an alien.

"You've been looking for me?" I asked Daniel, and he nodded.

"As soon as we got a hit on the location of the next secret keeper, we set out to get to them before Laous."

They'd almost done that too. Just missed saving my mom by hours.

"If you promise not to try and escape again," Daniel said, "I will answer all of your questions. It appears I'm staying in New Orleans for longer than planned, and you need to realize we're working toward the same goal here. I don't want to have to keep an eye on you at all times of the day and night."

Uh, yeah, I was totally not promising anything. If I felt at any point like my life was in danger being here, I would be gone so fast their supernatural heads would spin. So far I hadn't been hurt – by anyone other than myself – or raped or threatened. I felt somewhat comfortable being in their presence. But I would never trust them.

They weren't human. One of their kind kidnapped my mom. I needed to remain on guard.

At my silence, his grin extended a little further. "Close enough," he finally said, flashing me a full smile, all of those perfect teeth blinding me. And he had a damn dimple. Like he needed one more weapon to use against us. Despite my disgust toward him and his people in general, there was a moment where I had the clichéd butterflies-in-my-tummy thing going on.

Michaels took a seat on the edge of the bed, while Daniel and I remained standing. I continued to maintain at least a six-foot distance from them both. If I needed to fight or run, the space was important. At least the pounding in my head had finally eased a touch.

Daniel crossed his arms, which only emphasized the mammoth size of him. No doubt an intimidation tactic. "What exactly do you know about us? I don't want to waste my time repeating information you already possess."

Mimicking him, I crossed my arms, tilting my head to the side in a sardonic glare. "Would hate to waste your time, your royal highness, it's been a real worry of mine since we met." I continued on in the same drawling tone: "Let's see, what do I know. Number one: you're arrogant bastards who think humans are scum under your shoes." No reaction. No denial. "Number two, you're called Daelighters, you're not from Earth, but you somehow managed to infiltrate our world and control most aspects of it anyway." I was digging deep, going back to my mother's lectures. "You're from an alternate universe ... and your planet is called Overworld. There's been some sort of treaty with Earth since the late 1800s. Something keeping both planets alive? But in the end you'll probably take over Earth completely and kill us all."

Daniel nodded. "Except for the last part, you're on track. What else do you know about the treaty?"

Good to know they had no immediate plans for the annihilation of the human race. Maybe that was just one of Mom's crazy rants.

I shrugged, shaking my head. "Nothing else about the details of the treaty. My mom has spent my entire life warning me to go nowhere near your kind. All I know is that if you get your hands on me, very bad things will happen. She didn't spend much time telling me anything else."

His eyes darkened and deepened until they were reflective pools of emotion. Heavy emotions if I was judging correctly – anger, distaste, passion, fire. I tore my gaze away before it got too hard to handle. His eyes and voice did that same thing to my insides as jazz music and Jackson Square. Made me feel too much. And I needed the numbness right now.

Michaels sprawled out further across the bed, drawing my attention. "Your mother is greatly misinformed," he told me in his drawling accent. "The treaty was put in place as a mutual advantage to both worlds. Energy from Earth powers our network and keeps the four races of Daelighters from falling into war again, because now we all have enough power to be sustained. In return, Earth received a very special stone, one which stopped the weather phenomena of your world from ripping it to pieces. A starslight stone."

His voice dropped low, filled with reverence as he mentioned the stone.

Daniel added: "This stone is extremely powerful and

important to our people. It's the basis for holding the treaty together. When the overlords and the leaders of your free world first signed the treaty, it was agreed that humans and Daelighters would integrate. A hundred humans were brought in on the secret. Their offspring went on to be secret keepers for the starslight stone. There are always four, one for each house. Born in the same year."

"What's a house?" I interrupted.

Daniel didn't skip a beat. "In my ... part of Overworld, there are four sectors. House of Imperial is mine, then there is House of Darken, House of Leights, and House of Royale. We are all ruled separately by overlords – like a king and queen – and have unique abilities and traditions. You are the secret keeper born in House of Imperial."

I held a hand up, my mouth no doubt a wide O as I stared at him. "I ... I was born in Overworld?"

There was no way. Seriously. That would mean my mom went there, gave birth to me, and then came home only to poison me against these Daelighters for my entire life.

Michaels nodded, his expression somewhat serious. "Yes, you had to be born there to be a secret keeper. That's how your blood can lead to the next keeper. You have energy from House of Imperial inside of you."

My breathing was doing something weird, harshly drawing in and out, but my lungs were still starving for air. The men across from me let me have this moment to break down, and eventually the rest of the questions overwhelmed me, and I had to ask.

"So, there are four secret keepers ... I'm number two ... what happened to the first one?"

Daniel's expression softened, and for a moment I felt a stab of jealousy. Because it was clear he knew and cared about this number one.

"Emma," he said. "She was born in House of Darken, and she's my best friend's world."

Well, at least she wasn't dead. That had to be a good sign.

"Why did Daelighters trust humans with this secret?" I had to ask. "Wouldn't it be easier and simpler just to use your people?"

Daniel nodded. "Much easier, but humans felt they were at a disadvantage in regard to the treaty, because we have power and skills they do not. They insisted that while a Daelighter hid the stone, humans would be the ones to always know its whereabouts. The fourth secret keeper has a map on their body, which will change if the stone's location ever changes."

I got humans wanting that advantage. I could already tell that the Daelighters were way out of my league when it came to ... pretty much everything.

I sank against the side of the bed, trying my best to process it all. This new information ... it was a struggle to truly believe what they were saying. This had to be the "family business" my father had been part of. No wonder my mom was so angry. She no doubt got dragged into it.

"How exactly does this Laous fit into it all?" I asked, my voice raspier than usual.

Daniel's face went scary again. "Laous was the overlord of House of Imperial. He killed my father and somehow took the power which should have gone to me as the next overlord."

Michaels cut in: "He apparently did that to make sure he would have the power to find the first secret keeper. He's no longer overlord now. Got the boot when he killed the parents of the first secret keeper and then almost killed her as well.

Daniel is set to take over the role – which should have always been his."

I looked between both of them, blinking a stupid amount of times. It seemed to be helping me process. Or I had suddenly developed some sort of eye disorder. "Laous used Emma's blood to find me?"

They both nodded. "Emma's family was killed," Daniel told me, "and she was manipulated into coming to Daelighter territory by Laous. He managed to kidnap her..."

The sound of my harshly indrawn breath filled the room. Killed. Kidnapped. What the freaking freak was going on here? Maybe my mom hadn't been completely wrong about the danger in associating with this world. I just wished she'd given me more accurate information. Prepared me better.

"You're the second, and as I said, you were born in House of Imperial," Daniel continued, ignoring my obvious shock. "Your blood will lead him to the third, and we need to make sure that doesn't happen. If Laous finds the starslight stone, he will break the treaty. Both worlds could be destroyed."

I held two hands up, palms facing him. "Just ... hold up. I need a second to understand what you're saying."

A second ... who was I kidding? I wouldn't process this in a year. Everything he was telling me was important and scary and insane. But the bottom line was really about my mom. We had to save her, then I could deal with the rest.

"Okay, so my mom..." I said, trying to keep my voice and breathing even. "How are we getting her back? What is the plan?"

Daniel's head jerked up slightly, like he was surprised I wasn't asking more questions about Overworld and Daelighters and me being a secret keeper. But I just couldn't. *Not born on Earth.* Those words ran through my head over and over. It was too much. So I'd just deal with what my poor little brain could manage.

"We have a council in Overworld," he said. "They are made up from members of the four houses. They've ordered me to stay in New Orleans for another day or so, until we can determine if Laous is here or has fled. They want you to head to Astoria. They can protect you there."

I shook my head hard. "Not happening. I'm going to help you find my mom and kick Laous' ass. Will I be staying here in this house?" I didn't even give him a second to argue. "I don't have clothes or anything. Is it safe to go back to my condo? Should we be checking it out for clues?"

Daniel tilted his head to the side, eyes slightly narrowed. "I couldn't find out much on you or your family, but the little I did suggested you would be difficult and distrusting. Looks like my intel was somewhat accurate."

Research? If that didn't make a girl feel special. "Okay, stalker, did your research tell you that my mom is the only person I have in this world? It's my duty to get her back, and I will do whatever it takes, including but not limited to, trusting a few alien douchebags and putting myself in danger."

Logic told me it was going to be quicker for me to achieve my goals if I stayed close to the beings who understood what was going on here.

Michaels let out a yawn then, disrupting our stare-off. "I'm going to grab an hour of sleep before we have to head out. Can you wake this alien douchebag when it's time to go?"

I blinked at him as he wandered off. He was literally the most random dude ever, even when fighting. Which also made him hard to best. At the time I'd been so proud of my skills, drawing on multiple disciplines to confuse and beat him. It hadn't been easy, but I'd taken him down. Now I knew he had let me win, because these Daelighters were far stronger and faster than I could ever hope to be. *Bastard.* He'd thrown the fight. Throwing a fight was unforgiveable.

After Michaels left, Daniel continued to explain a few things to me. Mostly rules about what would happen if I stuck around with him. I was surprised that he hadn't fought me about staying; seemed he didn't care that much for the rule of his council.

I remained calm for all the new information, my brain processing as quickly as it could. It was kind of odd that I wasn't freaking out more, but my gut was telling me these particular Daelighters didn't mean me any harm. And I needed them. Keep your friends close and your enemies closer was really hitting home to me here. I'd never had friends, but enemies I was used to. I'd keep them as close as possible until I got all the answers I needed. I'd find my mom, then I'd figure out a way to ensure I never had to run from any of them again.

Even if it meant exposing them to the world. Or killing them all. Because I might be a secret keeper, but I never signed up for the job. They should have been more careful about who they entrusted to keep the worlds safe.

3

───────

he sun was just starting to peek over the horizon by the time we were done with "tell Callie about all the freakiness in the world." Daniel left me in my room while he went to deal with some Imperial business. He'd told me I could explore this house, but if I left, there would be a very good chance Laous would find me and kill me and my mom. With that sort of motivation, I decided not to act like I was too stupid to live and would remain inside. He'd said that he would do some recon later, and if I stayed by his side the entire time, I could go as well. I liked that we had a plan. It made me feel much more in control.

I could be patient until then.

Taking him up on the suggestion of checking out the mansion, I started with the room I'd found myself a temporary guest of. The house was by far the nicest place I'd ever seen in my life, with the feel of a building hundreds of years old, but which had been modernized throughout. The bedroom had high ceilings and rich burgundy walls, which stood out against the white crown molding. A white doorway led to a spectacular bathroom. It was tiled with slate and stone from floor to ceiling. The splashes of blue and gray went perfectly with the fluffy navy mat in the center, thick white towels in a small cupboard, and the large array of greenery in pots. Warm and inviting.

My eyes locked on the free-standing tub right by the window overlooking a garden, which I could just make out in the early morning light. The street was just beyond, and people were everywhere, heading home from the square. Despite the lack of privacy – because who would draw curtains on a view like that – I could easily imagine stretching out, reading a book, occasionally glancing out to the world beyond. It took a lot of control not to run a bath, but getting naked in a house of alien dudes didn't seem like the smartest move. I'd wait and see if any of them attacked over the next few hours before I flashed my goods.

Reluctantly leaving the bathroom I continued out of the bedroom, finding myself in a long hall. All of the open doorways I passed were bedrooms, painted rich, bright colors, with wood and antique furniture. I liked that they'd kept a few original touches of character. Near the end was a small library with thick beams across the ceiling. I lingered in the doorway, which was strange because I wasn't a huge reader. I preferred movies and television. Reading was actually something I struggled immensely with; words never quite did what they were supposed to. Letters didn't stay in the order they should, so reading was ... hard.

I'd mentioned the problem a few times to my mom, but she just told me I was lazy, and that if I wanted to get better at something I needed to practice it. After months of headaches and tears, I gave up on the entire endeavor. The world of books was not for me, even though I craved to know what was between each of the pages. Movies might be just the tip of the iceberg, but I had long ago accepted that I would never know the world below.

Tearing myself from the doorway, I tucked my dreams back inside. Nothing good came from wanting what you couldn't have. I'd been disappointed too much already. It was time for me to live in the reality of my world.

I traipsed down the stairs at the end of the hall, admiring the highly polished sheen of the wood handrail. Everything here screamed money. Lots of money. The upkeep on a place like this would be ridiculous. Michaels didn't strike me as the sort of guy who worked hard. His surfer bum vibe was from more than just his hair. Were all of these Daelighters rich? Or was Michaels just one of the lucky ones?

The ground floor was even more spectacular than the level above. It wasn't as open-plan as was favored in more modern houses – houses I'd only ever seen in magazines of course. This design had large distinct rooms, separated by archways and alcoves, with deep, bold colors, more burgundies, ochers, and even a teal dining space. The furniture was heavy and antique, like in the bedrooms, fitting perfectly to the era of this home.

It was really nice. Damn Michaels and his good taste in real estate.

After I'd explored, I ended up in the kitchen with its enormous rectangle island bench and an actual fireplace in the room. The fridge was modern, stainless steel, a three-door monster. Did these Daelighters eat normal food?

One way to find out.

Opening the door, I had to laugh. Inside was full alright, with a selection of beer and wine that would make a nightclub jealous. It was very clear why Michaels lived on the edge of the

Quarter, an area usually reserved for tourists and those who liked to make their money from tourists. Locals hardly ever went there, from what I'd learned, but clearly these Daelighters enjoyed the party life.

"Hungry?"

I jumped back from the fridge, swinging around to find Michaels leaning against the kitchen bench. He hadn't slept long, but definitely looked much more refreshed.

"I'm always hungry, but doesn't look like you have anything here that is actual food."

Michaels chuckled, moving around the other side of the bench to open the drawer. He pulled out a bunch of pamphlets, sliding them across to me. Walking over, I picked them up, finding that they were all delivery places.

"Order whatever you want. I have accounts with every single one of them."

I took my time flicking through them before finally meeting his eyes. "I thought you were sleeping?"

He shrugged. "Like I said, I only need an hour. I'll nap again later."

No doubt he was an expert napper.

Before I could say anything more, Daniel entered the room. I zeroed straight in on him, menus forgotten. "When will we be heading to Jackson Square?" I asked, not wasting time on pleasantries.

Daniel's heavy stare shifted between Michaels and me. Finally, he said, "We can go now, if you'd like. An early scouting trip. If Laous is still in the area, he'll make contact. He's no match for me, not now he's lost the overlord power, so he'll no doubt just deliver a message." He focused on Jason then. "Get your people ready, though. Later today we'll be the ones hunting."

The daelighter nodded, not at all annoyed by the order. "On it, boss. We'll be ready and waiting." Then with a wink in my direction, he left the room.

Daniel turned to me. "I need to grab a few weapons. Wait right here."

Like there was anywhere else for me to go.

He disappeared up the stairs, only to reappear a few minutes later dressed in similar clothes to before. He had changed his shirt for a long-sleeved black Henley that hugged his body and worked with the dark jeans, heavy black boots, and air of barely contained lethal power.

I wished I knew more about Daelighters and their abilities. Like the super speed thing. Could they all do that? What else could they do? Would any of my training actually come in handy against someone like Laous? There was nothing more annoying than stepping into the role of victim, being the one who had to be protected. I'd worked really hard to never be weak, but something told me I was going to be very outmatched by this alien species.

I needed more information. Knowledge was power. I was slowly coming to terms with everything I'd learned so far – the need to scream and freak out was fading – so maybe I'd ask Daniel some more questions when we were out.

As more of my fear faded, though, anger took over. This trickling urge to lose my shit was starting to churn inside of me. Fury was bubbling uncontrollably under my skin. I finally had somewhere to lay the blame for my years of shitty life – with these alien bastards. It was making me rage in ways I didn't know my numb, dead-inside body was capable of.

"Are you ready to go?" Daniel asked, interrupting my mental planning of how to take down an entire planet.

"Yes," I snapped back, pushing past him.

When he caught up to me at the door, he wore a half-smile, which only annoyed me more. Once he unlocked the door, he pushed it wide open and stepped back to allow me to exit first.

Just as I walked out, his hand wrapped around my arm. I tried not to react, but the heat from his palm branded me, along with the buzz of energy he sent into my blood. *Non-human bastard.*

"Don't run," he said slowly. "It's going to annoy me if I have to chase you."

I shrugged his hand off. "I want to find my mom. You're my best chance of that. I will stick around until that part of my life is resolved."

Keeping my word was important to me. I had so few things in my life that I could control; my moral high ground was one of them. Even these Daelighters would receive the same treatment. As we started along the street, I saw a sign. I'd been right before, Michaels lived on Esplanade Avenue, the street that bordered the Quarter and the Marginy. I had walked past it multiple times over my months here. No wonder I kept running into him.

Daniel was silent and predatory as we walked along. He constantly checked out the scene, keeping track of everyone and everything that moved around us. He scared me in ways – which I would never admit to out loud – I could not explain. There was just something so *other* about him, and yet at the same time, he looked human. Ish.

"How long have you been in New Orleans?"

His question took me by surprise, but it was an easy one to answer. "About two months. The longest I've ever stayed in one place was four months; Laous was lucky to catch us when he did."

We pushed through a large group of people stumbling home from a bachelorette party. They were very intoxicated, singing, dancing, falling down. It had been the usual *huge* night in the Quarter. The streets were filled with empty cups and trash, which we kicked out of the way as we walked.

"I know you hate my kind," he said, taking me by surprise again. "And I don't blame you for that. Sometimes life just deals us a shit hand. Trust me, I understand."

Something told me that he did. I'd known it from the first moment I stared into his eyes. Not to mention the wariness he wore like a cloak. It didn't matter how highly-trained a person was, they didn't act like they were in a warzone unless they had been in a warzone before. I didn't know what sort of battle it was, but Daniel had definitely been fighting for his life at one point or another.

Sympathy bloomed within me and I hated the connection that was there between us. I wasn't naïve enough not to recognize it. Whether it was that I was born in House of Imperial ... or something else ... there was no denying it any longer. Daniel stirred emotions inside of me and it was confusing as hell.

As soon as we stepped into Jackson Square, he closed the distance between us.

"Don't wander off," he told me.

Pressing closer to his back, I fought the urge to reach out and grab his shirt. I accepted I was human, vulnerable, especially compared to these creatures, but I was not weak. I would not rely on Daniel, but I could be cautious.

"Café Du Monde works for our cover," he decided. "Maybe we can drag Laous out from whatever shadows he's hiding in."

From my observations, it wasn't always that easy to get a table there, especially during one of the busy times. Right now, it would be filled with people looking for some early morning pick-me-ups after a big night. Somehow, though, the universe loved Daniel, because we walked straight into an empty double-seater.

"Sit," he told me.

I crossed my arms over my chest and tilted my head to the side as I waited for him to realize that I was not a pet for him to order around.

He let out a grumbling sound. "Could you please sit down, because if the server passes us by, we won't see them for another hour."

He'd said please ... good enough. Pulling out my chair, I dropped into it. Daniel took the other chair, sliding his massive frame in gracefully. I spent the next few minutes observing my surroundings, cataloguing exits, watching the people who sat around us.

My eyes ran over each and every individual, because even though I had no idea what Laous looked like, I felt like I would know him when I saw him. In my head, he was an evil, ugly asshole, and I should recognize that without any trouble.

A waitress skidded to a stop beside our table. "Ready to order?" she said.

I swung around to face her. She was tiny, her wild dark curls springing up on her head. She was lithe, built like a dancer, with huge blue eyes. There was no immediate accent – she didn't sound like a local, but clearly already had the swing of this busy job.

"We'll have a dozen beignets," Daniel said without preamble. "And I'll have a café au lait." He paused and turned toward me. "Do you drink coffee? Would you like something else ... tea ... or maybe hot chocolate?"

I snorted, managing to keep it low and under my breath.

But if the arch of his eyebrow was any indication, he still heard me. "If I don't have coffee I'm inclined to turn into a raging psychopath. Literally." Especially after being knocked out and waking with the headache of all headaches.

"That explains a lot," Daniel said with a half-smile.

Ignoring him, because it did actually explain a lot, I returned my gaze to the pretty waitress. "I'll have the same as ... him. Make it large." I jerked my hand in Daniel's direction.

"No problem," she said in a harried way. "Be right back with your order."

She was gone as quickly as she appeared, disappearing into the crowd. Off to the side, I could see a line was starting to form as people waited for tables. Actually, that line had probably already been there. Daniel had ignored it just like the locals usually did. Tourists were the ones who waited in line.

I tried really hard not to bounce in my seat, but I'd had no coffee or food for hours. And it was beignets and liquid-life – aka coffee – from Café Du Monde, a running fantasy of mine for the past eight weeks straight. My excitement could barely be contained.

"You're not as worried about your mom as I would've expected."

A flash of anger cut through me, wiping away those tendrils of excitement I'd stupidly allowed to build. I leaned forward on the table, my eyes no doubt flashing my fury at Daniel.

"You know nothing about my feelings." My rebuke was low and forceful as I emphasized each and every word. "My relationship with my mother is complicated. I don't want to see any harm come to her, especially not at the hands of a Daelighter. But just because she's my mom by blood, doesn't mean she's ever acted like a true mother."

Because we were so close, our faces only inches apart, I saw every emotion that crossed Daniel's face. His eyes blazed with gold, and judging by the angle of his jaw, he was clenching his teeth. There was a darkness in his gaze, and just like I'd known he'd been to war, in some way I also knew he understood what I was saying about family. On a personal level.

"Who in your family?" I asked, most of my anger gone now.

There was a long pause; I didn't think he was going to answer. Then, as the waitress reappeared with our order, he said, "The ones who cared are long gone. The rest are blood only. Not family."

That made sense considering he was related to a psycho like Laous. Another chink loosened in my cold, dead chest – my heart actually hurt for him. His confession had been matter of fact, like it didn't affect him, but I saw deeper. The wounds were still raw.

We were quite the pair.

Still, there was no way to be truly sad when I had coffee and beignets sitting in front of me. So why couldn't I take my eyes off Daniel? It was like for the first time in my life I felt camaraderie with someone. *Damn him!* Why did that someone have to be from an alien species that had been hunting me my entire life?

"I'm going to need you to tell me more about this world that I've been dragged into."

He nodded. "I will tell you everything you need to know, but not here."

I accepted that and was finally able to turn my attention to the food before me; the scent of coffee could no longer be ignored. Leaning forward, I closed my eyes and slowly inhaled the rich, dark aroma. When I picked up my cup and took the first sip, a low moan actually escaped from my mouth. I was no longer in control; my senses were firing, and this was probably the best coffee I'd ever had.

The plate of beignets, topped with their white powder, was my next focus. Reaching forward I lifted one, careful not to disturb the sugar. I really wanted to inhale as well, taking in their unique scent, but a nose full of powder was not my idea of a good time.

As I took my first bite, my next moan was much louder. Movement from across the table drew my attention, and I was surprised to find Daniel just staring at me. His coffee remained untouched in front of him, and he had not started on a beignet.

That was worrying – no one ignored these fluffy clouds of delicious. Had he seen something that I missed? Was Laous here somewhere?

"Everything okay?" I asked as I swallowed the last of the ball of magic.

He leaned back in his chair, crossing his arms. "I've just never seen someone quite so passionate about food before."

For a brief moment, I contemplated letting the embarrassment that was trying to well up take over. I didn't though, mostly because I sensed Daniel wasn't insulting me. There was ... interest in his gaze. I'd surprised him.

"Does your kind eat food?"

Since I was struggling not to shove the entire plate of beignets in my mouth, the only explanation for his reticence was that they didn't eat. Maybe Michaels' menus had just been for show. Or for the human girls they brought back from the Quarter.

Daniel answered by reaching forward and snatching up a

beignet and popping it into his mouth without spilling a drop of the white sugar.

Well, okay then.

A waiter passed by our table, his hand snaking out to grab my almost empty coffee cup. Quick as a flash, I latched onto his forearm. Narrowing my eyes on him, I said, "The only reason you should be touching my cup is if you plan on refilling it."

His mouth dropped open as he looked between me and my mug. "So ... so sorry," he stuttered, before quickly releasing the handle and hurrying away.

Shaking my head, I was reaching for my coffee – before another overeager staff member tried to remove it – when Daniel let out a low rumble across from me. The sound drew my attention, and as he tensed, so did I.

"He's here, isn't he?" I asked, no louder than a whisper.

Daniel inclined his head ever so slightly, and without another word, I quickly ate another beignet, because I knew this was going to be my last chance. Laous was here.

It was time to get my mom back.

4
___

It might have been my imagination, but it seemed the café got really quiet then – a lull, like it was holding its breath, waiting for a storm to hit. I couldn't see anything out of place, so Laous had to be behind me. I didn't want to turn my head and alert this asshole to our presence. Not until I knew the plan.

"Okay, so he's here. Has he spotted you?" I murmured, pretending to take a sip of coffee.

Daniel lowered his head, which in no way did anything to hide him. He was humongous, like the worst person ever to try to play hide and seek. "He's busy right now trying to set fire to the building."

"What?"

I couldn't stop from spinning now, scanning across the crowd. It took me about five seconds to spot him. He was standing in the main entrance, looking pretty unimpressive. Besides the fact that he had a shaved head with the dark red symbols tattooed on the right side like Daniel, I would never have thought that he was a Daelighter.

He was so ... ordinary. Squinty eyes. Weedy arms and legs. Roundish body. Like a bunch of body parts had been put together, but nothing actually went with the other. He took a step forward, lifting both of his hands on either side of him. When they were around shoulder height, I felt the first flickers of heat.

Daniel's chair crashed as he shot to his feet, his hands also filled with fire. I added that to my mental list of Daelighter abilities and moved myself even further down the evolutionary ladder. Some of the other diners started to react, but since a lot of them seemed to be drunk, they weren't panicking as fast as they should have been. Most of them probably thought this was some sort of NOLA show, but they'd change their tune once they felt the very real heat from the flames.

Laous shot out balls of fire, catching the nearby awning, which was almost immediately alight. It was then the patrons started screaming and rushing from the café.

"Guess he's not afraid of you," I quipped to stem my nerves. Part of me was thinking I should have taken the council up on that offer to go straight to safety.

"Just stay close to me," Daniel warned, positioning himself protectively before me, "until I figure out what he's up to. No Daelighter would make a scene like this in public, but Laous clearly does not care about any repercussions of his actions now."

Great, he was a complete madman and he had my mom.

"Remember," Daniel said, "Laous wants you. He needs your blood and will stop at nothing to get it. Protecting you is my first and only priority."

I could tell that Daniel was majorly regretting allowing me to stick with him, but it was too late to do anything but try to get out of this alive.

The café had emptied, flames roaring across the front of it, and ... Laous seemed a little scarier as he strolled toward us. Especially since there was nothing I could do against magic fire.

"I'd suggest leaving now," Daniel warned Laous. "Return Callie's mother to her home and get out of New Orleans." He sounded so casual. "You're no longer overlord. The power of our house is mine to command."

Laous paused, a disturbing sort of smile tilting up his thin lips. "I don't need the power from Imperial any longer. Did you know that the stone I procured from the first girl does a lot more than just lead me to the next secret keeper?" Before Daniel could answer, he continued on: "I'm going to find the original starlight stone, and there's nothing you can do to stop me. Soon, Daelighters will realize how stupid we were to place true power in the hands of these grubbers."

"Grubbers...?" I murmured.

"Ignore him," Daniel bit out. "It's ... a term that *some* Daelighters use for humans."

Should have guessed it was a derogatory name. Sounded like they thought we lived in the dirt and bathed in mud. It didn't bother me, though. The opinion of *Laous* was not going to keep me awake at night. What he did with my mother, on the other hand, was a different story.

"Where is my mom?" I asked, proud of how well I kept my cool. In my head I had already punched him in the throat six times. Twice in the balls.

He chuckled. The piece of shit actually laughed. "She's really enjoying her time with us, you know. I didn't expect her to be so..." He tilted his head to the side like he was trying to find the right word. "Spirited. She's quite spirited."

Rage filled me, but before I could reply, sirens filled the air, responding to the fire that was halfway to destroying one of the Quarter's most famous landmarks. The smoke was thick and black, and I was just worrying about being trapped in here, when Daniel took off. I finally got to see his speed in action. *Whoa.* It was almost like he disappeared and reappeared in another spot. In the same instant. *Superfast.* I added that to the list.

I watched, mouth hanging open as Daniel waved one hand across the six-foot flames and they instantly died off. He was back at my side in another moment, and the shock and awe on my face must have caught his attention. "House of Imperial specializes in fire. I can counter anything he throws at us."

The creep in question crossed his arms over his round chest. "That might be true, but don't forget, you've been overlord for days, I was the ruler for a lot longer than that. I know the power better than you."

He strolled closer to me and I braced for a fight, dropping lower into a stance more suitable to strike and defend myself. Daniel repositioned himself, standing between me and the crazy pyro.

They faced off at each other, Daniel definitely the more intimidating of the two. I liked his calmness the most; it gave me some confidence. Laous flicked his hand and an object flung free from the cuff of his jacket. A small stone, with a chain attached to one end. Like ... a necklace.

Laous whipped it out, keeping hold of the chain, while the stone slammed into Daniel's shoulder, cutting through the shirt and embedding deep. Ignoring this, Daniel took a step closer to Laous, wearing a look of complete loathing. Flames spread up over Daniel's arms, moving in increments across his body.

"I have the power of the justices now," he growled. "I will use them to end you. To end this before a war breaks out."

Laous shook his head. "You're missing the bigger picture, Daniel. You always did. Just like your father."

The flames were almost to his chest now. He was literally turning into a human fireball. On the edge of the café, suited-up firefighters spread out in all directions, and I was just about to mention something when Laous moved. He slammed a hand into the stone, pushing it all the way into Daniel's shoulder.

With a roar, the taller Daelighter dropped, his body shuddering like he was being struck by lightning, over and over. I just stared dumbfounded at Daniel, on his knees, with sparks of energy racing across his body. It even flickered through his eyes.

"Run, Callie," he grit out, trying to get to his feet, only to have the lightning power slam him down again.

Before I could scream, or react, or run – because that sounded like a great idea – a fist slammed into the side of my head. I dropped to my knees, ears and head ringing, blood filling my mouth, while stars filled my eyes. This wasn't the first punch I had copped, but considering I was still suffering from being knocked out earlier, I couldn't handle another. Rolling to the side, I got out of strike range of his feet, using a nearby chair to pull myself up.

Daniel was swearing and growling, and as I turned in his direction, I was astonished that he was up on one leg now, fighting whatever was holding him.

"Miss, are you okay?" A fully suited-up fireman stepped into the building for the first time. Through his mask, I could see concern creasing his face, and as he glared at Laous, I guessed he'd seen the punch.

I opened my mouth to warn him of the danger he didn't realize he was in. I'm sure he thought he could take Laous on, and in any normal *human* circumstances he would have. But these weren't normal circumstances.

Before I got the words out, Laous launched an arc of fire our way, completely engulfing the firefighter. It took me a minute to realize I was screaming, and I wasn't the only one. Other suited-up people rushed in to try and save their friend, and it was then that Laous launched into the second part of his plan. Something cold slammed into my cheek, so icy it numbed the spot immediately, while pain burst in my head, causing darkness. Wait, no, the darkness was because my eyes were closed. I couldn't open them again, I literally had no energy in that moment.

No. No, no, no. Shit, if I fell asleep now, it was all over. But what the hell could I do? Daniel was still being blasted with whatever weapon Laous had hit him with – though he was fighting it, he hadn't won yet. And the last human who had tried to help was engulfed in flames.

Concentrating as hard as I could on breathing and moving, I rolled. I'd mapped the layout of this building when I first walked in, so I knew where the exits were. Laous, who must have expected me to collapse immediately, reacted slowly. I heard the sound of chairs crashing as he tried to follow me. I stumbled to my feet, squinting as I deliberately knocked a table into him.

I took off in a rapid, unsteady gait. One of my eyes had closed again; the other remained in a half squint. I was bumping into lots of tables and chairs, but as long as I got out of here and back to the mansion, I could get some help. Michaels was there; he could contact others.

A hazy human came into view and I realized another brave

firefighter had stepped up to assist me. I had the vague idea that if I managed to collapse against him, he would be safe from Laous' flames, because the psycho needed me alive. Just as my arms went out, ready to dive, I was snatched up from behind. This time there was no fighting against the blow to my head. Darkness dragged me under and my scream was the last thing I heard.

~

BLOOD WOKE ME. Well, the taste of it. I choked and spluttered, trying to clear my mouth and throat. It felt as if there was a thick, bloody coating across my teeth and tongue. My head was screaming at me again. One day in the presence of these Daelighters and I'd been unconscious twice.

Seriously, this had better be the last time or I was going to do something drastic. What that drastic thing was, I had no idea, but it would be *huge*.

Focusing on useless threats was better than dealing with the thrum of fear coursing through me. I had no idea where I was; the room was dimly lit ... some sort of fancy condo ... nice wood floors, thick drapes, marble-topped furniture against a nearby wall.

These Daelighters had way too much money to play with.

Daniel. Worry for him was building within me, even though I was probably the one in the worst position. But I got the feeling that not much hurt Daniel, and whatever the stone was that Laous had hit him with, it did something unexpected. Laous might not be this *overlord* any longer, but he clearly had a range of techy little gadgets and inside knowledge on how to disable us. And a crap-ton of money. A scary combination.

I struggled against my bindings – I was strapped to a chair.

Every girl's dream, right? There was no give at all in whatever was tying my hands behind me. I had never been great with being restrained, but I refused to let the panic take over. I needed to keep a level head until I got out of here.

Continuing to struggle, I managed to wiggle my chair forward. It actually slid quite easily on the wood floor. Maybe I wouldn't have to get my hands free to get out of here.

Focusing on the door across the room, I started sliding forward. As I moved, I briefly contemplated calling out to see if my mom was here, but knowing I'd probably only alert the people I didn't want to alert, I remained quiet.

Halfway there, my head throbbed so badly that I had to stop for a moment. Breathing deeply through the pain, I gave myself only a few seconds before starting again, managing to find a good rhythm. Strangely enough, only one of my ankles was secured tightly to the chair leg; the other was quite loose, which meant I could use it for balance.

My eyes adjusted to the darkness. There didn't seem to be much in this room, which was working to my advantage. As the door came into clear view, my heart rate jumped into a thrumming pace. I wasn't exactly being quiet, scraping this chair across the floor, so the closer I got to the escape, the higher my chance of detection.

What if Laous was right on the other side of this door? What did he plan to do with me? I'd obviously been tied up in here for a reason.

There were just too many things I didn't know about this world.

That anger flared again. My parents should have prepared me better for this eventuality. Sure, my father had a somewhat decent excuse, being dead and all, but my mom had plenty of time to fill me in about the reality of being this stupid secret keeper, which I didn't even get a choice about.

The last few feet to the door took the longest. When I was only a few inches from the handle, I paused to decide how I was going to go about this. There was still no give at all in my hands despite my constant struggling, and one loose foot was not useful in opening a door. Tilting my head as low as I could, I tried to see more of the chair. Thick wood legs, carved and styled into roped elegance. *Crap.* It wasn't a cheap wooden rickety number that I could easily smash. It was one of those fancy solid pieces that would still be around a hundred years from now – and I would probably still be tied to it, a skeleton, with both hands and one leg bound.

A voice caught my attention, just a murmur really, and I leaned forward trying to hear what they were saying. At first the words were muffled, but then they started to yell and it got a lot clearer after that.

"Imperial is my land!"

That was definitely Laous. I'd recognize his slimy voice anywhere. The reply came from someone I didn't know.

"You will be taken by the council. They're looking for you – everyone is looking for you." The next words after that sounded like *resistance*, but I couldn't be sure because Laous laughed, drowning it out.

"I will have the starslight stone in my possession very soon," he said. "Two of the four secret keepers are found. Using the blood from the Imperial girl will lead me to number three."

The Imperial girl. He had to be talking about me.

Realizing I was wasting time – he was talking about using my blood afterall – I went back to my door dilemma. I stretched up as tall as I could in the chair, my hands and arms screaming as I strained them, and gained just enough height to use my chin and mouth to pull the lever down. As long as I didn't think about how many hands had been on that handle, it would all be okay.

The door clicked and I stilled. That sound had been deafening to my sensitive ears, but Laous and his companion continued talking, so I felt safe enough to hook my free foot into the gap and pull it back, shuffling my chair as I moved. Once the door was open, I realized that the voices had gone quiet. The sudden silence made me feel uneasy, but I really didn't have much choice. If I stayed, I was dead.

Shuffling forward again, I struggled to get over the edging between the bedroom and the hallway. That small piece of wood might have looked nice but it was freaking annoying when you were tied to a chair.

Eventually I got over, and then once I was in the hallway I looked left and right, trying to decide which way would lead me to freedom. Or my mother. I really didn't want to leave here without her, but I was outgunned, outmanned, out-aliened. I needed backup.

Making a split-second decision, I moved in the direction with the most light. The hall was plain, nothing in it to indicate what I would find at the end. I was lucky this entire place had wood floors, so far anyway. The moment I ran into carpet, I would be in trouble.

The light grew brighter and was almost painful after so much darkness. It wasn't the light of the sun though, definitely artificial. My mind was solely focused on just making it through this hallway. No point in worrying about what would come next if I was discovered here by Laous. At least it did feel like my headache was subsiding, making it easier to focus.

The hallway ended abruptly. I found myself in the sort of

kitchen that chefs dream about. High ceilings, long stainless-steel benches, multiple gas stoves and ovens, huge overhanging racks filled with every pot and pan imaginable...

I was no cook. I generally burned everything, myself included. My mom, on the other hand, could take three ingredients and turn it into something worthy of a restaurant. I guess everyone had to have some redeeming qualities. On one hand she treated me like the child of Satan, but on the other she could make a wicked omelet.

I had to lift myself up again to scrape across the tiled floors in this room. Tiles turned out to be a real pain in the butt, each of the grout sections catching on the legs, and I almost tumbled over more than once. As I passed some drawers, I wondered if there were knives inside. I could see some high on the walls, but they were way out of reach.

But these drawers...

Just as I was figuring out a way to pull one open with my mouth, a chuckle rang out through the large room. It startled me so badly that I slammed my chin against the partially open drawer, cursing loudly. Laous was standing in the doorway, the one on the opposite side of the room to where I had entered, looking amused, those squinty eyes locked on me.

"I wondered how long it would take you to try and escape. My companion thought I was crazy leaving you in there, but I'm constantly curious about human nature. Fascinates me the way you've ... dragged yourselves up. Battling with each other. Living so primitively. But you definitely shine as a species when you're backed into a corner."

Well, great, he was even crazier than I had originally thought. Disappointment welled so fast within me that it almost was a surprise. For one brief moment I had thought there was a chance I could escape, but Laous had been playing me the entire time.

"What do you want from me?" I said slowly, emphasizing each word. "Surely you could have taken my blood while I was unconscious, so there must be something else you need?"

He straightened, strolling closer, looking completely at ease. "Where is the fun in taking your blood while you are unconscious? Seems kind of rude."

Damn, I really hoped his sort of insanity wasn't something you could catch, because it was spilling all over the room. He paused right before me.

"Where is my mother?" I asked.

His happy geniality disappeared in an instant, to be replaced by a dark, stormy expression. In that moment, he was terrifying. My breathing and heart rate both increased, my body reacting even though my brain was calm. Laous closed in on me, leaving only an inch between us. "I will be the one asking questions here, not you. Right now you're alive because of me. Your life belongs to me."

Blah, blah. Heard the crazy dictator speech already. My mom was an expert at it, actually.

"Where is my mom?" I repeated.

He paused, staring at me, unblinking. "She's ... fine. Now that I have you, and your blood, I no longer need her to draw you out of hiding. So she's free to go."

"Show me her," I demanded. "If she's free to go, let me say goodbye at least."

He did that same pausing thing again, only this time I caught a flicker of ... worry in his eyes. The tight press of his lips gave me the same feeling. *What was going on?*

"Where is she?" I would just keep asking until he answered. "And where am I?"

"You're in Overworld."

Those words were enough to almost stop my heart. The sharp pain in my chest started rising toward my throat as I tried to digest the information. *Overworld? We're not on Earth?*"

He shook his head. "No, we're in a small section of Imperial which is not controlled by the overlord." He chuckled, and just like that his stormy expression was gone again. "I was smart enough to secure more than one location, knowing that eventually the time would come for Daniel to take his rightful place."

He raised an eyebrow in my direction. "Daniel was always meant to be overlord, did you know that? He has the true range of power at his disposal. But I needed the position for a short time. I needed to be able to vote for the overlord children to go to Earth."

That must have been what they were talking about with him finding the first secret keeper. Laous had a very long-term plan in place, which meant he probably had a plan B and C ready should anything derail this one.

"What did you do to Daniel?" I asked, hit with a mental image of how he'd been knocked down. An intense sort of worry bloomed inside of me and I was surprised by the strength of it. I had no idea why Daniel affected me so strongly. He'd done something no one else ever had. He'd gotten under my skin.

"I temporarily disconnected him from the network." Laous sounded very proud of himself.

He wasn't going to get a look of awe from me though. I was mostly just confused.

"Here in Overworld, we have a living network," he said. "Like your internet, but it's natural, running through our land.

Connecting us all. Giving us gifts. Powering the people. It's this network I plan to control when I find the starslight stone Earth currently possesses. Once I have the stone, I will control everything."

He'd used that stone on the chain to interrupt this "network" temporarily. What else could he do with it? And if that small sliver was starslight, I was afraid to imagine the power he'd have with a large stone.

Laous took a step closer to me. I'd been so busy watching his expression that I missed the blade in his hand. He rested it against my throat, and there was nothing I could do to resist. My hands were still secured behind my back.

"Playtime with the grubbers is over," he said. "I've enjoyed your fear and false bravado, but now I need to find the third secret keeper."

I knew what that meant. I tried to jerk back and twist in my chair. My entire body lifted as my chair went up onto two legs, before crashing back down again. That random movement startled Laous and the blade bit into my skin. Before I could do or say anything, he shrugged, and with a flick of his wrist sliced right across my throat.

5

It took longer to die than I would have expected. In the movies, a throat gets slit and then the person is dead almost immediately. Right? But that didn't happen for me. There was just pain, so much pain, and then blood seemed to be everywhere, making it difficult to breathe. I felt like I was choking to death on my own blood, in slow motion.

Laous must have released me from the chair. In my pain-filled state, I realized I was draped across the tiled floor, red washing across my vision, tinting the world into a single tone of death. There was a roar, loud, and then it faded away to leave nothing but an endless silence. I kind of missed the roar.

Why am I still alive?

The warmth of my blood disappeared as I was lifted, hazy white light replacing the red.

"Stay with me, Callie." The deep rumble of a voice was comforting, so I clung to it, letting that soothing sound and the haze of white take me away from all the pain. The rasping of my breath became more labored with each inhalation, echoing in my ears. Wetter. Blood spattering. There was one last shuddering breath ... then only silence. I didn't hear anything more. I didn't see anything more.

I expected to fade away. Only ... I continued to be tethered to life, despite the lack of heartbeat or breath in my lungs. Because even though I was not breathing, someone near me was, and it somehow filled my body with oxygen at the same time. The pain in my throat subsided; the blood stopped painting my skin red, and instead refilled my body, moving through organs, repairing injuries.

I wasn't unconscious. I wasn't conscious. I had to be dead, only ... that didn't feel quite right. Was there another state of being I'd somehow missed in the facts of life my mom taught me?

The hazy white disappeared from my vision, to be replaced by a bright blinding light. *Light at the end of the tunnel?* This had to be it, the moment I ceased to exist. The moment I faded from the world.

"Callie, open your eyes."

They're open! I wanted to scream. I had no voice to do so, but in my head I was yelling at the rumbly-voiced male. I was busy dying over here. Who the hell was he to order me around?

Out of nowhere, my heart started beating again; my chest expanded as air surged in and out of my lungs, this time by my doing. The white light faded, and I finally realized my eyes *had* been closed, so I let them spring open – only to find that there was still nothing but white surrounding me.

"Whhh-a..." My first attempt at talking didn't go so well, but as I tilted my head back to see the richest cinnamon and gold eyes staring at me, I finally found my voice.

"How ... am I not dead?"

It was almost impossible for me to read the expression on

Daniel's face. I had never seen anything like that look before, a blending of fury and pain, staring down at me like he was seeing more than just my face. He was seeing into the darkest recesses of my heart and soul. Usually I'd be trying to hide that side of me, but I'd just died ... almost. Or something had happened to me and I was feeling exposed and raw, unable to shield myself behind my usual barriers.

Feeling started to return to my arms and legs, and with that came awareness that I was cradled across Daniel's lap. He held me tightly, his long legs spread out in front of him, muscles visible through his dark pants.

I tilted my head back again, and I didn't even question how comfortable it felt to be resting against his shoulder. More feeling returned to my body, and I knew in a moment I would have to move off him. But until then I was going to let someone support me – for the first time ever. Reality could stay away for a few more seconds.

Daniel's eyes flashed a pure gold; I had to blink and make sure I was seeing that color correctly. "I'm so fucking sorry, Callie," he rumbled. "I never thought Laous could get the drop on me like that. I let you get taken. I let you down." His long lashes hid his eyes briefly, before he met my gaze again, the brown bleeding back through the gold as he tried to calm himself.

"He hit me with a piece of starslight stone, a very powerful piece which he stole from Emma. It malfunctioned my powers, knocked me off the grid, and disconnected me from the network. When that happens, our powers need to reset. Like a knockout punch. It takes some time for all faculties to come back into working order."

"Did you know the stone could do that?" I asked.

He shook his head. "Emma's necklace is a small piece of

the stone which is hidden on Earth. Like a tiny sliver of the power which Laous will have should he find that original stone."

This was why it was so important to stop him from finding it. He was crazy and evil. He'd tried to kill me.

I almost died.

As if he'd heard my thoughts, Daniel's arms tightened around me and I wondered why my chest suddenly felt like it had tightened, too. After a few seconds of contemplation, I realized what it was ... emotions. I was filled with a million feelings, and I didn't know how to handle it. I had been so used to numbness, but ever since New Orleans, where the soul and music of that city started to pierce my icy interior, things had been changing.

Daniel topped it off. He changed everything for me, and now he had somehow saved my life. I knew it was him. There was no one else who would bother.

"You saved my life," I rasped out, my voice not completely back to normal yet. My eyes were burning. Was I going to cry? I literally never cried. What was happening to me?

"I was too late to save you," Daniel replied softly, and suddenly he had all of my attention. "I did the only thing I could, which will allow you almost a full life."

A beat of silence, and then I was struggling against his hold, managing to roll out of his arms and onto the white floor. My legs were like jelly, but I didn't give up until I was standing before him. My skin was tacky with blood, and I didn't bother to look down because I couldn't bear to see the red staining my body.

"Explain?" Less rasp this time.

He was on his feet now, too. I had to tilt my head back to see him clearly. "As Jason told you back in NOLA, I'm the interim overlord of House of Imperial. I haven't had the initiation ceremony yet, but when I do, I will rule this house." He paused, as if weighing his words. "We're the guardians of the underworld." My heart rate picked up. Had he just said *underworld?* "When you died…" he continued, "I used the only power I had at my disposal to save you. I tethered your soul to me … and the land of Imperial. We're the house where souls come to be judged. To rest. So we have a unique power over them. You died in my arms, and I stopped your soul from leaving while I healed you."

I swallowed roughly. "Why didn't you just let me go through that … the rebirth?"

Everything about him went hard again. His eyes narrowed, lips tightened, jaw became rigid. "Because you would be gone." The words were ground out from between clenched teeth. "Gone, and a new version of Callie would be reborn in a new body. You'd have no memories. No connections. You'd start again."

I rubbed a hand over my face, trailing it down across my neck – which was no longer sliced in two – continuing down to press against my chest. "I have a heartbeat. I'm breathing. I feel alive."

Daniel nodded, still looking ten shades of pissed off. "For the most part, you are alive. But there's some things which will change. I'll do my very best to help you deal with it, but it's better you understand now."

I crossed my arms tightly over myself now, trying to hold it together. "I prefer my bad news straight up, so hit me with it."

He did.

"You'll have to spend a certain amount of time in the underworld. This world will renew your life essence, because its energy tethers your soul. A soul which has somewhat tasted the afterlife and will want to make its way back there."

Fuck. "Okay, what else?" Visiting here frequently was something I could live with.

"You'll also have to spend a lot of time with me. More than a few days outside of my presence, away from my energy, and you will fade away. Your soul will end up in our justices, and you'll be properly dead."

I couldn't read his face. It was blank for the first time since he'd saved me. Which sucked, because there was no way for me to know how he felt about his sacrifice to keep me alive.

And in all truth, right then I was struggling to think about anyone but myself.

A roaring filled my mind, like a tornado had just sprang up. I wanted to yell and scream. I'd been a prisoner most of my life already, and just when I was planning on some freedom, I found myself in an entirely new sort of jail.

I knew I was an ungrateful bitch, but I couldn't look past it right now.

"What are the justices?" I asked, my words echoing weirdly in my mind. I sounded detached. I felt it, too. My body wasn't my own anymore and that had my brain struggling to comprehend who I was in this moment.

Daniel stepped closer to me, and I would be a liar if I didn't admit that my body reacted. It wanted to crawl back into his arms. I couldn't just pretend it was because of our new bond; I'd been wanting to crawl into his lap since I first saw him. Too-good-looking alien bastard.

I would be stronger than this new dependence I had on him, though. I might have to be around him, but I didn't have to touch him.

As I stepped back, he paused. "I'll show you." His voice was flat. He turned and waved his arm, and the white-walled dome we were in opened with a pop that left a low ringing in my ears.

My nose crinkled as I stared around trying to figure out where the hell I was. It was a room of egg-shaped pods. Everything was very white, like I could barely make out another tone or shade in the place. Daniel stepped out of the egg we'd apparently been in, and started making his way through the other pods, which were closed, but I could see shadows within them. Were they…?

Holy crap. This place was filled with dead souls, or dead … Daelighters. Whatever the hell they were. It was taking every ounce of my willpower not to start freaking out. I just kept telling myself I was stronger than this. I'd faced struggles my entire life. I could manage this next little hurdle.

Hurrying after Daniel, I caught up to him in moments. When the long white room ended, we exited out into a dark world. I couldn't see what was above us, but I got the feeling that it was not sky up there. That panicked feeling returned, so I forced my mind to focus on the rest of this world around us.

We were on top of a cliff. The white building behind us was tall, seeming to hold many more floors than the egg one. There were a few other scattered buildings further back as well. In front of us was a series of staggered cliffs … levels, like a staircase for giants. I moved forward, trying to comprehend what it all was.

"The Cascading Justices," Daniel explained, his voice low. "When someone dies in Overworld, they come here. They end up in the incubation level first, where we just were. There they are weighed. Their good and bad deeds are tallied, and then they are given choices. Those who have pure souls are allowed to be reborn, or they can spend their days in the utopian land at the base of the justices. Those who have darkness in their soul are dropped into the justices. The purer of a soul you have, the lower you'll start. Eventually you'll get to the bottom level. The truly terrible souls, like my uncle's, end up on this first level."

He pointed down over the cliff to what looked like a ton of trees below. "It's next to impossible for them to journey to peace from here, so they get stuck living out their days in one of these levels."

The top levels were filled with monsters, and lava, and creature-infested water. All the things which were not going to make the afterlife easy or comfortable or fun.

"They can die again?" I asked, trying not to stare at the screaming souls in the level with the fire and lava.

Daniel shook his head. "No, there's only one death. This is their afterlife, where they can enjoy torture over and over without relief."

Whoa. "Remind me not to be an asshole during my life, because I really don't want to end up there."

Daniel actually smiled at that one. "Most beings have more purity than darkness in their souls. These upper levels of the justices are reserved for the truly evil. If you land in one of the bottom three, you'll eventually make it to utopia. To redemption. You just have to work a little harder for it."

"What's the normal lifespan of a Daelighter?"

Daniel's expression turned contemplative; there was a decided spark of something in his face then. Amusement, I would guess. "We're long-lived, let's just put it that way. Age is not something that brings death."

That was amusing. And terrifying. And impossible to comprehend. Tied to him and this land now, I wondered if I too would be "long-lived."

"So Laous killed me..." It was the elephant in the underworld, what had happened to me. I was starting to wrap my head around it ... around what I had become. I was ready to learn more. "He got my blood. I'm sorry I didn't stop him."

Daniel's arm brushed mine and I wanted to touch him so badly I had to clench my fists and plaster my hands to my sides.

"None of this is your fault," he told me.

I changed the subject. "How did you find me? It seemed like you appeared from nothing as soon as he cut my throat." The roar had been Daniel, I knew that now. Without a doubt.

He hesitated briefly, and some of the fury was back in his expression. "The council knew he took you to Imperial. They can track him through the transporter and network, even though they're often a step too late to actually stop him. So I was already here, searching for you. Then when he tried to kill you, he dropped his warding. I know your energy; I found you through the network. I came straight for you."

He'd saved my life. His quick actions and sacrifice of his own soul, or whatever happened, had brought me back to life. This was the part of the story I truly couldn't understand. "Why did you save me?" My voice was doing some sort of stupid breathy thing, but Daniel had literally saved my life. It was a big deal. When he didn't answer, I hurried on, "Surely it's going to be inconvenient to have me attached to you for eternity."

Or however long I was going to live now.

He turned away from me to stare out across the world he was the ruler of. I didn't push; there was no rush. He would either answer eventually ... or we could just live in this awkward silence.

"It was my duty to keep you safe," he said without inflection. "I failed at that duty."

I thought he was going to leave it at that, but then he continued: "I've been left for dead before." A hard murmur. "Discarded on the floor like I was nothing. When I saw you there, all of the blood surrounding you, I just ... couldn't let you die like that."

No part of me believed he'd been a victim like me. Even when he was hit with that special stone, his energy shorting out all over the place, he'd still fought against it.

But maybe he was talking about a time when he was young. Which had all of these soft feelings hitting me again. Baby Daniel should have been protected, and I hated that he had lived a life where that wasn't possible.

"What is the plan now?" I asked, straightening. Death had rattled me – understandably so – but I was ready to take this asshole down. I also needed to know where my mom was. Laous had been weirdly cagey about that.

Daniel turned to face me, expression somber. "The council is taking immediate action. They've called a meeting, and all overlords are required to attend. They've been trying to keep this under wraps, but they're starting to see that it's bigger than they can contain. It's time for everyone to know what's been going on, to prepare for the fallout should Laous succeed in breaking the treaty with Earth."

"If I'm with you, I can leave the underworld?"

He nodded. "Yes. I have the energy of House of Imperial within me. I will keep you tethered. The strongest tie your soul has is to me – Imperial is second – because I was the only thing there for it to cling onto."

It was his heartbeat I heard when mine stopped. His heart keeping the blood pumping in my body.

"Thank you," I said, with more passion than I usually showed. "I'm sure I've seemed a little ungrateful, but I know you did everything you could to save me. I'll forever be in your debt."

Daniel just stared at me, and again I was getting the sense that he didn't know how to feel about his new burden either. With a final nod, he turned to head back to the egg building.

I hurried to follow after him, not wanting to be left behind in this strange world. As we stepped back inside, I noticed there were Daelighters everywhere. *Whoa.* Either they came out of nowhere, or I totally spaced the first time we walked through.

As we passed, many of them lowered their heads to Daniel, some placing hands on their forehead in what looked like a gesture of respect. For all I knew that was their way of flipping each other off, but it didn't feel like that.

Daniel nodded to each in return, and I sensed his discomfort as he continued forward in long graceful strides. I had to take three steps to keep up with each one of his. At the back of the room of eggs, there was a sink next to another doorway.

"You might want to wash up best you can," Daniel said, before he pushed open the door.

Glancing down, I shuddered at the red staining my skin and clothes. Hurrying forward, I let the thick water run over me, and without almost any scrubbing it sucked the blood from my hands and arms. There wasn't much I could do about my clothes, but by the time I stepped into the room after Daniel, most of my skin was blood free.

The new room was a small, stone-lined area, nothing like the white, sterile environment of the eggs. The only thing in there was a ball of light ... actually, it was more like a ball made up of lots of strands of light, that moved about constantly.

"This is a transporter," Daniel explained when I joined him, close to the lights. "This is just a small one, which will take us to the large permanent one between Earth and Overworld. That transporter is the one which gives us power and keeps our network functioning. Most of my council and advisers have gone on ahead, so we need to hurry."

"I really should change first," I said, waving my hands across my bloody clothes. Thankfully my Converse were dark, so if there was blood on them I couldn't see it.

He shook his head. "Most of it is off your skin, which I needed to happen, because seeing you coated in blood was not doing much for my control. The rest can wait. We don't want to be late. I need to hear what they have to say. I need to be there to keep my house in order." He held out a hand and I stared at it. "You'll have to hold my hand. You can't navigate the network without me."

Okay, then. My independence was pretty much toast anyway. Might as well get used to being a puppet. I reached out and his hand engulfed mine. He was gentle for such a huge guy.

"Do your tattoos mean something?" I asked, catching sight of them as he turned.

I wanted to know all the things about him, and this world I was now in. Maybe there was actually a chance at the freedom I had always craved, if I could just learn my place.

He ran his free hand across the maroon marks on his head. "They're the symbols of an overlord. Each holds different meaning, written in the old language. Most Daelighters who are fit to be overlord are born with them. Some develop them later, or like Laous have them marked on their skin with ink." He ran a hand across his shoulder and down his chest. "My marks are all the way down to my waist on one side. We're the only House to have this happen."

"What do yours mean?"

No doubt that was a hugely personal question, but what the hell. Our souls were tied together. Did it get any more personal than that?

Daniel let out a derisive sound. "Bringer of light. Keeper of souls. Unification of worlds."

Those words hung heavy in the air, like they were more than just words. Like they were a prophecy of sorts. They suited him, though ... felt right.

Daniel pulled me a little closer and I let him do it. Before I knew it, we were stepping toward the ball of light. He reached out, grabbed one of those strands, and my cry was lost as we were sucked into the brightness. Immediately I closed my eyes, because the sensation of travelling along this stream of energy was disconcerting and nauseating. I felt like a wimp not taking it all in, but I was also trying to give myself a break from the pressure to be perfect all the time. A break from having to always be strong. I'd lived in a world of fear and anger and control for eighteen years. Then I died. It could have all been a waste. I would not squander whatever time I had been given now.

"You can open your eyes." Daniel's rumbly voice sounded mildly amused.

When my eyes flung open, I immediately tried to take in everything around us. Which was impossible, because there was so much to see. Hundreds of Daelighters were already gathered, but they were standing a little away, clearly waiting for this all to start. Moving past them, I focused on everything else. We were on a huge circular platform with a diameter of at least a mile, or maybe even two. A ball of light – the permanent transporter we'd just stepped from, I would guess – was right in the center of it all.

The platform appeared to be made of metal, and carved into the metallic-like surface were lots of symbols like those marked on Daniel's neck and side of his head. More of their ancient language, no doubt. Moving away from Daniel, I remembered my almost-death – and new dependency – and halted before turning back to meet his hooded gaze. He seemed to know exactly what was worrying me.

"You don't have to stay by my side, Callie. As long as you are within a few hundred feet of me, you won't fade away."

I sucked in a relieved breath. That was a win, because I'd freaked that maybe I'd literally have to stick to his side at all times. "It will get easier," he added.

"What do you mean?" I asked, wondering if he meant that figuratively or literally. Because in lots of aspects, I was already coming around to the entire concept. Maybe I'd have a break-down later, but so far, I was okay. I'd always been very good at taking things in stride. As long as I understood what was going on, that there was a logical reason for what was happening, my brain could deal.

He took a step closer to me and I tilted my head back to keep his face in my line of sight. It was odd for me to have to look up at someone like this; my height usually gave me the advantage.

"I don't know for certain," he said, "because this sort of bond has never happened in my lifetime, or to my knowledge, but we did learn during our schooling years that a soul link can charge up over time. Your soul will grow stronger again. Eventually, you'll be able to spend extended periods of time away from me and my land."

OhmyGod. I didn't think, I just launched myself at him,

hugging my arms around him. "Thank you," I murmured. "Thank you for that sliver of hope..." My voice caught, but I pushed through to add, "And thank you for being the only alien I could imagine being bonded to."

It was an irrefutable truth. There had been a comfort with Daniel right from the start. I'd never given Michaels the time of day, but those inner securities never kicked in with the Daelighter I was hugging. Fate had doubly blessed me, because without Daniel I would be dead, and if another Daelighter had been the one to bond me, I might have wished I was dead.

When I pulled back, there was a moment of awkwardness there, but then it drifted away in the breeze. I turned back to stare out across the view, and he stayed at my side.

"That's House of Darken," he said, pointing toward a land filled with snow-topped mountains, and gorgeous valleys and streams. It was so pretty that I let out an exaggerated sigh of appreciation.

"I've never seen anything like that before. It looks almost like a fairy tale," I murmured, awe lacing my words.

Daniel made a sound of agreement. "My best friend is the overlord minor there. He will take over from his father one day. Lexen and his draygone are the rulers of this land, and they would not tolerate anyone hurting her."

Draygone? That had sounded an awful lot like dragon, only all drawled out and slow. But surely they didn't have dragons ... that would be ... *impossible?* The fact I was on an alien planet and still somehow thought things were impossible was not speaking highly of my intelligence.

Only one way to find out. "Is a *draygone* ... a dragon? Like the myth on Earth?"

Daniel's lips twitched, probably at my lame attempt of

mimicking his accent. "Yes, they would be closest to your dragon. Daelighters have been crossing to Earth for thousands of years, long before our treaty arose, creating the similarities in our language."

Okay, that was pretty cool. Also, the fact he had a best friend with a pet dragon ... yep, Daniel would definitely be the quarterback in my high-school fantasy.

"So, overlord minor is like ... second in line?" I asked, trying to piece this world and its leaders together.

"Yes," he confirmed. "Overlord major is the highest leader of the house, together with their partner. The overlord can be male or female, depending on who is more suited to the crown. But always in the same family group. There are other roles for members of the overlord's family, but the major and minor are the most important."

And Daniel was an overlord major. Almost. Which was a really big deal. Before I could freak out more, he pointed toward his left.

"That is House of Royale."

There seemed to be three distinct landscapes surrounding this disc, all of them extending out into the distance with no end in sight. House of Darken was the largest, taking up a decent portion of the space, but the House of Royale, where he was pointing now, was a close second.

It was a world of only water, beautiful blues and golds mingling together in a long calm line of tranquility. My heart started to hammer hard in my chest as I stared and stared. "Daelighters live there?" I asked, taking a few steps forward.

"Yep, they're our legreto ... water dwellers. Able to exist on both worlds."

Wait a freaking minute. "Water dwellers?" I choked out. "Like ... merpeople?"

I loved mermaid movies when I was young – literally my favorite for years. I knew every line of the few I owned word for word, and watching them were some of the only times I could remember being happy.

Before Daniel could stop me, I was sprinting toward the edge of the round circle, heading toward the world of blue, green, and gold. Low, heady laughter followed me as I ran, my heart almost bursting with joy as I let the beauty of the water entrance me. Somehow, Daniel was right at my side when we reached the edge. I stared down into the clear depths, trying to see something.

"Xander Royale is another one of my best friends," he explained, and I tore my gaze from the water to him. "He's the overlord minor of Royale. I'll make sure you meet him, one day, when everything calms down. He might even be able to show you some of their world below."

I gasped and reached out to grasp onto his shirt. "I would love you forever."

He chuckled again, tilting his head to the side, examining me. I swallowed roughly, suddenly feeling a little exposed. Probably a little too soon to throw out the L word, even if we were soul-bound.

"What?" I asked when he continued to stare at me that way.

"You're just really different to the person I first met in NOLA. You should let your guard down more. It's a good look on you."

Heat filled my cheeks. I willed the blush away, but as usual, my bodily functions never listened to my mental commands. Feeling like he was waiting for me to respond to his last statement, I shrugged. "I almost died – I mean, I'm still covered in my own friggin' blood." My eyes went back to the water. "It changed me. I'm feeling everything so much stronger, and honestly ... I can't find the energy to continue holding onto my anger and fear any longer. None of that stopped my mom from being taken. Or stopped me from being killed. All that happened was I missed out on the life I could have had."

I allowed the water to fill me with joy again. "I'm doing things different this time around, even if I'm still a prisoner to some extent."

Daniel didn't reply, but he did settle in closer to me, his side pressing against mine, our arms brushing against each other as we stared out into the distance.

"Daniel!" The call jolted us from that moment of peace.

Standing a dozen feet away from us was another Daelighter. I knew this because one, we were in Overworld, and two, he was as tall and beautiful as Daniel. His skin was a perfect shade of dark brown, eyes much lighter, although I couldn't make out the color from this distance. Daniel started walking and I felt a new sort of happiness coming from him. He was genuinely pleased to see this other guy.

As we got closer, light green eyes – sparkling unnaturally – met mine. A sense of calm and peace weaved through my body, and I wondered if this new guy had some sort of hypnotic power. Whatever it was, he carried an ancient energy. Those sparkling eyes saw everything.

He, too, had symbols in his dark hair; one side was shaved short, the other had these long braids interwoven with glittering bands of material. His skin was completely flawless, as was the rest of him.

"Hello there." His low voice was as rich in tone as his skin. "I'm Chase, from House of Leights."

He pronounced it like "laights," dragging the "la" part, letting it roll off his tongue.

"Nice to meet you," I replied, letting a genuine smile cross my lips. "I'm Callie, from almost-died-so-now-I-have-to-stay-close-to-Daniel." I paused. "And Earth."

Chase looked momentarily disconcerted, his gaze lifting to his friend. Daniel started to fill him in on all the events from the past few days, and while they talked, I ran everything I knew over in my head. Daniel had now mentioned three best friends, all of them overlords. Lexen, Xander, and now we had Chase.

My impression had always been that their houses didn't get along with each other, the mention of war between the houses had happened more than once, but this group of guys was proving that wrong.

"I had no choice, she was going to die," Daniel finished. "Laous..." He growled, angry and low. "We need to figure out where he is going to hit next. We need to stop him before he makes it to the next secret keeper."

Chase just nodded, and this time as our eyes met, his were softer. "I'm very sorry for what you've been through, but there's no better Daelighter for you to be bonded with. Daniel will keep you safe."

I snorted, startling them both. "I don't rely on men to keep me safe. I keep myself safe. I'll also look after Daniel when the time comes."

I felt their amusement, but both of them managed to refrain from laughing. Arrogant aliens. There was a shift in the light ball then and we turned to stare. Chase took a step away from us, heading back toward the area of this world that was filled with trees. That was a section I hadn't had a chance to observe yet, but it looked as if it was just one huge forest.

"The four houses have been at war for centuries. This is the first time of peace," Daniel explained to me, confirming my previous feelings. "For some reason, despite the tensions between our families, Xander, Lexen, Chase, and I have always been best friends. Brothers. As the overlord minors, we were often thrown together during meetings and such, and we bonded. Years ago, we decided to hide the true nature of our bond. We were afraid our parents would disapprove and keep us apart." He shrugged. "I don't know why we do it anymore. No one could control us now."

"Old habits, I'm sure," I said, and he nodded. "Are you going to try for total peace when you're all overlords?" I asked, taking a step closer to his side.

He tilted his head in my direction. "Yes, that's exactly what we hope for in the future."

Before we could speak more on it, the ball of light sparked and another group of Daelighters appeared. They dispersed quickly, moving toward those already waiting.

Before we could move closer to the council, though, we were ambushed by another overlord, and a chick who didn't have the same look as most of the Daelighters I'd seen. In fact, I was pretty sure she was ... human. Blinking a few times, I suddenly knew who I was about to meet.

Secret Keeper number one. Emma.

6

---

*E*mma Walters stared at me. I stared back. Both of us taking a moment to assess the other. I felt a spark of something between us, same as I had with Daniel, but different. Like camaraderie, a sense of kinship because of who we were and the things we had gone through. Plus, she was wearing Converse shoes, which in my books was a very good start to any friendship. We matched. That was a thing, right?

I could be way off base, though; it was hard for me to understand friendship. If I ever did get friendly with anyone, it was usually a guy at the local gym where I trained. I'd never told my mom, of course, but I'd been sexually active since I was fifteen. Not a part of my past I was particularly proud of, but there was a time that I tried to assuage my loneliness through sex. I'd stopped that just before my seventeenth birthday, vowing the next time I shared my body would be because I wanted to share my heart as well. Blame that on my obsession with romantic comedies; those movies were always my go-to when I was feeling down. If the Hallmark Channel had a group for addicts, I'd be a member.

"I'm so happy to finally meet you." She startled me by speaking out loud. Before this our conversation had been mostly body language and eye contact.

She kept her voice low – the meeting had started, but so far the council was just going over old news, so we had a few moments to chat.

"Happy to meet you, too," I said, and I really meant it.

I felt eyes on me, and I knew they were going to be cinnamon and gold. Somehow I always knew when Daniel was looking in my direction. This time, though, he wasn't the only one. I met the gaze of the huge male standing behind Emma. Lexen Darken, the overlord minor of House of Darken.

Dragon lord apparently.

Just like Daniel, this guy gave off scary, badass vibes. Unlike Daniel, I did not feel comfortable with him. He *was* gorgeous on a scale that should be illegal – I was starting to see a pattern with these aliens – but he was also dark and brooding, with eyes so black they were almost reflective. The way he moved was otherworldly. Like an animal, assessing me and all my weaknesses. Teaming that with the fact that I already knew he had a dragon friend meant Lexen was going right into the box where I kept things that frightened and fascinated me.

Emma cleared her throat and I managed to turn away from her scary boyfriend. One might think that an Earthling and Daelighter together would be an odd couple, but they made it work. It didn't hurt that Emma was adorably pretty, with long auburn curls and stunning blue eyes. I could see why the Darken overlord had fallen for her.

She lowered her gaze, brow pinching. "You're covered in blood. What happened?"

Oh, right. That little thing. I gave my clothes a rueful

glance. "I kind of … died today. Apparently having your throat slit is messy."

Emma gasped, her head flinging up as she glared at Daniel. "You were supposed to get to her before Laous."

Lexen placed a hand on Emma's back, and it was hard to tell from my angle, but it almost looked like he was stroking her spine. As she tilted her head to smile at him, his irises flashed with what appeared to be a white light, just for a moment, then it was gone, so fast I wondered if I imagined it.

"Laous used the stone in your necklace to temporarily disconnect Daniel from the network," Lexen explained to her. "We didn't know it could do that, so Dan was not prepared." He paused, as if choosing his next words carefully. "If we are disconnected from the network, our powers…"

"Reboot," I supplied, excited to know something for once.

Emma didn't gasp this time, she growled. Fire leapt in her features, lighting up her eyes and skin. She had a temper to match the red in her hair, I could see that now. It made me like her even more. Perfect people were not something I dealt well with, mostly because I was always a mess.

"So Laous obviously got Callie's blood, which means he's going to be heading for secret keeper three. What does the council think they can do now?" Emma asked.

"Hopefully *the council* will tell us soon," Lexen grumbled. "So far this is a repeat of useless information about the treaty."

I'd been half listening, because it was new to me, but there really hadn't been anything important said by the council so far. Just that both worlds had been dying, that this treaty was about peace, and that we needed to do everything to protect it.

Most Daelighters around us were having conversations amongst themselves. It was easy to tell who was from which house; they tended to stick to their own, standing in front of their territory. Lexen and Emma were currently in the Imperial section – Chase had left to rejoin the Leights – but very few others were cross-mingling.

"Do you live here, in Overworld?" I asked Emma, far more interested in this interdimensional relationship.

She shook her head. "Nope, I live in Daelighter territory, back in Astoria."

"You'll be staying there as well," Daniel informed me. "I still have to keep up appearances. We have to go to school on Earth as part of the treaty." Something I just learned from the council update. "You're going to have to remain with me. I'll bring you back to House of Imperial periodically to recharge."

Narrowing my eyes, I looked between the three standing across from me. Emma was the only one shorter than me, but she didn't look remotely intimidated by my anger. I supposed after dealing with these overlords I was nothing. "I don't have time to go to school. I need to find my mom and kill Laous. In that order. Or either order. I don't care."

Emma chuckled. "I knew I was going to like you. Us secret keepers need to stick together."

Warmth bloomed in my chest, dimming some of my anger.

"We'll find Laous and your mother," Daniel assured me. "But none of us can shirk our responsibilities. It's the unfortunate part of being an overlord."

Letting out a ragged breath, I just nodded. I was going to have to accept that there was no rushing in this situation and be grateful that everyone was still working to find my mom.

"Come on, Em, it's time for us to get back to the Darkens," Lexen said to her, wrapping her up into his huge body. The way he held her ... it was like she was more precious than anything else in the world.

Damn you, romantic comedies. You've given me unrealistic

expectations, and now I wanted a Lexen. Not him, exactly, because he wasn't my type. Too pretty, too broody, too in love with another woman. I did not poach. That got you a straight punch in the boob.

"I'll find you after," Emma said, then she surprised me with a hug before they left.

I turned confused eyes on Daniel. "Emma is a great friend for you to have," he told me. "She understands what you're going through. Ever since her family was killed by Laous, she's been struggling."

Those words triggered a visceral reaction within me. Daniel responded to my pain by capturing my hand and squeezing it. "I'm so sorry, Callie," he murmured. "That was thoughtless. Your mom could still be alive. Laous is very good at keeping his victims alive but miserable."

I let out a long breath, before a snort of laughter hit me. "That's really not much better. 'Hey, Callie, your mom is probably alive while an evil former-overlord tortures her daily.'"

Daniel rubbed a hand across his head and I couldn't stop from following the path of his overlord symbols. I kind of wanted to touch them too.

"I'm not the best at comfort," he admitted, dragging my attention back to him.

"Have you ever been shown comfort?" I asked, curious.

His jaw turned to granite as he gritted his teeth. I was about to apologize, because clearly my question had hit on a nerve, but then he let out a long breath. "My mother and older brother were the only good things I had in my life. My brother disappeared when I was young. He was the oldest and had always looked out for me. One day he was there, and then he was gone. No one has seen or heard from him since. We presume he is ... dead." He growled at the last word. "And my mother died when I was in my second metamorphosis burst. So ... around ten."

I didn't even want to know what a *metamorphosis burst* was. It made me think of a caterpillar turning into a butterfly or something. I focused instead on the number. He was ten. Just ten when he lost the only decent member of his family. His mom.

"How did she die?" I asked softly, my heart already hammering at the possibility of his answer. Not only had he lost his brother, but his mom right after. It was so unfair.

Daniel lowered his head briefly, shuttering those eyes from me. I found myself a little bereft ... I was growing far too accustomed to staring into his depthless irises. They helped me understand this man. His expression hid a lot, but his eyes were clear as day.

"She died in childbirth, having my youngest brother," he bit out, and I could feel the hurt in each word. "When my father told me what happened ... it almost destroyed me. I blamed Fraizer. Unfair of me, I know that now, but at the time I couldn't see past my pain. It ruined our relationship forever."

God, he'd basically lost two brothers and his mother almost in the same hit.

I followed Daniel's line of sight then to a Daelighter with his arms crossed over his chest, staring daggers at us. There was no doubt in my mind that this was his brother; he looked like Daniel. A less rugged version of him anyway. He was a pretty-boy with a slicked-back faux hawk – shaved on the sides but longer on top – and long-runner muscles. He had a few marks, signs of the overlord family. About a quarter the amount Daniel had.

"Fraizer?" I asked softly.

Daniel nodded, before turning away from him. "We're the

last remaining members of the overlord family, my true blood brother. I started the destruction between us. Then greed, jealousy, and our father – who turned into even more of a complete and total asshole after Mom died – were the final nails in that coffin."

What a sad freaking story. So much loss in his life already, and now he was dealing with everything I had brought to his world, with being tied to a stranger. I wanted to apologize again, but my words wouldn't change anything.

My heart ached so badly it almost felt like I'd been punched in the chest. I was trying to figure out what to say, because comfort was not my thing either, when another member of the council stepped forward. A woman this time.

"It's time for us to speak frankly," she started. "To speak about the dark days ahead for our people."

This got everyone's attention. Imperials pushed forward, while always maintaining a respectful distance from Daniel. I eyed the shaved-headed aliens around us. Even the women had very short hair; the longest were only brushing across the bottom of their ears. All of them looked hard, wore a lot of black, and had a lot of attitude. Despite this, the expressions shot in Daniel's direction were a combination of respect and fear. Of all the badasses, he was the scariest of them all.

No one looked at him like a friend, though. Not the way Lexen and Chase had, which helped me truly understand that softening of his face when they had come over to us. True friendship. I'd never had anything like that ... like an unconditional love. I pretty much didn't believe in the concept, but there was no denying the truth of what existed between Daniel and the other overlords. And also Lexen and Emma – that had an epic feel to it. Maybe Daelighters were just more evolved than humans. Hopefully they were.

The council member's next words were filled with emotion. "At the last meeting we touched on this subject, but we're afraid this situation is growing out of our control."

I shifted uncomfortably in anticipation of her next words.

"Carestima lostin aroutina forlessit."

Okay, then, no need to worry about that bad news.

Daniel helped me out by translating. "Laous has approached members of the human government in the hopes to entice them to join 'his side' of this war. One member is now missing, presumed dead."

My heart and pulse racing, I couldn't stop a rasp from emerging, a prequel to tears, which I was definitely not shedding. I didn't know the politician who had possibly died, of course, but Laous had my mother. *She's already dead, Callie.* It was a reality I needed to wrap my head around, but it was difficult when my emotions were such a mess. Should I be devastated that a woman who made my life miserable was gone? Part of me still loved her, she was my mother, but I had never liked the person she was. That didn't mean I wanted her to have suffered a horrible death. I just wished I had some answers.

"The treaty is in great jeopardy." A different council member spoke this time. Back to English. "Over the next week, overlords will head to Washington to try and smooth this over, and it's possible that we'll have to sign new agreements. None of which will mean anything if Laous gets his hands on the starslight stone. We have put word out to the Draygo people, hoping the one who transported the stone originally will come forward. We need to get to it before Laous does." Another long-extended pause, then the crowds started to talk again. High pitched words of worry and fear.

More council voices burst out, attempting to calm the

Daelighters. "We need you all to prepare for what might eventuate," a man said loudly. "Prepare your people. Search for traitors. If we lose the connection to Earth's energy, our network will weaken. Over time our abilities will disappear..." He trailed off.

Overworld was in trouble, and Laous was determined to push them all the way to the edge.

"If this is going to destroy your network, why is Laous doing it?" I asked Daniel. That was one part of the story I didn't get. Laous was a Daelighter. Surely he wanted his world to be as powerful as it could be.

"Laous doesn't believe that will happen." That reply did not come from Daniel, but from another man behind us. Fraizer strolled closer. "His theory is that we're actually weakening ourselves with this alliance. That by returning the starslight stone here, it will boost our network to mammoth levels."

"A theory I believe you subscribe to also, Fraizer," Daniel bit out, not staring directly at the slightly smaller male.

Fraizer joined his brother in scanning across the crowds of Daelighters around us. "You've always thought the worst of me, brother."

"When have you ever given me reason not to?" Daniel replied, but without anger. More like resigned sadness. "You've gone out of your way in the last few years to side with Laous and create as much suffering for me as you could."

Fraizer scoffed and walked away before anything more was said. I was frozen, staring between Daniel's rigid jaw and Fraizer's retreating back.

"Do you think your relationship is salvageable?" I asked, unable once again to mind my own business.

A tic started high in Daniel's jaw; his words were rough when they emerged. "I don't have evidence of it, but I believe

Fraizer has been in on Laous' multiple attempts to kill me. He's working toward the same cause as Laous and is never to be trusted. If you find yourself alone with him, get away as soon as possible."

The urgency in his words was enough to have my fear spiking. I just stared, bug-eyed. I had not gotten a murdery vibe from Fraizer at all, but Daniel had no reason to lie about something like that. His eyes remained locked on my face, and I knew he was waiting for me to promise.

"You got it," I said, "no heart to hearts with the crazy part of your Imperial house."

His muscles relaxed, and I was gifted a rare full smile. "Going to be quiet back home for you, then. Crazy runs quite deep in the Imperial sector."

"I'm sure I will fit in just fine," I said blithely. "Crazy I understand."

The meeting appeared to be wrapping up. The council added a few closing statements, along the lines of "the world is going to shit," "hide your kids and jewels," "every Daelighter for themselves if the apocalypse hits..."

The final statement was a little more positive: "We have multiple plans in play to try and thwart this," a female council member said. "As we've mentioned, we're working with the humans, and we're hoping to find the secret keepers before Laous. We will continue to work on finding the Draygo people as well. Keep us informed of anything you learn within your own houses."

Noise erupted around us in crazy bursts, and I was getting the general vibe that Draygo people were all kinds of awesome, scary, and lethal. "Lexen is one of the last remaining members from that race," Daniel murmured.

I snapped my head up and blinked at him. "Are you telling

me that Lexen is not only a dragon lord with a pet dragon, but he's ... what ... part dragon as well?"

Daniel nodded before he slammed a hard look onto a nearby Daelighter who was inching closer to hear our conversation. With a squeak, the shaved-headed male turned tail and dashed away.

Daniel turned back to me. "Lexen takes a half-man, half-beast form. He's pretty much indestructible when he is morphed."

Shut. The. Hell. Up. *Was he serious?*

"Would he have any idea where the one who hid the stone went?" I asked, somewhat breathlessly. My question made sense, right? It takes a dragon person to find another dragon person.

Daniel didn't seem as convinced. "I have no idea. Lexen has never spent much time developing that side of himself. He's the first Draygo to also be born overlord minor, so he's been rather busy."

Everyone started to disperse after that, until eventually there were only a few scattered beings left on the platform. Escaping Lexen again, Emma made a run for me. I was really starting to like her. She felt like a kindred spirit, and it was such a foreign feeling ... having an ally – this had to be the only reason for the bursts of warmth and happiness pressing into my chest.

Who knew dying would be the best thing that ever happened to me.

The thought was so insane that I actually shook my head. *Really, Callie? The best thing?* I needed therapy.

"Are you coming back to Astoria now?" Emma's words sounded like a demand directed at Daniel.

He shook his head. "Callie needs to return to the underworld for a short period first, to recharge. We'll be back in the morning. In time for school."

Emma's face fell and she turned to me. "I'm so sorry about what happened to you. Shit, this really sucks!"

Lexen, who had strolled over to his girl, ran a hand across her shoulders. "We will figure something out to help Callie. There has to be a way so that she has some freedom from Daniel."

Emma got this weird dreamy look on her face then. "This is just like Hades and Persephone. Which maybe means it will all work out for the best."

She winked at me. Two blank faces from the men, but I got her reference exactly, and had to laugh. "You're right. I've now tied half my life to Daniel and an alien underworld."

I'd always kind of thought Lucifer had an evil, hot, scary appeal. Daniel rocked that same dark vibe, just with less of the crazy – despite his insistence that Imperial House was not the most stable. Like I said, I knew crazy, and it wasn't him.

"You need to study up on your Greek mythology, Lex." Emma narrowed her eyes on him. "Told you that having one history class on the 'founding houses of Starslight Prep' was a little limiting."

He shrugged. "Human stuff is not exactly top of my lists of interes..." He trailed off at the look on Emma's face. The grin which pulled at the corner of his mouth turned his good looks into something scorching. "Except for you, mate."

Mate. Like a soulmate. Damn, Emma. Lucky she was so awesome, otherwise I might hate her. Just a little.

We were one of the few groups left on the platform now, and both of the overlords were getting really odd looks. "Why don't you four just come out with the friendship?" I suggested, looking between them. They were standing as far apart as they could, while still being able to hear the other speak. "You said that there was nothing really holding you back but habit. I think now is the time."

"Yeah," Emma chimed in, being the great ally she was. "The council has far bigger things to worry about, and I think some unity could be good for the four houses."

"I agree." That statement came from Chase. He'd wandered over, leaving the remaining members of House of Leights.

Before anyone could say another word, we were joined by another overlord. He had blond hair, with dark marks visible on one side. He was also rocking a broad, tanned chest, with water peppered across it, and a cool confidence.

"I'm adding my agreement to this," he said, and I knew then that this was Xander, from House of Royale.

My eyes met Daniel's, searching out those inner thoughts. For some reason his mind fascinated me, not in a zombie, I-want-to-eat-your-brains way, but more ... what was he thinking now?

I decided to push: "Is there any reason for you to keep your bond secret? What could happen if you allowed the world to know that you four are brothers, friends, allies?"

The gold deepened in the rings of his light brown eyes. "I actually don't know. As I said, when we were kids we had no power. We were afraid our parents would separate us if they found out."

"So we snuck around," Lexen added.

Emma stepped into her mate's huge chest, wrapping her arms around him. He got this look on his face when she did. It was a nice look.

"You're now adults," Emma said to him, before turning around to us. Lexen pulled her back, so she was pressed right to his front. "You thought that being mated to a human would cause a huge problem, and so far it hasn't. Daniel is already overlord, no one to stop him in House of Imperial. Roland is not going to be angry about it, I don't care what you think."

She looked at Xander and Chase. "What about you two? Will your family be okay with it?"

They exchanged a glance before shrugging. "Probably not, but I for one don't care." Chase was straight up.

"Me neither," Xander said.

Emma clapped her hands together. "Well, it's settled, then. Tomorrow at school, we're sitting together at lunch."

She looked so excited, and the four overlords were clearly enchanted by the human in their midst. Before I could let jealousy rear its ugly head – because I'd always been an outsider – Daniel turned to me, changing the subject.

"How are you feeling?" he asked, and I was so disarmed that I forgot how to speak for a beat. Did he ask that because he cared? Had anyone ever asked me that before?

"A little tired, actually." I realized how true that was as soon as I said it. There was this weight pressing down on me. I'd been ignoring it pretty well, but it was getting a little more uncomfortable now.

He nodded. "We need to get you back. Say goodbye to badass, you'll see her tomorrow."

I tilted my head in Emma's direction. "Badass?"

She threw a withering glance at Daniel. "I impaled myself on a tree when I fell into the first level of the justices. And didn't die. He's been calling me badass ever since."

On instinct, I reached out and grabbed her hand. I had no idea where it came from, I wasn't a touchy sort of person. I'd grown accustomed to never being touched. Had to be the death thing again. "You were in the justices?"

She nodded. "Yeah, Laous tried to kill me blah blah – we both have that badge. I only survived because of Lexen and Daniel. Together the three of us made it to the final level. Redemption."

I shook my head. "I'll be honest, that world scares me. Those justices were like nothing I've ever seen before. I can't even imagine being stuck trying to navigate through them."

"Let's hope you never have to find out," Lexen said smoothly. "But if you do, Daniel and I will come for you as well. We're a team."

"We'll be there as well," Chase added, gesturing to himself and then Xander, who was nodding resolutely.

My heart stuttered. It took everything inside of me not to cry like a baby in front of them all. What was this world I was in now? *What was it?*

Daniel's chest rumbled at my side, distracting me from the overwhelming emotions. When I lifted my head to see him, his expression was hard, eyes swirling. I raised one eyebrow in his direction – a skill I'd been perfecting over the last two years; it was cool to have a chance to use it.

"You will never end up in the Cascading Justices," he told me, his voice almost as hard as his face. "You're going to live for as long as I do, so you have no need to fear death. Not to mention that I'm the acting overlord major. I control that land, and I will not let you suffer for even a second in that place."

Well, I guess that answered my question about my lifespan. Those tears I'd been trying to hold back surged forward again. A huge ball of emotion lodged in my throat; it was only years of control that stopped the waterworks.

Even harder to control though was my urge to reach for Daniel. Something strong stirred in my chest every time I looked at him now. No doubt the soul link, tying us closer. Whatever it was, resisting him was growing harder.

I had to though. I knew touching him would tip me right over the edge into obsession. And the last thing I needed was to grow obsessed with a guy who was only around because he'd literally been forced to tie our souls and life forces together to save me.

He was definitely a good guy, and would make a perfect mate one day to some Imperial Daelighter. I'd have to be satisfied with the friendship which seemed to have sprung up between us.

Forcing a smile across my face, I said, "Thank you. Thank you for protecting and saving me."

Xander interrupted then, his voice deep and smooth: "What exactly happened with you and Callie? How did you two become bonded?"

Daniel explained it, starting from the moment he found me in NOLA, my mom's disappearance, Laous' attack, and finished up with the details of my death and our new bond.

I tried to block most of it out again. It was bad enough going through it the first time, so I instead focused on the House of Royale territory, or sector, or whatever they called it. My obsession with the beach started during a three-month stint in Los Angeles. I think I was about five years old at the time. Mom would walk me to fight class along the beach, and I would be staring at the water the entire time we traveled. By the end, she knew to never let my hand go or I was likely to wander right off to sit on the sand.

Something about the play of light and color in the waves, the way the water moved and mingled together, so fierce and yet also able to be perfectly calm. Sometimes it felt like my soul was born of the ocean. At times there was no emotion inside me at all, and then other times everything crashed together, unable to be contained.

My insides were definitely tumultuous now. It started in New Orleans – that damn music. Then Daniel was the icing on the cake. He'd ignited emotion inside of me from the first moment his arrogant face appeared in my condo doorway. Then he saved my life. Now my ocean was raging at me, wanting to be released, wanting to flow toward this male.

Dammit, just stay where you are.

"Callie?"

Shaking my head, I focused on the group again, only to find that everyone was staring at me. I'd clearly missed something important. Deciding I didn't care if they thought I was a weirdo, I just shrugged. "Sorry, I zoned out. What did you say?"

Daniel took a step closer to me, and before I could protest, he swept an arm around me. My legs gave out, like they'd only just barely been keeping me up. "You've been away from Imperial for too long," he said, a rumble in his voice. He lifted me with ease, holding me close to his chest.

With almost laughably pathetic strength, I pushed at his arm, before letting out a sigh and falling against his hard chest. "How is she going to function in Astoria?" Emma asked, and even though I couldn't see her face, I could hear the concern in her voice. "She's only been away from Imperial for about an hour."

Daniel shifted me higher on his body. I realized my eyes had closed. I tried to pry them open, but I couldn't.

"She almost died today. Her body and energy need rest. Tomorrow she should be able to stay away for a lot longer."

I missed more of what was said, as that heaviness which had been pressing on me increased. I regained some consciousness as we started to walk again. Part of my brain was screaming at me to get down and walk on my own, but there was no way for me to fight against the fog in my head and body.

For the first time in my life, I was going to have to trust someone other than myself to take care of me. In some ways, that concept was scarier than the fact I had died today.

7

*A*wakening in a strange place was becoming part of my norm lately. So when I opened my eyes to find myself in a bedroom that wasn't mine, my heart barely skipped a beat. Scooting higher on the pillow, I looked down the bed. It was huge, bigger than any I'd seen before. I ran my hands across the navy comforter, thick and luxurious, enjoying the high quality and silky feel of it. Sign me up for a year of sleep in this bed. Not only was the bedding quality, the mattress might have been made from magic. Alien magic.

Unfortunately, it wasn't in my nature to laze around, so I pulled myself up even further, sitting up straight. It looked as if I was still dressed in my bloody clothes from yesterday, which was totally gross, but I was also glad Daniel didn't undress me without my permission. I appreciated that about him. Even if he would have to change his sheets now.

I stretched my arms above my head. I had a few aches and pains, but nothing to indicate I'd died yesterday. Standing, finally, I gave the rest of the room, which was as large and decadent as the bed, a quick look. There was a seating area filled with cushy couches, two dressers, a tallboy, and multiple other heavy, dark, wooden pieces.

Noticing a door, I dashed toward it, hoping it was the bathroom. I needed to pee. Badly.

Success!

The room, tiled in white with charcoal accents, had a shower and a deep tub. Ignoring these, I hurried to what looked like a toilet. It was different to what I was used to, smaller, lower to the ground, and square. But it was the closest thing to a toilet in the room, and I was at desperation level.

When I was done, I looked around for some paper. There was no holder or rolls that I could see. Just when I was about to give up searching, resigning myself to the old "drip-dry" method, there was a whoosh and the toilet flushed. Before I could move, a blast of icy water shot at my bare skin from all sides and I let out a low shriek as it hit me.

What in all the worlds?

That was the opposite of paper. I was now soaking wet.

Warm air followed right after, and just like that I was dry and clean and completely freaked the hell out. Scrambling off the alien toilet, I pulled my pants up and backed away from it slowly. I had no idea how it did that, because I sure as hell didn't press any buttons or anything. I was hoping it was a sensor, and not some robotic-toilet coming to life thing. That would be really shitty. Pun intended.

Crossing to the sink, I had to search again for a way to turn the water on. Eventually I figured it out. One thing learned, twenty million to go. When my hands were washed, I lifted my head to the mirror.

My gray eyes were brighter than usual, the streaks of blue in them quite prominent. My skin, which was normally quite pale, looked positively ghostly. I was probably anemic after losing almost all of my blood yesterday. I'd always been tall and thin; athletic stuff came easy to me – I was generally healthy and well-toned. Today I looked frail. I didn't like it.

A knock at the door startled me. I turned and rested back against the bench. "Yes," I called out, hoping it was Daniel and not some rando. I did not feel up to dealing with an Imperial alien today.

The door cracked open and my heart did that stupid fluttery thing when a familiar face appeared in the open space. Daniel was dressed all in black, the slightest of dark stubble on his face, adding even more sexy to his appeal.

"Hey, was just checking in on you," he said, leaning against the doorframe. He focused completely on me, eyes intense on my face. "We need to head to Astoria soon if we want to make class today. If you feel up to it."

I forced myself to stop staring at him like he was a cool drink of water in the desert and rubbed a hand across my hair. "I feel fine, so far. Being here seems to have restored my energy." Clearing my throat, I added, "And thanks for looking after me yesterday. You know, putting me to bed." Dammit, that sounded far sexier than I had intended.

"I wanted you in my room, so I could keep an eye on you." His voice was a caressing whisper across my senses. "I trust most of my people, but we know there are traitors. Logic says that a lot of those will be Imperial. Until I weed them out, I'm going to be keeping a close eye on you."

Daniel's bed! No wonder it was so awesome. Overlords probably got all the awesome things.

I must have been glaring and blinking rapidly, because Daniel lost some of his cool and actually smiled at me, that damn dimple creasing his cheek and sending my insides crazy. "I slept on the couch. No need to worry."

He had it all wrong, I had not been worried about that at all. My mental images had gone straight to me sharing a bed with Daniel, and worry had not been the emotion that thought evoked.

Shaking it off with a grin, I tried to lighten the mood. "You don't have to do that on my behalf. If we need to stay close for awhile ... well, your bed is huge. I'm sure we can share. Just don't hog the covers."

The gold rings in his dark eyes felt like they were burning into me, raising my body temperature. And, of course, in that moment I lost my mind completely.

"I need a shower," I blurted out.

Smooth, Callie. So freaking smooth. God, I was a moron at times. If only my mother had cared as much about my people skills as she did about my ability to roundhouse kick a dude in the head. She should have made it a priority to not make me this awkward.

Daniel didn't react, even though I knew he was laughing at me. His lips might have been pressed in a firm line, but his eyes were sparkling with mirth. "I'll show you how to use the shower. I'll leave some new clothes and such outside the door." He pointed to a low white cabinet just before the stall. "Everything you need to wash is in there. We use toothbrushes here as well. We stole the idea from Earth. There are some new ones in there."

Daniel soon had cascades of water and steam filling the glass cube of the shower, and he turned to leave the room.

"Hey," I called out, halting him. When he turned back, I smiled. "Thank you for not removing my clothes while I was asleep, even though I'm sure you didn't want these disgusting rags on your sheets. It's just that I ... I was in a vulnerable position, and you didn't step over the line."

His eyes burned into me, leaving me feeling as if I *was* completely naked and exposed in front of him. How did he do that?

"Trust is more important than a bit of blood on my sheets," he said, words deep and low. "I would never risk yours."

Then he left the room, and I wasn't sure if he might not have just taken a small piece of me with him.

When I finally pulled myself together – and it took way longer than it should have – I wasted no time stripping off my filthy clothes and tossing them as far from me as possible. I never wanted to see them again. On top of the fact they were beyond yuck, they also represented everything that had been taken from me over the last few days. My mother and life topping the list.

Stepping into the warm spray, I let out a low moan. It was steamier than I expected, but Daniel had explained that the water here – the *legreto* – was not exactly like Earth's. Something I had learned yesterday, but it was even more different when heated – thicker, becoming an even mix of steam and water.

I found it quite soothing, and it cleaned so well, without me even using soap or anything to wash myself. The water that ran off me was red at first. The sight of that sent me into a bit of a frenzy. I attacked my body with a coarse scrubbing block that had been in the new supplies Daniel pointed out. Then I used a minty smelling wash for my hair and body, and by the time I was done, there was no blood – or layers of skin – left on me anywhere.

Stepping out, I grabbed the large webbed material that they used here to dry themselves. It absorbed the water quickly, much better than the ragged towels we had back in the condo. My hair fluffed out around me, thick straight strands falling naturally to my shoulders. I cut my own hair most of the time, and I'd gotten very good at mimicking simple but fashionable hairstyles.

When I was dry, I crossed to gently ease the door open. A pile of clothes was sitting in front it, just as Daniel promised, so I quickly gathered it up and shut the door again. A black bra and panties were on top, and I stared at it for many long moments.

Okay, how the hell had he managed to find me underwear? Was this some stranger's underwear? Could I be picky and not wear it? I mean, it looked clean – it looked brand new actually – but it seemed kind of weird.

As I lifted the bra up, a white piece of paper fell out. Bending over, I picked it up. It was folded in half, and when I opened it I realized it was a message, hand written. The flowy words did not work well with my stupid inability to read like a normal person, but after about ten minutes I figured out that the note was from Emma and she was writing to tell me about the clothes. I managed to read the entire thing and by the end, I was more than a little impressed with myself.

Hey Callie, Emma here, it started.

Dan asked me to send some clothes over for you, but of course I am in Astoria, not Overworld, so I asked Star, Lexen's sister and a great friend of mine, to procure something. She's always giving me clothes. Somehow in my size. I hope you like what she sends.

p.s See you in school

p.p.s The underwear is brand new. It freaked me out at first, too.

THE WARMTH in my chest was strong enough to be worrying,

but I was starting to recognize the sensation. Friendship. It was nice.

I slipped the underwear on, marveling at how comfortable they were. The material was very fine, almost like silk, but it wasn't shiny or slippery. I personally had never been a fan of silk, not in sheets or clothing. I didn't like the texture. This was the perfect mix, though, just smooth enough to be the most comfortable thing I had ever worn.

The clothes were very similar to what I wore yesterday. Jeans, which somehow fit me perfectly, just as Emma had said. And a simple white shirt – also in a similar high-quality material to my underwear. There were socks, but no shoes. Which was fine, because I was not giving up my Converse. They were a staple in my wardrobe.

One last glance in the mirror was enough to show that I no longer looked like a murder victim. I ran my hand across my throat again, images of Laous' blade slamming into my mind. I wondered if I would ever forget that sensation of being cut, of the fear and cold which filled my body as the blood dripped out of it.

"You ready to go, Callie?" Daniel called through the door, startling me from the memories holding me in their thrall.

With a shake of my head, I turned from my reflection and hurried across to open the door. Daniel must have been right on the other side, because we were suddenly face to face. I tilted my head back. "Oh, hey," I said. "All ready to go. Just need my shoes."

He didn't say anything, but he did run his gaze over my newly-washed hair and face. When those pretty eyes settled on mine, I sucked in a low breath, hoping he didn't notice anything odd in my gaze. I didn't want to talk about what happened yesterday, I just needed time to deal with it. In my own way.

"You look a lot better," he said, a husky murmur of words.

I swallowed roughly. "I feel better," I mumbled, awkward as always. "Thanks, again."

He nodded, taking a step back, and I felt like I could breathe again. How did he take up all the space and air in the room when he was in it? It wasn't possible for people – even alien people – to do that, right?

"Your shoes have been cleaned. They are over on that stand." He pointed to a small table near an open door. I was just reaching out to grab them when a travel mug emitting a delicious smell stopped me in my tracks.

Before I could think, I was diving on the cup, cradling its warmth to my chest. "Oh my precious," I cried. "I have missed you."

Daniel let out a low rumble of laughter. "I figured you might need that to start the day."

He had no idea; the scent of the coffee was actually bringing tears to my eyes.

"My mom got me addicted," I said, lifting it to my lips. "When we would move towns in the middle of the night, she'd ply me with coffee so I'd stay awake and make sure she didn't sleep. It was the start of a beautiful friendship."

The first sip had my eyes closing; a sigh escaped. Holy God above, they made good coffee here.

"Do you think you can drink that and walk?" Daniel sounded amused and I opened one eye to glare at him.

"Could you maybe leave us alone? You're interrupting a perfect moment."

His grin was lethal. I was starting to think that between Daniel and coffee, there was too much stimulation going on right now. Placing my precious cup down just for a moment, I wasted no time pulling my shoes on, then we were off, moving along a hallway. I took sips as we walked, and with each mouthful I started to feel more like myself. The hall continued on for some time, and I kept expecting to see other doors, or rooms spanning off it, but there was nothing except some very fancy pieces of art.

I made a comment about that, and Daniel flicked his head to me. "This is the overlord's wing," he said. "We're on top of the incubation level of Imperial; no one else lives here. It changed itself to my preferences when Laous had his title removed."

I blinked a few times, stumbling and grinding to a halt. "What do you mean it changed itself?"

He had walked a few more strides before he realized I wasn't following; he spun to return to my side. "This entire world is formed from a powerful energy..."

"The network, I know that," I interrupted.

His lips twitched slightly. "Yes, the network. Imperial, being below the surface of Overworld, makes its connection stronger than any other land. My house literally changes with the whim of the overlord. I could rewrite everything here. The only thing which saved us when Laous was overlord is that the council monitors our activities, and any abuse of the system would start a war."

Un-freaking-believable. "He probably kept his crazy contained because he thought he had bigger fish to fry with this secret keepers thing."

Daniel nodded, eyes narrowed. "Yep, it was his plan all along. Kill my father. Somehow confuse the system and take over. We still don't know how he did that, but there was something in the way my father died ... I think Laous absorbed his energy, which made the network believe he was the next overlord."

That sounded like a horrible way to die, and I wondered if Daniel had seen the body.

"He was a husk, drained of life and blood and energy. Like petrified wood."

Guess that answered that question.

"My father was killed, too." *Oh, for fu—*

Why did I over-share when I felt upset by something? This was not about me, it was about Daniel. He focused on me, concern creasing his forehead.

"What happened?"

I shrugged. "Workplace accident was what they told my mom. I wasn't born yet, so I never met him. Apparently, he used to work in factories. The forklift malfunctioned and pinned him against a huge shelf. It was instant death."

I still felt a pang for the man I had never known. In my mind, I always believed that he would have made my life better. He would have brought me love.

"Do you think the 'accident' had anything to do with the secret keepers?" I asked Daniel. It was something I couldn't just disregard; too much was happening in my life that seemed to be connected to it.

He considered it, before shaking his head. "I doubt it. The secret has not been in jeopardy until recently. Most likely it was just an accident."

I sighed. "Apparently my dad was the one who brought me into this crazy life. Probably why my mom has always been so angry with me."

Daniel surprised me by stepping a little closer, his heat warming my exposed skin. "Did you know you were born in the springs which run through the bottom level of the justices? Redemption."

I tried to swallow down my shock. I'd known bits of this, but the more I learned the crazier it seemed. I'd thought I was born in Austin, Texas. My mom was a little off on her geography.

"I'm still human, right?"

Daniel nodded. "You're still a human. Just a more advanced version than the rest of your species. On top of the longevity of life, which you share with me, you should also have an increased ability to heal. The network helps us heal quickly, which is how your throat is no longer sporting a blade mark."

On instinct I reached for my neck, those damn images of my death springing up again to torment me. Pushing them away, I said, "There's at least three others like me. We can be a human super-squad, kicking asses and taking names."

Daniel almost looked pleased by my words. "The four secret keepers this time are all female, according to the council."

So, four secret keepers, all born in the same year, all born here in the different houses of Overworld. And all female. I liked the girl-power side of it immensely. Still, it was a freaking lot to take in, especially with my upbringing. My mother had tried to poison me toward these Daelighters, but she hadn't counted on Daniel. From almost the first moment I heard his voice, he had soothed my distrust. Now, I was open to the possibility of being part of their world.

"Come on," Daniel finally said, walking again. "We're going to be really late if we don't make it back to Earth soon."

I hurried after him, trying not to let all of my confused thoughts and emotions overwhelm me. Lifting the coffee to my lips, I could have cried at how empty it was. One cup was never enough.

"Tell me about this Hades and Persephone fable."

I was so caught up in mourning my coffee that I almost missed the question. It surprised me that he remembered that from yesterday, but it was nice that he had. The story was one of the few myths I was well-versed in. A favorite of my mother, who liked to push the consequences of messing with bad boys who needed a woman to change them. *"Will never happen, Callie!"* she'd yell at me over and over. *"Just stay away from them. Men like that don't change."*

Whoops. *Sorry, Mom, I didn't listen and now I'm tied to a powerful alien that rules the underworld.*

Holding my cup with both hands, I smiled at him. "It's a Greek myth. Hades was the god of the underworld – he ruled over the dead. The myth said that one of the rare times Hades left his domain, he caught sight of Persephone, who was the daughter of a goddess." I paused for second to think. It had been a while since I heard the story. "I'm not actually sure what her mother ruled over, but something to do with nature. When Hades saw Persephone, he fell instantly in love with her and kidnapped her – as you do – bringing her to the underworld. I'm not sure exactly what happened after that, because I'm crap at reading and my mom liked to only tell the parts she enjoyed, but I believe that Persephone's mother ... Demeter ... was really upset, for obvious reasons. Hades ended up making a deal with her that Persephone would stay with him six months of the year, and then go back to her mother for the other six. I think that's why there's beautiful weather like spring and summer for half the year, and winter for the other half. Persephone's mother mourns the loss of her daughter and brings the icy weather."

We had reached the end of the hallway now. Daniel hadn't looked in my direction since I started talking, but I knew he was listening. He hit a button on the wall and finally turned to me. "Did Persephone always hate Hades for what he did? For how he trapped her with him for six months of every year?"

Gold burned into me, those eyes too much for an almost-mortal human to stare at. Swallowing the huge lump in my throat, I cleared it and said, "No, actually, she fell in love with him. She saw past the mean, lonely bastard and ... well, gave him her heart." My voice was way huskier than I'd ever heard it before. "She mourned the six months she was away from him." There might have been another version where she hated him, but I preferred the one with the love.

I could not tear my gaze from Daniel's. I yearned to know what was carving his face into such an intense expression. I couldn't tell if he was pleased or not with the final part to the myth, the happyish ending of their story. Before I could ask, a ding had him turning away.

A door slid across the wall, and when Daniel stepped inside, I followed. He pushed a button on a side panel and I realized this was very reminiscent of an elevator, only we shot up in the air so fast that my stomach rolled. I was not losing all of that coffee, though, so I closed my eyes and tried to focus on keeping my stomach contents in place. If I'd had some food to go with it, I might have been less nauseous.

"You need to eat."

I jerked my head up. He was staring ahead at the wall. "Can you read my mind?" I asked, a little horrified by all of my recent thoughts. *Dammit.* They should have told me that from the start. I could have guarded my random internal conversations then.

Amused eyes lowered to meet mine. He lifted a hand and

brushed his thumb across my cheeks. "You're blushing. What have you been thinking to put pink in these cheeks?"

I shook him off with a huff. "Uh, it's really rude to read people's thoughts. I did not give you permission for that."

He laughed then, his head tilting back. I glared at him until he finished, flashing me another dimpled smile. "I can't read your thoughts. You have your hand pressed to your stomach, and I can hear it grumbling. I also haven't seen you eat since New Orleans."

The box we were in slowed and another ding signaled that we had reached our destination. I waited for the door to open in front of us, but when the whoosh sounded, it was the roof that slid across. I stared up at the emerald sky before turning to the Daelighter.

"I'll go up first," he said, striding toward a metal ladder built into the side of the wall, a ladder I had not noticed until then. "To make sure it's all safe." He scaled the side in about a millisecond.

I waited with one hand on the ladder, and the second his head reappeared, I was already moving. Climbing was easy. I could scale the rope all the way to the top in my gym, also vault and hurdle ... I loved stretching my muscles and using my flexibility.

When I pulled myself over the top, I stood to find we were back on the huge metal platform, the one with the sparkling transporter. "So this permanently exists between my world and yours?" I asked him.

He nodded and held a hand out to me. "Yep, for some reason this transporter is allowing Earth to power our network. Which is why the treaty cannot fall."

With a deep sigh, I took the proffered hand and then we were off, heading back to Earth. The journey was longer than the last time I'd been in a transporter, but I enjoyed it more. Knowing what was going to happen made it less scary to watch the streams of energy zipping past. An experience I knew I'd never forget.

At the end we landed in a stone courtyard, then we walked along a rose covered walkway. There was an early morning feel to the sun when we stepped out onto a pretty street, and it was actually colder than I expected. "What's the date?" I asked. It kind of felt like a million years had passed since I found my mom missing.

"It's October 30th."

Disappointment hit me. I tried not to let it show, but I must have failed, because Daniel was giving me a look of inquiry.

"Tomorrow is Halloween," I said. "I thought I would be in New Orleans for it this year. I wanted to see all the crazy."

Understanding blossomed over his face. "Maybe we can go next year, if the worlds are still spinning."

I chuckled. This was definitely one of those "laugh or you'll cry" situations. As another burst of cold air hit me, I shivered. Daniel surprised me by reaching out and running a hand along my bare skin. A trail of heat followed his touch.

"How can you use your power here?" I asked him. "Away from the network." He'd been strong even in New Orleans, but I didn't understand how. My understanding was that their powers were directly linked to the network. Which was on Overworld.

He sent more heat along my body. "The network does cross into Earth, thanks to the permanent transporter. But we're much weaker here. In fact, most Daelighters have no power on Earth at all. Overlord families carry a lot of their own energy inside. As long as we connect with the network on occasion to recharge, we're always pretty strong."

"Does everyone in your house have the same fire power?"

"A small measure of it," Daniel told me. "But it's nothing compared to the energy I control. Each of the houses has a specialty, something which ties them closer to a certain part of the network. Darken can control electricity and storms, like lightning. Royale has control over legreto; the water is theirs to call and shape. Leights are all about nature. They have a hybrid side that they share with the trees – which is a formidable weapon..." I was trying to picture how they could "hybrid" with the trees, but I had no idea what he meant. Hopefully one day I'd get to see it in person. "And Imperial is all about the fire. As you've seen."

"So, overlords are very strong, but the rest of your house has only small amounts of power..."

He nodded. "Pretty much." His hand lifted to run across his marks. "These symbols give us extra power. They allow us to channel much more of the network without being over-whelmed."

That explained the strength and lethality that Daniel exuded. Before I could ask anything more, he steered me further down the street, picking up our pace.

"We should stop at my house and grab you a coat," he said, his fingers wrapping around my forearm, branding more heat into me. "Keep you warm until you get a uniform."

I nodded, even though I was feeling quite heated all of a sudden.

My coffee was long gone, but I still held the cup in the hope it would be refilled at some point. We continued along the most picturesque street I had ever seen – rose bushes, chirping birds, pruned hedges, huge mansions with gates and landscaped gardens.

"This is Daelight Crescent," Daniel told me. "This is the

spot where humans and Daelighters coexist. It's actually the location which is closest between our two worlds. That's why the permanent transporter is here."

As I opened my mouth to ask which mansions were occupied by humans, I noticed the tiny rundown shacks. They were grouped together, starting about halfway down the street, on the opposite side to the mansions.

I jerked to a halt; his hand released me. "Please don't tell me that you make the humans live *there*?" I said, pointing, anger giving my words a ragged sound.

His gaze flashed across there for a beat, before it came back to me. "Yes, it's not something I agreed with, but this was all put in place long before I was part of the world. As you've already discovered, it's not in the best interest of humans to interact with Daelighters. It's dangerous, but part of the treaty states that we must mingle our two people. This was the compromise. We rent to those who will not ask too many questions, who will obey the rules, rules which are in place to keep them safe. We've never had an issue with this until Emma moved in. She's not a fan of rules."

Something else I had in common with my fellow secret keeper.

"You're trying to tell me that part of the reason you treat humans like shit is because you're protecting them...?"

Daniel shrugged. "Sounds bad when you put it like that."

I snorted, amused despite my irritation. "It's bad, whatever way you put it. But..." Now it was my turn to choose my words carefully. "But ... I do sort of understand. Most of the time, I feel like I'm way out of my league, living in a dream world. Once you get a taste for that sort of life, it's hard to walk away."

Daniel acknowledged this with a nod. "There have been cases of addiction," he confirmed. "The energy within us is attractive to humans. Some of my fellow Imperials have had to be reprimanded about overstepping boundaries with human girls. Obsession can get ugly fast."

He wasn't kidding. "Would that happen to me?" I asked, suddenly wondering if that might explain my *thing* with Daniel.

"No," he said without pause. "You're not a normal human. You can hold your own with us."

Well ... relief on one hand, but on the other ... still feeling a little obsessed and no explanation for it. Turning back to the mansion side, I had to shake my head at the sheer opulence. Did these aliens understand the meaning of overkill?

"Are you all rich?" I asked with a sigh. Logically, I knew money wasn't everything, but did they have to have money, amazing looks, height, intelligence, cool light transporters, everlasting life...? Come on, share the gifts, people ... aliens.

"In terms of human currency, then yes, all Daelighters have millions. The overlord families have billions. We could literally buy the human world, which is something your leaders do not realize. We have investments and interests in almost every industry. We hide them within shell corporations."

I blinked a few times at him. Not only did he just say *billions*, which was a number too big for me to contemplate, he was also sharing the sort of information that Daelighters would no doubt kill to keep.

"You trust me?" I blurted. For the first time, I wondered if this pull I felt to Daniel went two ways. Did he think of me as more than just a burden he'd been stuck with? A forced friend?

Daniel captured my hand, pulling me to a stop. I stumbled into him, our bodies pressing close, and I almost closed my eyes at the delicious warmth seeping into me. When I realized he was speaking, I forced myself to pay attention.

"I do trust you. I can feel your intentions through our bond." *Say what?* I didn't know he could do that; I certainly didn't feel his intentions or emotions coming back. But maybe that was a good thing. I was pretty new to this "feelings" thing and was barely handling my own.

"I won't lie to you about anything," he continued. "I hope that even when we've reached the point of being able to be separated for long periods of time, you'll still always rely on me ... come to me when you need someone in your corner. We're going to be tied together forever." He paused, and I held my breath waiting for his next words. I needed to hear them. "We're still getting to know each other, but ... I've been alone most of my life, never able to rely on another Daelighter. It feels a lot like fate that *this* bond fell in my lap."

My chest was really tight; we had grown up so similarly. Always alone. Always searching for something. "You can rely on me, Daniel. You can trust me."

As soon as the words left my lips, I felt the real truth behind them. Daniel had done everything to prove he was an honorable being, and I would make sure I lived up to that in my actions with him. His thumb brushed my cheek and my body trembled. He broke contact with me, almost roughly, before he turned to walk again. But he kept hold of my hand.

As we passed another beautiful mansion, I caught a glimpse of towering white turrets through gaps in the fence. "That's where Lexen and his family live," Daniel said. "My house is next door."

Next door turned out to be like a block away, but technically he was right. Daniel's fence was at least twenty feet tall, shiny and reflective, no way to see in at all. He keyed in a code to a small pad by the entrance and the gate swung silently in.

"Whoa," I whispered, completely enthralled by my first glimpse of his home. Daniel pulled me through, because I was too busy gawking to walk.

"It's one of my favorite places in both worlds," he said quietly. "I had it built when Laous decreed that all overlord minors had to spend a two-year term at the school here."

"They must have built it quick," I said breathlessly. "Seriously, it's amazing."

I was catching more glimpses of his house through the trees, the full picture getting clearer as we walked closer. It was a log cabin. Well, cabin was a vast understatement, but I couldn't think of another word. Two or three stories high, with dark timber panels and wide wraparound decks on the lower and upper levels. Surrounding it was a forest worthy of a fairy tale: tall trees and a trickling creek. It was perfect. I was instantly in love with this cabin in the woods.

"I dreamed of owning a home one day," I told him breathlessly. "A place which was just mine. Didn't have to be huge, as long as I could put my own touches on it. Make it feel homey." And there I went, over-sharing again. Before he could say anything, I segued to a random question: "How many Daelighters live here on Earth?"

He paused on the front porch, just before the main huge, wood door. "A few hundred thousand live out in your world." I was surprised; I would have expected far less. "And about a hundred live here on this street. Daelight is generally reserved for those attending the school here. Or those wanting to slowly transition to Earth within a safe, controlled environment. Overlord families have their own territories here, and the rest share all the mansions near the back of this street. Keeping to their respective houses, of course."

He released my hand, opened the wide door with a click, and then let me step inside first. Part of me mourned the loss of his touch. It was getting harder and harder for me to remember that we were just friends. My "newness" to this emotions thing had to be the reason. Surely this was too soon to care so much?

The cabin interior did distract me nicely though; it was as opulent and stunning as outside. It held a rustic charm, but the kind of rustic charm only a billionaire could afford. There was a lot of wood, broken up with accents of slate and tile and brick – of the old red and whitewashed variety. There were wide beams across the ceiling, open rafters, and so much charm.

Everything on this floor centered around a fireplace; barn doors led to a kitchen. "Can I live here forever?" I asked, jokingly.

Daniel didn't laugh as I expected. He nodded. "What's mine is yours. You don't even have to ask. We have a bonded soul. My houses and money are nothing in comparison."

I coughed, trying to figure out which of my emotions was strongest right then. Confusion, elation, fear ... and something thick and warm which was wrapping around my heart.

I decided to share something of myself with him. Because he had shared so much with me. "Until recently, I was very alone." I didn't look at him, because I was nervous. "I shut my emotions down and never felt anything. It just seemed easier than hoping for a different life." My mom's haggard face flashed across my mind, and the familiar pain I associated with her flared with it. My voice was rougher now. "Life was just about running and training. Fighting was my only escape

... until we moved to NOLA." I sucked in a deep breath. "That city ... it set me alight. It made me feel. The music touched my soul. The people filled my heart. I haven't been able to shut myself down since. And almost dying only made it worse. My world before all of this was very black and white, maybe some gray at times, but it was always dull." My voice was shaking, and for the first time in years, I was going to cry. "You brought colors and life to my world. You made me realize that if I had died at Laous' hands, then I would never have lived at all. I wasted the first eighteen years. I won't waste the rest." Hot tears slid down my cheeks, and I choked on the last words, letting my head fall forward. Gravity stole my tears, pulling them down to land on the polished wood at my feet.

Movement had me lifting my head slowly, and my breath fled in a huff when I realized Daniel was standing right in front of me. His expression was fierce but somehow tender. He raised his hand and tilted my chin up with one finger, his other palm cupping my face as our gazes remained locked. My lungs were screaming at me, but I couldn't make myself suck in any air, lest I break this moment.

Something had changed between us, a fundamental shift. I suddenly couldn't wait to see what he did next.

"You'll never be alone again, Callie," he told me. It was a promise, I felt that in every word. "Your mom didn't deserve the bright, smart, funny girl she got. But I won't make the same mistake with the woman who fell into my life."

I wanted to kiss him. The urge came at me so hard that I actually rocked toward him. His arms wrapped around me and I sank into the hug. It was the perfect thing in that moment, drying up the tears and sadness in my heart. Sure, no kiss, but that was okay.

In truth, we were going to be in each other's lives for

hundreds of years ... or more. There was a real chance that a romantic relationship could lead to hurt feelings and resentment. In that case, logically, we were better off staying friends.

If I kept telling myself that, maybe one day I'd believe it.

After that, things felt lighter between us. Daniel led me up to the second level of his home, explaining the artwork on the walls as we passed. He was a big fan of industrial era paintings, teamed with lots of handmade metal work. Outside of the multiple art pieces, there were three open doors on this level, each of them leading into a huge bedroom.

When we finally reached Daniel's room, it took up almost half the entire floor. My shoes squished into the thick rugs draped over wood floors as he led me into a large walk-in closet. It took him about five seconds to pull out a sweater for me; it was thick, warm, and dark gray. I had to roll up the sleeves multiple times, but otherwise it was so comfortable I could have snuggled into it and gone to sleep.

And that had nothing to do with the fact that it smelled like dark spice and wood-fire, just like Daniel. Absolutely nothing.

Back downstairs, we stopped in the kitchen, so Daniel could grab us some food. He whipped up a few grilled cheese sandwiches. "It's my go-to breakfast," he said, putting the plate in front of me.

I practically snatched it up. "My favorite," I moaned, already anticipating the cheesy goodness melting in my mouth.

Just as I took my first bite, he placed a newly-filled mug of coffee down for me. I was starting to think I was becoming more than a little addicted to having Daniel in my life. Seriously.

"How do you know the way I like my coffee?" I asked between mouthfuls.

He took the seat next to me at the kitchen bench, his own plate full. "I remembered from New Orleans," he said simply.

He started to eat, and I just stared at him. He remembered that? Remembered and made sure he brought it just the way I liked it. Daniel was too good to be true. I was starting to worry that one day, when my soul was strong enough to be without him, I would find that another part of me couldn't be separated from him.

My heart.

8

———

*A*fter breakfast he led me down into his underground garage. This was the only section of his house, so far, which wasn't "rustic billionaire." Under here it was all chrome and stainless steel, every inch shiny, including the twenty or more cars he had.

"Let me guess, you're a bit of a fan of motor vehicles?" I asked drily, staring at the gleaming machines filling the space.

Daniel grinned, running his hand across the smooth lines of a dark purple Mustang. It was one of those old school ones, '69 Fastback, I was pretty sure. I wasn't a big fan of classic cars, I liked mine modern and sleek. He had a few of those scattered about too. I saw an Audi R8, a Rolls Royce, and a lime green Lamborghini Aventador ... which was one of my favorite cars.

"Everyone needs a hobby, right?" He patted the car one more time. "Cars are one of the best things about Earth. We don't have them back in Overworld, so here I indulge my love."

Another thing we had in common. "Can I choose?" I asked, unable to hide the anticipation in my voice.

Daniel's grin grew, and my legs got a little shaky as he

crowded closer, pressing me back into the Rolls Ghost behind us. My body ached, lifting of its own accord to push against his. He was killing me here – I had just found my ultimate aphrodisiac, Daniel surrounded by expensive cars.

"You like cars?" he asked, and I swear he dipped his head low then, brushing his face close to mine, like he was breathing me in. By the time my eyes fluttered open again, though, he was back to where he had been standing before, inches of space between us.

I tried to find some oxygen, but I couldn't seem to fill my lungs. "Yes," I choked out. "The faster and more modern the better."

This time I didn't miss the movement. He cupped my face, tilting my head back so we could lock eyes. "You, Earthling, were definitely put in my path to tempt me," he murmured, a bite to his tone as a flash of darkness turned the cinnamon of his eyes murky.

He let me go then, turning away, and I sucked in some deep breaths, filling my starving lungs. Daniel was such an enigma. There were two sides to everything he did, and I was starting to crave both of them. His kind side nurtured my soul, and when he turned hard, it made my body burn. I never feared him, mostly because there was a control he carried at all times, and he rarely directed his anger at me.

Fact of the matter: I had always liked my guys rough around the edges.

I might actually need therapy.

Recovered, I walked to where he stood in the center of the huge garage. He lifted both hands out on either side of him, palms up. "Pick your poison."

"That one." I pointed, no hesitation in my tone.

He briefly rested his gaze on the gun-metal gray Audi R8

and gave a nod. It wasn't my favorite of the cars in here, but it was the one that fit my mood today. Daniel was happy enough with the choice, if the look on his face was any indication. The doors opened smoothly, and I couldn't help but sigh as I slid in, the leather bucket seat wrapping around me. The interior was a stark white, with dark gray accents.

Growing up on a limited income, I obviously had never sat in a car like this before, but I had seen all the pictures. Pressed my face to the showroom windows. None of that compared to this moment. There was no way to truly understand the feel and smell and opulence of the car until you experienced it.

"The 5.2L V10?" I said in a rush. Daniel, now in the driver's seat, turned his head lazily in my direction. His eyes were very dark again.

"You know your cars," he finally said, hitting the button to start the powerful engine.

As it roared to life, vibrations ran though my body and I had to stifle the moan that wanted to escape. Best. Day. Ever!

"If you let me drive it, I will be the best soul-sharer you've ever been attached to. Promise."

Daniel didn't even hesitate. "You can take the cars out whenever you want."

I fought against my sudden instinct to climb out of my bucket seat and into his, and not because I wanted to drive.

Daniel backed out, heading toward the triple set of garage doors that guarded his precious cargo down here. I buckled my seatbelt and sank back to enjoy the ride. I'd never actually lived in this part of the Pacific Northwest, so it was interesting for me to take in the scenery as we drove. We took a road along the ocean, and I loved that as far as I could see was water. I pressed my face to the car window, before jumping back as it started to lower. I flashed Daniel a smile and then arched my neck so I was just hanging out of the car. I breathed in the salty air, letting the coolness whip across my face, invigorating me.

Turning to Daniel, I knew there was a beaming smile on my face; my cheeks were actually hurting. "Can we drive this way home?"

"We can go any way you want. I've missed quite a lot of school recently, so my appearances are mandatory for some time, but once I clock in some human hours, I'll have more freedom. I'll take you wherever you want to go in the world."

I had to shake my head. I'd never had a person in my life who actually cared about what I wanted, who cared enough to try to make me happy. It was messing with my brain.

Twisting in my seat, I actually turned my back on the water so I could see him better. "How does it work, you being over-lord major but not being in House of Imperial to keep it running?" He was a king, of sorts. Surely he didn't really have the time to take me anywhere in the world.

Daniel shot me glances between focusing on the road. "As long as I make frequent trips to House of Imperial, the rest of the day to day running is done by other members of my house." He turned a corner then, away from the ocean. "At the moment we're in a transition period. Laous caused a lot of problems, and there is anger and resentment going around. I want to be with my people as much as I can, bring us back together as a house, but I also have to make these trips to Earth. The balance is getting harder to maintain."

"Does someone keep you updated?" I asked.

"I keep track of it via the network."

This network thing was hard for me to comprehend, so I was mentally picturing it as a cell phone with internet access. "Will you explain this network to me one day?"

Daniel chuckled. "It's difficult to explain without experiencing it. But one day we can try."

Good enough for me.

We arrived at the school far too quickly for my liking. I felt comfortable, safe, in my bubble with Daniel, but the sight of hundreds of uniformed students streaming into the school was enough to jolt me right out of it. The concept of going to school was something I had accepted. I needed to be around Daniel, and he had to go to school. Made sense that I would go too. But now that we were sitting here in a parking lot, so similar to the many I'd seen in teen drama shows, the reality was hitting me hard.

Just as Daniel went to open his door, I reached out and grabbed his forearm. "I have never been to school," I blurted out quickly. "Like ... in my entire life. And I'm also ... stupid or something. I can't read. Words are a jumble. My mom said I was born stupid. I guess she wasn't wrong, because it has never gotten easier, not even when I worked my ass off to get better." I forced my words to slow down, because they were a jumble. "I ... I just don't want to embarrass you."

Admitting that was difficult for me. But I trusted Daniel not to use my weaknesses against me. Which was never a trust I had with my mom. If she knew I was sensitive about something, that was the very thing she used to hurt me when I didn't conform. Or just because she felt like it.

Daniel made a derisive sound before shaking his head. "You're not stupid. I don't need a textbook to tell me that. Nothing you do will embarrass me or House of Imperial." His voice got low then as he leaned in closer. "You could parade through here, naked, singing the national anthem, and I wouldn't give a shit."

I laughed, still feeling like a moron, despite his words. "Right ... naked? Really?"

He let out a rumble, before he sighed. "You got me there. But not because I'm going to be embarrassed. Human males don't always show the respect that they should. Especially teenagers."

"You're not a teenager?" I asked, wondering exactly how old he was.

He wore an amused look then. "Haven't been a teenager for a long time. In human years, I'm probably sixty years old. But in Daelighter years, I'm the equivalent of ... a twenty-year-old, I would guess. Hard to tell with the way we age."

This was too much to deal with on top of going to school, so I let that vague explanation go. Realizing I was still holding Daniel's arm, I released it and sucked in a deep breath. *You can do this, Callie.* I really did want to try school. This would be the last chance I ever had. Technically, I should have graduated already. I'd turned eighteen in June, but no one here knew that.

"Let's do this," I said, opening the door and pulling myself up and out of the low-slung car.

Daniel was at my side in an instant. With a shake of my head, I had to wonder how these Daelighters managed to keep their secret. They shed their human façade far too often to hide their otherness. It was lucky for them that most humans didn't notice what was going on outside of their own little worlds.

As we stepped up to the path, I stared at the school. The parking lot might be exactly like the movies, but the building itself was nothing like I expected. No boxy brick building, it was all steel and glass, with a bulbous center and sleek lines along each side ... like arterials leading off the main hub.

This had Daelighter technology written all over it. "This school is the territory of your people, right?" I lifted my head, so my murmur could only be heard by Daniel.

He nodded, leading me up onto the path and past a center statue of four imposing men. "When we first crossed from Overworld, we ended up in Astoria. This town has been our center point ever since. Its close proximity to home and the transporter is useful for those of us having to making the trip across frequently. The school, Starslight Prep, was put here for the families who decided to raise their children on Earth. They needed a safe education institute, a place they could control."

I still couldn't believe these aliens had been here with humans for well over a hundred years. It made me wonder how many other beings might be here on Earth, too, blending in, biding their time. The Daelighters were, for the most part, peaceful, but knowing they controlled a lot of the global money ... it was scary to think of ... that power. If they ever turned on humans, we wouldn't stand a chance. I guess that's exactly what Laous had done, and one rogue Daelighter could do a lot of damage apparently.

Inside the main building I was getting an airport, space station vibe. Lots of metal, moving sidewalks, high windows, and security. I noted all of the cameras, because that was something I was trained to do. Always figure out who was watching. More training from my mom.

Thinking about my life with her brought up the long-suppressed feelings of hurt, but knowing she was out there right now possibly being tortured ... or worse ... dead, was too much on top of everything else. My breath sucked in and out harshly as mild panic took me over.

"What is it?" Daniel asked, gently gripping my biceps as he pulled me closer and away from the gawking crowds.

Yeah, I noticed all of the students staring at us. The hall was full of open mouths and wide eyes. Most of them were looking at Daniel and then me, wondering who this strange girl with him was.

"Callie!" There was more urgency in his tone and I snapped my attention back to him.

My voice was monotonous, only a twinge of my upset showing. "My mom is being held prisoner somewhere, or dead ... who knows ... and I'm just here going to school, acting like life is normal..."

Some of the tension eased out of his broad shoulders; his expression softened, thick lashes partially obscuring his eyes as he took a deep breath. It looked like he was trying to get himself under control, and I realized that I'd really scared him. Probably should have been more circumspect in my random freaking out when there was a psycho on the loose.

"The council assured me that they're doing everything they can to find Laous." He didn't remove his hands. "Until we have some leads, there's no way to track your mom down. But the second we know something..."

My return whisper was laced with sorrow. "He has no more need for her, right? He got what he wanted from me. She was only leverage for that. We're kidding ourselves to think that she's still alive."

He released me, and then in the same instant wrapped his arms around me. The gasps that filled the entrance to the school were loud. Whispers started after that. *Who's the new chick? Another one stealing a founding son.*

Founding son? Really? Were they referring to the fact that the four houses founded the school? Was that actually a thing here?

"I don't know if your mom is still alive, Callie," Daniel said close to my ear, his body so warm and firm against mine. "But we won't stop searching until we figure out what happened to her."

I heard his assurance, but was distracted because ... I was being hugged by Daniel. Again. This time it was unlike any hug I'd ever had. He was wrapping me up tightly, holding all of my broken pieces together. My eyes burned as I pressed my face into his soft shirt. I never wanted to leave his strong arms. I wanted to stay there, warm and safe and hidden from the world.

And not alone.

That's all I ever wanted from life. To not be alone.

Eventually, I had to pull away. The whispers were out of control, it kind of felt like everyone was standing in a circle around us. They dispersed as soon as Daniel narrowed his eyes on the groups nearby, and then he nudged me forward, toward a double set of sliding doors.

"We'll talk more about it later," he said. "For now, let's get you enrolled."

My heart was still racing like crazy, so I worked to control my breathing as we entered the office.

"Daniel Imperial, how are you doing, sweetheart?"

That overly chirpy voice belonged to a blond woman. She was impeccably styled, not a hair out of place in her tight chignon. She had a lot of makeup on, which didn't disguise the fact that she was in her forties. Forty but trying to look twenty was exactly how I'd describe her.

Her heavily made-up eyes were locked on Daniel, and I was pretty sure she'd just licked her lips. Seriously ... she could be his mother. Or probably not, since in human years Daniel was older than her, but she didn't know that, so my point remained. Crossing my arms over my chest, I leveled my very best resting-bitch-face on her.

Daniel either didn't notice or didn't care. And he was far too polite. "Good morning, I have a new student to enroll today, Callie Channing. All of the paperwork should have been sent through last night."

Blondie made a disparaging noise, her watery blue eyes locking on me. "Callie, is it?"

Before I could nod, or flip her off, which is what I wanted to do, she dropped her eyes to the computer in front of her and started to type. It seemed to take her an extraordinarily long amount of time to find my file, but eventually she figured it out and set me up in the system.

While she explained my class schedule, she continued to stare at Daniel.

Eventually I had to clear my throat. Loudly.

"I'm sorry?" she said, blinking and finally turning in my direction.

"You're talking to me, right?" I was all fake politeness. If I'd been Southern, I'd have said "bless your heart" to her multiple times already. "Daniel already knows his classes, so there's no need to tell him."

She blinked a few more exaggerated times, and if her forehead could move, it would have been wrinkled in shock. "I'm sorry..." she spluttered out once more.

I took a step closer, leaning over the bench so that our faces were only a few inches apart. But before I could give her a piece of my mind – subtle just wasn't me – Daniel wrapped one arm around my waist, picked me up, and dropped me behind him. He then grabbed up the paperwork the cougar had been waving around before directing me out of the office.

Laughing eyes met mine, and I was relieved that he didn't look too upset. "Come on," he said with a smirk. "Let's get your uniform."

My annoyance dissipated quickly, and I hurried after him. The uniform turned out to be some sort of torture device with skirts and tights and a fitted shirt. They even made me remove my Converse for these shiny, slippery, uncomfortable shoes.

Just as I was stepping out of the seamstress' room, a familiar face skidded around the corner.

"Callie!" Emma shrieked. "You made it."

She hugged me, and this time it almost felt natural. I even returned her gesture without having to think too much about it. Before I could offer a greeting or anything, she had my arm and was already turning to Daniel. "We'll be back in a minute. Watch our stuff, okay?"

She started to drag me, and before I knew it, we were in a nearby bathroom.

9

This room looked exactly like the movies, starkly white, tiled, with a row of stalls and a row of sinks. Emma flashed me a huge grin and I chuckled at how mischievous her expression was. She then turned to stare at the closed door. "Three ... two ... one..."

Bang, bang, bang.

"Emma, get your scrawny butt out here. Callie needs to get to class." Daniel sounded annoyed but not angry.

"Give us a minute, this is girl stuff, Dan," Emma shouted back, rolling her eyes at me. "These Daelighter dudes are so predictable. I hoped that this was the one place I might get a second alone with you. But even being a girl's bathroom, it won't keep them out for long."

The door swung open then and I almost expected Daniel to stroll right in, but it wasn't him. A stunning, dark-haired girl stood in the doorway. She looked somewhat familiar to me, but I couldn't figure out where I knew her from. Anyone that beautiful was going to stick in my mind, but ... I really couldn't remember where I'd seen her before. Maybe she was from a television show or something.

"Star!" Emma waved her over. "Come and meet Callie. She's the second secret..." She trailed off then, clearly realizing we weren't exactly in a private place.

From what I could see, all the stalls were empty. "I think we have the room to ourselves," I said.

Star quickly checked and said, "Yep, all clear." She then stepped over to me, the sweetest smile on her face. "It's so nice to meet you, Callie. I'm Star Darken, Lexen's sister."

Ah, well, that explained the supermodel good looks and familiarity. Now that she'd mentioned her family, I could see she had the same shaped eyes and nose as her broody brother. But she was definitely not of the broody variety. If anything, she seemed unnaturally nice and friendly.

Emma quickly pulled me toward the sinks. "We need to hurry. As I said, our guys aren't going to leave us alone for long. Until Laous is caught, we're under strict guard." She really didn't sound too upset by that. "But I figured you wouldn't have any makeup or the essentials, being stuck in Imperial with Daniel, so Star and I brought you some supplies."

For a moment I wondered if I'd heard right. Star pulled a small purple bag out of her expensive leather satchel and handed it to me. It was a half-moon shape, with a zipper right across the top. Swallowing the lump in my throat, I opened it. *Whoa.* They had packed in a veritable beauty shop, enough makeup and supplies to last me months. Or years. I had very little experience with beauty products, except when I'd managed to steal some of my mom's.

Blinking rapidly, I stared down at the bag longer than was really necessary in an attempt to get my emotions under control. Finally, I was able to say without my voice breaking: "Thank you, this was really thoughtful of you both."

"You really don't need much makeup," Star said, and my head shot up to find her examining me closely.

It was clear that she was very into this sort of thing. Her eyes were lined, sparkly shadow above her gorgeous blue irises. She wore the uniform, but it was all fancied up, with a scarf, and pins, and a ton of other adjustments.

"But every girl likes a little battle armor, right?" she said.

Emma grimaced. "I don't wear much either, but ever since Lexen and I started hanging out in school, it's been nasty-bitch central around here. So now I always put mascara and eyeliner on. Stupidly enough, they make me feel more confident." She met my gaze and said, "They will try and undermine your confidence. Don't let them get in your head."

Looking between the two of them, my heart felt like it was about to literally burst from my chest. This feeling ... the warmth and kindness and caring, I wasn't sure I knew how to process it.

"I'm pretty good with keeping my fight-face on," I replied huskily. "But thanks for the warning. If you two get into any trouble, let me know. I've got your back."

My tiny, secluded world was suddenly filled with so many people. I was going to have to work triple time to make sure they were all safe. They both beamed smiles at me, and I wondered if maybe I could actually do this friend thing. Like ... it seemed easy enough – be nice, care about them, and don't treat them the way my mom treated me. Simple rules worked best for me. I didn't like to complicate life with too much else.

I wasn't an idiot. I knew we all had human feelings ... except for Star, but from what I'd seen, Daelighter emotions worked similarly. Emotions did confuse things, but if I stuck to my core three rules, then everything should be okay.

The bell rang then, and I wondered how we'd managed to keep this bathroom to ourselves for so long. Quickly rifling through the makeup bag, I pulled out mascara and eyeliner, as well as a pale pink lip gloss and some pressed powder.

"My mom loved makeup," I said, placing those items on the sink. "I have never owned my own, but I would sneak hers on occasion. Most of my attempts resembled a clown face."

"Do you need some help?" Star asked.

Gripping the sink with my free hand, I nodded jerkily. "Yes, thank you."

In an instant my face was being held in one of her hands, the eyeliner in the other. I just closed my eyes and let her do her thing; it really didn't matter what I looked like. No one here cared. In what felt like thirty seconds, she was done.

"Perfect," Emma exclaimed, clapping her hands.

Turning to the mirror, I tilted my head to the side and assessed the face staring back. "I have eyelash envy," Emma admitted, fluttering her own dark lashes at me.

My lashes did look insanely long and thick with the mascara. The gray of my eyes was stormy against the thin line of kohl, and my lips were all shiny. Whatever blemishes my skin might have had were gone now, covered in a thin sheen of powder. It was all subtle enough that it wasn't even obvious I wore makeup; I just looked more polished.

It made me feel ... not like me, but I understood this battle armor thing, so I would just suck it up and enjoy the pampering.

"Is it okay?" Star sounded unsure, her gaze flicking to Emma for a moment. I wondered then if maybe she was really new to this whole friend thing too.

"It's perfect," I said, placing my hand on hers. "Thank you so much."

Emma straightened, helping me throw all of my makeup back in the bag, which she then stashed in her backpack.

"I'll give it to you later to take home," she said, before turning to leave the room. "Come on," she called, "I can feel Lexen pacing outside." There was laughter in her voice; she clearly knew her guy well.

When she pulled the door open, we were met with a wall of muscles. Literally. Two broad backs covered the doorway and I now understood how we'd managed to hog the entire bathroom. Lexen and Daniel had stood guard, stopping anyone from entering.

Looking at the pair of them – tougher and more menacing than any human men I'd ever seen – I doubted they'd had much trouble from the locals. They used pure intimidation to get what they wanted, no need for words.

As we stepped out, Lexen only had eyes for Emma. She smiled cheekily at him. "Thanks, babe. Appreciate the assist."

He shook his head. "One game of basketball and suddenly you're a sports expert."

Emma huffed. "One game where I didn't fall down or injure myself. Pretty sure that makes me an expert. In anyone's definition."

She threw me an annoyed look. "I'm completely athletically challenged. Lexen keeps making me run, and throw stupid things—"

"Like a ball," he interrupted drily.

She snorted. "Right, like his balls."

Star let out a groan, and everyone else just shook their heads. Me, on the other hand, I was loving it. They were couple goals. The realization that I wanted what they had hit me hard. I'd never thought that love and family and children were in my future. I expected my life would be empty, but I'd always held out a secret hope for more. That's the reason I stopped the casual sex. I was tired of being empty.

My cup runneth over. I prayed then, harder than I ever had before, that I would never go back to my old life. That if ... *when* ... we found my mom safe and sound, she would be happy to let me go. Both of us free, finally.

My eyes shifted to Daniel before I could stop them. He was staring at me in a way that made it difficult for me to breathe. I wondered what he thought about my makeup. I hoped he didn't think I'd "prettied myself up" for him. If I ever found myself in a position like Lexen and Emma, I would want to be loved for my natural self. With all of my flaws. I mean, he could love me in makeup, too, but the natural thing was non-negotiable. It would be way too tiring to try to look perfect every single day.

So the makeup was not for Daniel, it was for me. Because Star was right, sometimes a girl just needed some battle armor.

"Looks like Star got to you." He sounded amused.

I shrugged. "Apparently school is akin to a warzone. You have to go in with your camo on or you'll be shot dead instantly."

He just shook his head. "You looked just as beautiful before you walked into the bathroom."

My brain stopped working when he called me beautiful, so if he said anything else it was just a jumble. The bell rang again, startling me. I quickly brushed down my uniform and tried to mentally prepare. It was time for class.

"Come on, you're in math with me and Lexen this morning," Emma said, reaching out to link our arms together.

"These guys don't use books or anything. They're already old and smart enough. But you can share mine, because there's no time for you to stop by your locker."

I tilted my head toward Daniel. "Do I have a locker?"

"Yeah," he nodded. "But you can just use mine. It's easier to access and there's nothing in there anyway."

I narrowed my eyes on him. "Bitch face in the office put me in the furthest locker she could find, didn't she?"

Emma snorted. "Blond and mean, right? Bitch face is the perfect description."

I turned to see her grimacing expression. "Oh yeah, cougar-bitch. She appears to have a thing for Dae—"

Star cut me off with a squeak when she tripped, which was probably a good thing. I'd almost – stupidly – said Daelighters out loud. Lexen moved super-fast, catching his sister before she hit the ground. There was a scuffle behind, and when I spun around I found Daniel holding another guy up against the wall, his forearm lodged in the stranger's throat.

"I will not tolerate that bullshit in my house any longer," Daniel snarled, and it almost looked like the marks on his head had started to glow, swirling red.

It was also getting really hot in the hall.

"What happened?" I whispered to Emma.

She tightened her hold on me. "That's a member of Daniel's house." I guessed as much from his shaved head and attitude problem. "I think he pushed Star. Imperial and Darken do not get along, not at all."

And yet Lexen and Daniel were best of friends. I was really glad that was the case, because I already thought of Emma and Star as friends. The guy against the wall was starting to turn purple. A pretty color, except it probably meant he was dying. Pulling away from Emma, I crossed to Daniel, moving cautiously when I got close. He was giving me "wild beast" vibes.

"Dan," I said slowly, hoping to draw his attention.

Lexen moved to stand on the opposite side to me, close enough to intervene if he needed to. He seemed content to let this play out, though. Clearly it wasn't a done thing to step in on another overlord while he was dealing with his people. But I didn't want Daniel to kill anyone today.

"Daniel," I said more firmly.

His head snapped to the side and swirling eyes locked on me. "This is not exactly discreet," I murmured. "You've made your point. Can't you deal with him back home ... later?"

The word *home* slipped out before I could stop it, and even though it was stupid for me to think of a place I'd only spent a few sporadic days in as home, it was the truth. I had bonded to the land of Imperial. To Daniel. My body had adjusted to that fact long before my mind.

With a final rumble of anger, Daniel jerked his arm down, letting the Imperial fall in a heap to the floor. He scrambled up quickly, letting out a groan as he wrapped his hand across his throat. Hatred burned from dark eyes as he snarled at Daniel. "You won't have followers for long. Laous knew what was right – he would never have tied a human to our world."

The hatred was directed at me, but I didn't flinch. No need to be scared when I had an Imperial and Darken bodyguard on either side of me.

"And on top of that, now you're hanging around the Darkens?" This time the accusation was said in a shout. "No one will stand for this! You're not going to be the overlord for much longer."

He stormed away then, pushing through crowds of students, scattering them across the hall.

Calming myself using my favorite breathing techniques, I waited for someone to speak.

Lexen finally did: "We knew there was going to be fallout from this, but I still believe the time is right for us to show unity between our houses. They will get used to it."

Daniel didn't disagree, but his hard gaze remained on the end of the hall where the angry Imperial Daelighter had disappeared.

"Xander and Chase are supposed to meet us at lunch," Emma said, sounding unsure. "Should we maybe take it slower than that? I don't want to be at war by last class."

Lexen wrapped her up in his arms. "It's going to be fine. This is the best course for the future. Daniel's house was always going to be the hardest. Laous left him a real mess."

"Lexen's right." Daniel words were clipped. "I have let this go on too long. Imperial will fall into line or I will make them." Before I could blink, his arm wrapped around me and I was pulled closer to his side. "You're with me this morning. I wouldn't put it past any of them to try and punish me by hurting you."

I shook his arm off, needing to maintain my independence. "I accept that I'm batting out of my league here, but you don't have to throw me around like a caveman."

Emma laughed. It was such an unexpected sound that whatever tension was riding our group dissipated. A semblance of a smile even quirked up the edges of Daniel's lips.

"I adore you already," Emma said, between chuckles. "Let's hope the last two secret keepers fit in just as well."

Lexen cupped her face, his lips pressing to hers. "I love your happiness," I heard him murmur, "but I don't want you to be disappointed if the four secret keepers don't end up as one big happy family."

Emma looked a little drunk when he stepped back. Lexen's hands slowly left her face, sliding down her body to capture her hands.

She recovered enough to say, "I might read a lot of fantasy books, but I know how to live in reality as well. My hopes aren't that high." She paused and tilted her head to the side. "Still ... it's hard to deny that there's something fate-like at play here. For the first time in your history, we have four overlords who are friends. Best friends. Brothers in arms from a young age. The four secret keepers are tied to each other as well, and to each of the houses they were born in, and therefore tying themselves to the overlords. Your dragon soul..." Her voice got very low. "Chose me as a mate. Daniel tied his soul to Callie's without even knowing her, just because he couldn't let her die. We're all soulmates or soul bound, whatever you want to call it. The council said the last two secret keepers are female, and I also believe that somehow Xander and Chase will end up ... connected ... to the girls born in their houses. It's fate."

I expected Daniel and Lexen to laugh and dismiss this perfect world she was painting, but the pair exchanged a glance and I was startled by the fact that they seemed to be seriously considering her theory. Was she on to something? Was there any possibility that I had been tied to Daniel long before Laous' attempt to kill me? Was that why I'd just accepted this bond so readily? I'd thought it was because I craved the feeling of having someone in my life, someone at my back. But could it go even deeper than that?

"And," Star chimed in, "don't forget that this is the first time in a long time that the overlord minors are all male." Her voice had the same awestruck quality as Emma's. "It's very fate-like."

Emma gasped. "Exactly. This is just how I would play it if I were fate. How better to protect secret keepers than to tie them to powerful overlords." She clapped her hands together like it was all settled. When Lexen shook his head at her, she wrinkled her nose in his direction. "You'll see, I'm rarely wrong about these things. I've read too many books."

It sounded like he let out a low grumble then, and in a flash, his arms were around her. My heart skipped a beat as his lips crashed into Emma's, kissing her like he couldn't help himself.

I had to turn away, because one, it felt weird watching them, and two, I was a little envious of their perfect relationship. Emma didn't seem to care that her bond to Lexen might have been set up by fate. I guess she went with the theory that our path was predetermined, and that meant Lexen was always hers. Did that mean Daniel was mine?

I was fast coming to the realization that I would be more than okay if that was the truth.

Emma was very flushed when she finally removed herself from Lexen. The hallway was completely empty now. We were officially beyond late for class.

"I think we should all stick together today," Star said, and her suggestion seemed to return focus to the group.

No one disagreed, and I fell into a spot between Star and Emma. They led us to a moving walkway – which seemed weird for a school, but what did I know? When we reached the classroom door, Lexen made us stop, so he could go through first.

Daniel remained behind us, protecting the back.

"Overkill much?" I muttered, sort of wanting to laugh.

Emma groaned, pink still high in her cheeks. "This is nothing. We're literally going to have Daelighters all up in our business until this shit is resolved."

I gave her a side eye. "Seems to me you aren't averse to one particular Daelighter 'all up in your business.'" One side of her mouth pulled into a quirk as the pink darkened.

"You have no idea, Callie," she said quietly. "There's nothing in either world which could compare to being loved by Lexen."

I had no doubt. I'd seen it with my own two eyes.

As we filed in as a group, the teacher's expression didn't change, remaining somewhat pleasant. Lexen started toward a back corner, but Emma stopped him with a hand on his forearm. She gestured toward a blond girl and lanky, curly-haired guy, who were waving to her from the front row.

"I'm going to sit with Cara and Ben." I heard her murmur. "I haven't spent any time with them lately."

It looked like Lexen wanted to argue, but he just sucked in a deep breath and nodded. "Yes, it's better that we don't act out of character right now. Just ... don't leave the room without us, okay?"

He phrased it like a question, but I was pretty sure it was a command.

She returned his nod. "I promise."

"Do you want to meet my friends?" she asked me quietly as the other Daelighters started to move.

I hesitated before deciding I'd rather stay with Daniel. "Thanks, but I'll just stick with our group."

She squeezed my hand, before turning and hurrying over to the front where her friends were holding a desk for her. The rest of us took our seats, and I kept waiting for some sort of reprimand from the teacher, but she didn't say a word. Once we were all sitting, she just picked her lesson back up and continued on, like there had not been an interruption at all. *Well, okay, then.*

I followed enough of her lecture to know they were focusing on algebraic equations, but since I hadn't made it past eighth grade math with homeschooling, the finer concepts were gibberish to me. With math, I knew enough to work out my groceries and pay someone for a job.

My body remained in a semi-tense state as I waited to be singled out or called on to answer a question. But the teacher didn't say a word. In fact, she never asked a single question of the class; she just taught her lesson. Wrote everything on the white board. Handed out a few pieces of paper. Then dismissed us early.

As everyone filed out, I headed toward Emma. She was waiting by the door, her friends had already left the room. I had to ask: "Is this sort of class ... normal? Shouldn't she, I don't know, ask some questions? Check to see if everyone understands the work?"

Emma shook her head. "It's weird as hell. I've never even had homework. Or anything more than a little pop quiz. Most of the classes involve frank discussions about life, and then when you get to one like math, which is more technical, they just hit you straight up with the facts but never check to see you're actually learning it." She took a deep breath. "I'm getting used to it now, but honestly, I'm getting straight A's here, and I haven't even had a real exam." She swung her head around and glared at Lexen. "That's nothing to do with you, right?"

Her question was soft, but there was a ton of undercurrent there. Which Lexen definitely picked up on, if his somewhat amused expression was anything to go by. "Whatever grades you're getting have nothing to do with me. There will be exams closer to December, and then again before we graduate. But for the most part, you're getting the good grades because you participate. You take notes. You demonstrate your understanding throughout the class discussions. Teachers use their own judgment with that sort of thing."

She gave him an extra-long measured look, before nodding. "Another reason to love this school. That and the food."

My stomach growled then, despite the fact it hadn't been that long since breakfast.

"What time is lunch here?" I asked, suddenly starving.

"It's after the next class," Daniel said. "But if you need to eat now, we can go grab something. I've made my appearance today. They won't mark us off again until this afternoon."

Emma reached out, smacked him in the arm, and then yelped and shook her hand in the air. "I need to learn to never hit you overly muscled ali—" She cut herself off but continued to wave her hand.

Daniel smirked, and my eyes went to his dimple. Stupid perfect dimple. "Lexen needs to toughen you up," he said to Emma. "Got to keep your badass title." She flipped him off and he full-on laughed. "That's more like it."

Ignoring that, Emma turned to me. "You can't leave until we try this experiment with the four houses sitting together at lunch. We need to get that ball rolling."

I agreed with that. "No worries. I think I can last another class before expiring from hunger. I've never been a huge eater, but the last few days I feel like I'm starving all the time."

As I said that, I caught sight of Lexen and Daniel exchanging a look, and I let out a huge sigh. "What?"

"Your body is adjusting to the new bond," Daniel told me.

"It's using a lot of energy, especially while you're not in House of Imperial. You'll need to keep your food intake up. I should have thought of that and brought you some snacks."

Emma quickly grabbed her leather satchel, opened it, and pulled out two bars. "It's not much, but hopefully they help." She held them out to me and I shook my head.

"Wait, no, I can't take your food."

She laughed. "Don't even stress about it. I was hungry a lot before I met Lexen." She took a really deep breath and her eyes grew haunted, shadows dancing over her face. "My parents ... they were killed in a fire set by Laous. I had to move in with old family friends, and we never had much money." She hugged herself closer to the massive guy at her side. "But everything is different now. Firstly, Lexen feeds me all freaking day. And secondly, my guardians, Michael and Sara, work for House of Darken now. We have plenty of money and lots of food at home. It's great."

She went on to explain why her guardians used to move all the time, chasing rumors of Daelighters. But since they'd found out the truth – and almost died because of it – they were happy to give that lifestyle up. By the time she finished her story, I'd eaten the first bar, and we had arrived at the next class.

I knew that not all of us were supposed to be in art class, but again the teacher did not ask a single question when we filed in. It was becoming very clear who ran this school, and it definitely wasn't the humans.

I had no experience with art. Supplies were expensive, and my mom had never been interested. Today the class was on pottery, but it wasn't hands-on yet, just learning about the property of the clay, temperatures, movement to shape, setup of the kiln, and more information like that. It was much easier for me to follow than math, and I was surprised when the bell rang.

Nerves had my stomach jumping. It was lunchtime. We were about to try the great overlord minor experiment. Maybe we would start a riot. Or maybe, just maybe, this would be the beginning of something better for Overworld.

Change was coming no matter what. It was time to see which way the dice rolled.

10

———

The cafeteria was unbelievable, bigger, brighter, and more luxurious than I would have ever expected. There was a long buffet on the ground level, and the line of kids moving through it was almost mesmerizing. They had it down to a fine art, hundreds of students moving through and collecting food without any issue.

I started to head in that direction until I realized Lexen was leading us away from it, toward a set of stairs in the center of the room. Stairs that led up to the first level. As I stepped out onto this landing, my eyes got very wide. *Holy fancy pants.*

It was a six-star restaurant up here: black and white linen tablecloths, wine glasses, cutlery. There were no waiters I could see, but there was another long buffet. Their own private buffet.

"They call them the elites," Emma said to me. "The humans think all Daelighters are from the families of the "founding fathers," because their last names are the houses' names. There are about fifty of them in the school, and they all get special treatment."

"Your friends don't eat up here with you?" I asked, wondering if this new life she had with Lexen had caused issue for her.

Emma shook her head. "No, this is elite only." Her face screwed up, eyes sad. "It caused a lot of problems at first, with my human friends. The words "traitor" and "stuck-up-bitch" might have gotten thrown around a few times, but eventually we sorted it all out. I try and spend time with them in class, but they know Lex is my priority. Neither of them blames me, they both think he's hot as hell."

Lexan's lips twitched, but he refrained from saying anything.

We were not the first ones on the elite level. There were a few small groups already eating. It was immediately clear that they had split themselves into houses. In one corner they were almost all blond, tanned, and broad shouldered, just like Xander.

"House of Royale," Emma confirmed.

In the opposite corner were the brown-skinned, brown-haired individuals. High cheekbones and lots of pretty eyes were a common trait there. I mean, they had unique and individual looks, but you could tell they were from the same house.

"House of Leights," Emma said, following my line of sight.

Which left House of Imperial and House of Darken in their own respective corners. Imperials were glaring absolute daggers in my direction, and I realized that this was the first time I would come face to face with a group of Daniel's people.

Outside of passing through the egg room.

So far, it was going as well as expected.

My dreary thoughts were cut off as we arrived at the start of the buffet. I wiped at my mouth, just in case any drool escaped while I stared at the array of dishes artfully displayed in stainless steel trays. Normally I had simple tastes in food. As I'd told Daniel, grilled cheese was my favorite, but I was more than a little impressed with their selection here.

"Daelighters don't eat much meat," Emma told me. "But they make fruit and vegetables into the most delicious meals."

I shrugged. "I've never been a huge fan of meat. Especially red meat."

Her eyes widened. "Me neither. I think it's because we were born in Overworld."

Hmmm, that would make sense; we'd definitely taken on other traits from that world.

When it was my turn to walk down the line, I started to scoop food onto my plate. A creamy sundried tomato pasta, pumpkin and spice salad, fruit cup, and to finish it off, mashed potatoes with a creamy mushroom sauce.

I skipped most of the next dishes; my plate was pretty much full anyway, but right near the end I hesitated over the vegetarian pizza. Daniel, who was behind me in the line, laughed when I pouted. "You can come back if you finish what you have and want more. We'll stay here until you've had enough."

I blasted him with my brightest smile. It actually hurt my cheeks and made me realize how rarely I used to smile. I needed to work on that, finding the joy in the small things – once we dealt with Laous, and I found my mom. My smile faded away, and I wondered if I'd ever be able to just feel happy without guilt. I supposed that was pretty much life; happiness and guilt often went hand in hand.

Daniel and I were the first to finish filling our plates and took a seat at a large round table right in the center of the room. I had no idea who usually sat there, since territories were very clearly designated. The moment Lexen, Star, and Emma joined us, the entire floor went deadly silent. We ignored this, continuing to talk normally while eating the mouthwatering food.

It took a while, but eventually ninety percent of the Daelighters surrounding us went back to their conversations as well. A few of the Darkens even threw smiles in our direction and gave slow head nods to Lexen. The Imperials had the most attitude, especially when Xander and Chase joined us, but no one said anything outright.

"Well ... that went okay," Emma said after about twenty minutes. She looked between the four overlords. "Right?"

Xander, who had one eye on the blonds over in Royale's corner, shifted his body back toward her. "They're actually taking it quite well."

Daniel, who had hardly touched his food, more focused on the Daelighters around us, crossed his arms, leaning back in the chair. "Only time will tell," he said. "If there is any fallout, we won't know about it for some time. But at least this is a step in the right direction."

I agreed with him. It was time for this change. I just hoped their people were able to deal with it. I only had the potato mash left, having finished everything else on my plate. Scooping up a mouthful, it slid across my tongue and I let out a low groan. "Holy sweet heaven above ... this is amazing."

Amused expressions were directed at me, but I didn't care. They could laugh all they wanted; this was me enjoying the little things. When the bell rang fifteen minutes later, I could barely move, dreams of a food-nap playing in my head.

I perked up a little when Emma started to whine. "Seriously, why is gym class mandatory? Why? And right after lunch ... surely they could give us some time to digest our food."

Lexen, clearly used to her hatred of gym, just pressed a quick kiss to her lips. "We have a study period first. You'll have plenty of time to digest."

"Besides," Star piped up, "today is self-defense classes. You keep saying you want to learn how to defend yourself..."

Hell, yeah. "I love training in self-defense. Is there an advanced class?"

Star nodded at me. "Yep, advance students mix between defense and fight training. I think the teacher said it was a M-style of fighting or something."

Oh, fingers crossed it was MMA. I adored mixed martial arts.

Emma picked up on my excitement and let out a choked sound. "God, no, you're athletic, aren't you? And we had such a beautiful friendship going."

A snort of laughter escaped me. Her dry wit was perfect; it matched my own sarcastic tendencies. "I do enjoy pushing my body to its limits. I've been fight training most of my life. It was the only activity outside of the home that my mom allowed me to do."

It was the only thing I had to stay sane.

Sympathy and revulsion warred in Emma's dark blue eyes. "Sorry about your mom, but nothing you say will convince me that exercise is good for you. Scientists are wrong. Doctors are wrong. Everyone is wrong."

"What if I can prove *you* wrong?" I said to her. I had no idea where those words had come from, but they were out now, and I couldn't take them back.

She gave me a suspicious look, one eyebrow raised in my direction. "Listening..." she replied.

"I'll do some fight and self-defense training with you, and once you learn how to take control of your own body ... own your power ... kick Lexen's ass when he needs it ... I bet you'll love it. Once your body is strong, you'll feel stronger in all ways."

The raised eyebrow wasn't going anywhere, but I knew she was thinking about it. Finally, she nodded. "You know what, I am going to take you up on that offer. I know I'll always be weaker than most Daelighters, physically at least, but it doesn't hurt to arm myself as much as I can. A few skills might have come in handy when Laous kidnapped me the first time."

As we all turned the corner then, heading toward study hall, I really should have known my world was about to go to shit. The karmic scale only allowed so much happiness before yanking it away.

It started with a whisper of my name.

At first I thought I was hearing things, but as I turned to follow the sound, I locked eyes with a set of familiar dark ones.

"Mom..." I said slowly, swallowing hard as I took a step in her direction. She was thirty feet away from me, just visible at the end of the hall. Her long mousy-brown hair hung in matted strands, her too-thin body swaying visibly as she tried to remain standing. She was much shorter than me, about five-foot-four, and right now she seemed even smaller.

Melony Channing was in her late thirties, having had me young, but she looked like she was sixty, her face haggard and lined, head drooping forward as she gripped the side rail.

"Mom," I whispered again, with more urgency. I lurched forward, ready to take off in her direction, but before I could, Daniel reached out and captured my hand.

"Wait," he said, murmuring in my ear. "This is probably a

trap. We need to move cautiously. Laous is no doubt some-where close by."

Of course it was a trap, but that didn't mean I was not going to help her. Daniel had a minute to come up with a plan or I was taking my chances. Turning from me, he said something to the group and Lexen immedi-ately moved Emma and Star back. The four overlords changed positions, so they were surrounding us protectively.

"I need to go to her," I bit out, at the end of my already limited patience.

A hand landed on my shoulder and some of the tension inside of me eased. I waited for him to order me to stay. That's what I was expecting. In my head I was already formulating an argument.

"Go slow," he warned, surprising the hell out of me. "We're right with you. Laous will not get his hands on you or Emma again. I promise."

Thank you, I mouthed at him, grateful that he was acting like we were a team. Doing this together.

As I took the first step toward my mom, all of the food I'd just eaten swirled in my stomach, threatening to come up. "Callie, I'm so sorry," my mom said as she took a step forward. One of her arms had been crossed over her chest, and she let it fall forward now, billowing out her sweater.

That's when I noticed the device strapped to her chest. My feet halted. I blinked and blinked, trying to wrap my mind around the fact that my mom was standing there, her chest covered in wires and metal.

"I think it's a bomb," I said, my voice low and wavering.

I heard curses from behind, and my hand was suddenly in Emma's, who gripped it tightly, and I squeezed back, grateful for the support. "We need to get everyone out of the school," she choked out in a panicked wheeze.

"What do you want, Mom?" I called out. She almost fell as she stumbled another step forward. We were about ten feet apart now. "Why are you here? What does Laous want?"

I'd never seen her look this weak; it made me sad in a way I didn't expect. This was a woman who had never loved me ... never hugged or comforted me ... who did nothing except lecture, and hurt, and belittle me ... but I couldn't stop the tears from silently tracking down my cheeks. Inside there was a young girl who just wanted her mom to love her, who had no one else in the world and needed someone in her corner.

"He needs you, Callie." Her voice was thin and reedy. She sounded nothing like her normal self. "Your blood was tainted last time. The floor must have had a substance on it which degraded the blood. He promises that if you come with me now, he will not hurt anyone in the school."

We were starting to attract a lot of attention. Students milling in the hall realized something was going on, and when someone noticed the bomb, screams rang out. Bedlam erupted as students started running and pushing, everyone panicking as they tried to escape.

Except for the Daelighters. Members of the four houses started to gather, some behind my mom, others to my left and right. For once, none of them were segregating themselves. The four houses were mingling, forming an alien barrier.

"All of the houses have minor powers," Emma murmured, reiterating what Daniel had told me this morning. "Each is different, and they're pretty weak this far from their network, except if you're an overlord. But they might be able to help contain the blast if Laous does detonate."

That was not going to happen, if I could help it. "Why don't

I just give you more blood to take to him," I suggested to my mom.

She shook her head. "My orders are to bring you to him ... alive." She stumbled, almost falling. "He won't wait much longer."

As she held her hand out, I centered myself, reaching deep for composure. "Okay, Mom, I will come with you."

I tried to take a step forward, but Daniel wrapped an arm around me, lifting me off the ground and into his body. "I will not let you go with her," he said, voice no more than a growl of fury. "Not on your own. We're a team." His eyes bored into mine. "You don't have to sacrifice yourself. We can contain the blast."

Freeing one hand, I lifted it up to press against his face. This might be the last time I saw him, and I needed to touch him. "You know I have to do this. I can't risk all of the humans. I won't risk them. Please don't ask me to."

His jaw clenched, and I could tell he was having trouble speaking through his rage. Finally he said, "Okay, here is the plan ... because I can feel your energy, I think I might be able to track you. You're going to lead her out of the school, and then stall as long as you can until I get to you."

He was working with me. He truly meant it when he said we were a team. "I can do that, or try at least. If Laous is there, this might be our best chance at taking him down once and for all."

He dropped his forehead down to gently rest against mine, and that action had my insides rolling. "Don't freak out on me," he said softly, "but I need to tell you something ... I believe Emma's theories. You and me, this is about something so much bigger than even our souls being bonded. You captured me from the first moment I saw you. I can't ... I won't let you go now."

My heart just about beat out of my chest in that moment. I could barely breathe, but I had to tell him how I felt. "You're the first family I've ever had," I said with conviction. "Now that I've found a *home* with you, I won't give it up without a fight."

I lifted my face and pressed my lips to his. If this was my last moment – again – I didn't want to miss out on kissing Daniel. I needed to know how it was, at least once.

He parted his lips, and before I could react, he took control of the kiss, his tongue stroking mine as our mouths moved together. The life and death situation faded from my mind and I lost track of everything but this moment.

Was there a way I could kiss Daniel forever?

With a growl, he pulled away and I had to fight back tears again. It had been short and fast, not a classically "perfect" first kiss. It was so much better than perfect. It was real.

"Do not antagonize him," Daniel warned as he lowered me back to the ground. "Stall him as long as you can. I will be right behind you."

He pressed his lips to my forehead one more time and then released me. I shuddered, taking one last look at his face before turning to my fate. A tearful Emma and Star caught my eye.

"Stay strong," Emma whispered. "Laous is going down this time."

I liked her confidence, but we all knew there was a huge chance Daniel's ability to track me would fail. Laous seemed to be multiple steps ahead of us at all times; he probably knew a way to block our connection. But I had to try. I had to hope.

As I took a step forward, there was a blast of heat at my back but I didn't turn around. It was only as I reached my mom's side, when a rumble shook the ground, that I looked back. Lexen, Xander, and Chase were all holding Daniel, who appeared to be fighting his resolve, trying to come after me. He was actually gaining ground, even against his three powerful friends. His marks were swirling; flames danced across his skin. I let out a gasp as he shook his friends off and fire rippled up his body. Lucky the humans had all taken off earlier, because no doubt someone would be filming him right now.

Before I could say anything or go back to him, which is what my instincts were urging me to do, my mom wrapped her bony fingers around my wrist, and then, moving at unnatural speed, had me outside in a blink.

How ... what ... how in the hell did she just do that?

Two minutes earlier she had barely been able to stand, and now she was moving like a ... Daelighter. My head hit something hard as I was shoved into a car, and in the next breath we were screeching away. *Shit.* So much for stalling them. We'd expected a human to be taking me out, and instead I got...

Light rippled across my mom's skin; it started to jiggle ... like Jell-O, before it split, tears spreading across all the surfaces I could see. I almost vomited as she literally shed her skin, ripping it off in large chunks and throwing it out the window, all the while managing to keep the car on the road.

Within thirty seconds, my mom was gone and another woman was in her place.

Still not the weirdest thing to have happened to me in the last week.

"Who are you?" I asked, trying to place the shaved-headed woman before me. She was clearly a Daelighter ... House of Imperial probably. Heavily muscled, with thin lips that were pressed together as she glared at me.

She tilted her head in my direction, expression almost bored. "I'm no one of concern."

The bomb was gone now, too. It must have been part of her illusion. Dammit. She tricked me ... I'd thought for a second my mom was alive. I'd thought I could still save her. All of that hope crashed down. I bit my lip to stop a whimper escaping.

"Get back in your seat," the woman snapped. "Laous wants you in one piece, and I'm going to be driving fast."

Reaching out, I snagged the belt and yanked it down just as she pressed her foot to the floor. Whatever car we were in, it was heavily modified, moving at racecar speed. "Where is my mom?" I asked, fearing the answer.

Imperial bitch just laughed. "Stupid, grubber. Your mother is dead, she's been dead since the first time Laous grabbed her. Heart gave out and she died before we could get anything useful from her. I shaved off some skin, so we could use her cells to build a skinsuit, because Laous knew we might need her as incentive, but other than that ... she was left down in Louisiana. I believe she was cremated as a Jane Doe."

Everything inside of me went cold and numb, like I'd just been sliced with a blade, but the pain hadn't kicked in yet. I'd toyed with the idea that my mom was dead, but I guess I never truly believed it. Because I couldn't believe it. She was my mom.

God, Mom, I am so sorry. There was some comfort in knowing she didn't die horribly in an alien torture chamber. That had been one of my greatest fears. Thinking of her suffering had been killing me. And maybe later, when I came to terms with what happened, I'd be able to smile at her getting one up on the aliens. Dying before they could touch her.

Laous still managed to use her, though, even in death. He

really didn't have to bother. It could have been anyone wearing that bomb and I would have left. I didn't walk out of that school just to save my mom. I walked out to save everyone. All of the Daelighters, the innocent humans. Every single person in there.

I didn't ask any more questions. I stared out the window and tried my best to track our path, all the while praying Daniel was behind us somewhere. I didn't recognize any landmarks, but it looked like we were heading out of the town. It was all trees.

Daniel's face remained a burning beacon in my mind, the memory of our kiss strong. Being away from him was making me feel weak and clammy, my heart beating far too rapidly as beads of sweat formed on my forehead and along my hairline. My stomach growled, and I couldn't tell if it was hunger or unease, but whatever was happening, I was all out of whack.

I was going to be at a very real risk of fading away if I didn't get back to Daniel or House of Imperial soon. The bond was too new for this sort of distance. Before I could freak out further, the bitch wrenched the steering wheel, did something with the clutch and gearstick, and let the car spin in a one-eighty degree turn before coming to a halt on the edge of the forest.

"Get out," she growled, not looking at me.

Unclipping myself, I stumbled out of the car and she was gone in a flash, tires kicking up gravel. *Okay, then.* I turned to look around, trying to determine the reason she'd dumped me here, but before I could do more than catch a glimpse of approximately a million trees, a swirl of light appeared before me and Laous stepped out of it. Dressed all in black, there was no expression on his face.

When he crooked his finger at me, I remembered I was supposed to be stalling.

"Why did you bring me here?" I asked, allowing the fear I felt to creep in my voice. No doubt this loser loved the sight of other's fear, and I wanted him happy and relaxed.

His face crinkled, impatience shining in those cold eyes. "The network is being watched very closely, so the only way I can open a transporter is if I grab a random one. That way it's too quick for them to get here before I'm gone. Cherise just stopped when she felt the energy. She knew I was almost here."

Bitch was a far better name than Cherise.

"Come on, grubber. I need to get you back to my place, so I can extract the blood."

He waved at me again, but I remained where I was standing. "Will you kill me as soon as you get my blood?"

He'd tried to kill me the last time, so I pretty much already knew the answer to that. This was just to keep the talking going on.

He surprised me though. "Actually, I've decided not to kill you keepers. After this last fiasco with your blood, I realize now that my original plan was very shortsighted. I might never have been able to find the third if you had died, and I still don't know what might be required from me to retrieve the stone once I have the fourth secret keeper. With that in mind, I'm going to hedge all bets and keep the four of you alive. I have people readying right now to pick up the Darken grubber."

Good freaking luck with that. Lexen was not a dude to be messed with, but then again, neither was Daniel. I'd forced his compliance, but in the end, he hadn't been able to let me go. Only his friends holding him back gave the changeling a chance to drag me out – using her super Daelighter speed.

"How can *Cherise...*" I growled her name. "Change her shape like that? It's not a normal Imperial power, right?" I asked, desperately searching for another topic to keep him here.

"Mix of human and Daelighter technology. With the right combination, anyone can become a changeling. The longest part is growing the skin she wore, using a human cell. Unfortunately, it's a once-only deal. But I got what I needed, so..."

"So, where are you taking me?" Next topic of stalling.

His fist snaked out then; I hadn't been expecting it at all, which gave him an advantage. I jerked to the side, but his knuckles skimmed my jaw and smacked me in the ear. I reacted instantly, and despite my fatigue, managed to land a right hook, followed by an uppercut.

Training kicked in, and the next time he threw a swing, I side-swept his legs, knocking him down. Laous might have the speed of a Daelighter, but he was clearly used to other people doing his dirty work. Fighting was not his thing, which gave me a sliver of a chance.

As he jumped up with a roar, I went on the offensive, jabbing and kicking, changing up my style and stance to keep him off guard. He blocked a few, but most of my shots landed, and I was excited that his right eye was already darkening, blood seeping from his nose.

"Enough!" he finally bellowed, and that's when I kneed him in the balls.

He dropped to the ground, a groan escaping his lips, and I wasted no time in slamming my shin into his temple, knocking him out.

"I'll say when it's enough," I crowed at the unconscious Daelighter.

Panic hit me then because that had been way too easy. I

wasn't sure what was coming for me now. I started to walk away, preparing to run for it. At the last minute I backtracked, deciding to quickly search him for Emma's necklace. It was giving him way too much advantage over us.

As I hurried to his side, I noted the odd array of clothing he wore. Looked like he'd scavenged through someone's dirty laundry to piece together an outfit. An old and faded cotton shirt that had been dark blue but was now a washed out gray. His pants were surf shorts, which he'd teamed with long socks that almost met the bottom of them. Leaning down, I quickly searched his pockets. No way Laous trusted anyone else with his precious stone. He had to have it on him. *Paranoid, dickface.*

In my haste to search him, I missed the giant behemoth stepping out of the transporter. The next thing I knew, a heavy blow landed on my head, knocking me forward. I was barely conscious enough to immediately vomit down the giant's back as he hauled me up in one arm.

Light sent screeching pain through my head as we stepped into the transporter.

Daniel wasn't going to make it in time. I was heading to wherever Laous had just come from.

11

———

Mammoth man turned out to be kind of a rough ride. Thankfully, in a completely non-sexual way. By the time we reached our destination my ribs were screaming at me from being slammed across his shoulder. Laous was still unconscious over his other shoulder and I was starting to freak out about what he might do when he came to. Probably my ribs would be the least of my worries.

The transporter spat us out in a weird world. It almost looked like there was nothing around here but … clouds. Literally. Just a world of clouds. The huge scary dude dropped me not very gently onto the cloud ground, Laous landing next to me.

Scrambling back, I got my first real look of my attacker and had to swallow down my unease. His face, and the skin I could see leading into his dark shirt, looked like someone had taken a blowtorch to it, melting and burning and scarring. I felt a pang of sympathy for whatever he had been through, but at the same time, I was not going to let my guard down. Not at all. He was working for Laous, which made him the enemy.

Lying on the ground made me feel extra vulnerable. The urge to get up was strong, but I was afraid I'd get knocked down again. I focused on inching away from Laous. Being this close to his slimy ass was giving me the creeps. The giant watched me but made no move to stop me from shifting out of Laous' reach.

"I ... sorry I hit you."

I was startled by his gruff apology, his voice raspy, words stilted, like he hadn't used them in a long time. Clearing my throat, I wondered if maybe I could use this to my advantage. I desperately needed an ally; maybe he also needed one.

"That's okay," I told him. "It only hurts a little."

I pressed my hand to my cheeks and winced. Okay, so maybe a "little" was kind of an understatement. He followed my movements and his face dropped, eyes downcast.

"Where are we?" I asked, wanting to keep him talking.

He looked around, as if he was only just noticing that we were in this weird cloud world. I couldn't see any end from where we stood, but with everything white and fluffy, it might have all been an optical illusion, making it next to impossible to tell the size of this place. I mean, was this in Overworld? Or was it somewhere else altogether? It didn't feel like we were in Imperial, because my energy had not returned.

"Safe place," mammoth man finally said.

"What's your name?"

I startled him with this question. His mouth opened to form a silent mime of the word "name."

"What do I call you?" I tried again, not sure how much he understood. He spoke broken English, but I sensed that was not because he didn't know the language.

He straightened. "I am called Rao, Rao Imperial." He

pointed down to Laous, who I was pleased to see was still unconscious. "Father."

I blinked a few times, trying to see an ounce of similarity between the two men. Rao was twice as wide and a foot taller than his father. More like Daniel, who until now had made everyone look scrawny. Rao might be the one Daelighter who was bigger than him.

"Daniel never said he had a cousin." I tried to keep the surprise from my voice. Hopefully they called them cousins here also.

Rao shook his head. "Secret."

I swung my head around and nailed Laous with my bitchiest glare. Piece of shit asshole of a father. Hiding Rao away. I wanted to ask him why, but I was afraid it was about his face, and then I was afraid I might stomp on Laous' throat. Which might get me hit again.

"Daniel is a good man," I said to Rao. "He would have been a great friend to you. Laous should not have kept you apart."

His eyes glittered at me and I realized they were a golden brown. I hadn't noticed before now, because he was so tall and tended not to look directly at me. The color was like Daniel's, but less cinnamon and more gold. Truly beautiful eyes.

When I told him that, he started to shuffle his feet, and my instincts were to hug him tight, but that was not going to happen. I didn't hug strangers who had hit me, no matter how much they tugged at my heartstrings.

Laous stirred beside me and I sucked up as much energy as I could, jumping to my feet. As I expected, I wobbled like crazy once I was standing; my legs just didn't want to hold me any longer. Heaviness pressed down on me, like darkness seeping into my soul, and I ached. My eyes burned as I fought back tears.

The weariness was one thing, but this ... depression ... which was closing off my mind and sucking away all will to live, was the most worrisome of all. I knew what I needed, what my body needed.

Daniel. This was the side-effect of the bond he'd mentioned.

"He won't hurt you now," Rao said, distracting me, and I realized he thought I was shaking because his father was waking.

I tried to smile. But there was nothing happy inside of me, so it no doubt looked more like a grimace. "I need to get back to House of Imperial," I mumbled. "I am tied to that land, and not ... strong enough ... to be ... away ... yet."

I was back on my knees, but at least I was about six feet from Laous, who had his eyes open, right hand rubbing across his forehead. Rao blocked my view, his strong hands sliding in under my armpits as he lifted me up.

I slumped against him, desperately wishing I could stand on my own, but knowing there was no chance. "Don't let him touch me," I murmured.

I felt Laous' presence as he stalked toward us, that malice he carried drifting just ahead of his angry stomps. "You're lucky I need you alive, grubber!" He was a few decibels short of shouting. "But you will be punished. Plenty I can do to keep you alive and unhappy."

I'll bet. From the corner of my eyes I could see him looking around, seeming to notice where we were. "Why have you brought us here, Rao? Was this the only transporter you could get? How long have we been here? The council could be on their way right now!"

I remained slumped against the big guy's chest, and when

Laous went to roughly haul me off, his son moved me just out of reach. "No," he said firmly. "You hurt her."

Laous snarled then, very animalistic. "I didn't give her that black eye. So maybe you should be more worried about your temper."

I patted his chest. Gentle taps was all I could manage, but he felt it. "You didn't ... hurt."

Yeah, I was done with the forming and speaking of the words. How annoying. I could handle a lot of things, but not being able to talk was not one of them. Angry glaring did not sufficiently portray my true annoyance. I needed witty one liners.

"Give her to me, or you will find yourself in the cell next to hers."

I wanted to punch him in the head again. So badly. Rao just moved me even further away. "No."

I was cheering him loudly in my head, as another wave of darkness pushed in on me. "She needs to get out of here," Laous told him. "I will use one of my pre-arranged transporters to the edge of Imperial. I planned it that way, because I know she needs the energy. So hand her over right now. Otherwise she will die and end up in the justices. Her soul ... it's fading away."

At least the council was doing something right. Laous was struggling to get around without being able to use this network freely. Still, he'd obviously figured out some way to get to House of Imperial undetected if he needed it.

When Laous' cold, hard grip wrapped around my forearms, I shuddered. His touch was probably the worst thing I had ever felt, but my fight was gone for the day. If I had been more in my right mind, I might have freaked out by how close I was to death. I felt it rattling around inside of me, the slow wheezing of my breath the only sound I had left to focus on. But I sort of just accepted that if it was my time to go, it was my time to go.

Would Daniel die too?

Something I really should have asked him before now. Our souls were bonded, his keeping mine alive. But did it go back the other way as well? I seriously hoped it wouldn't. The thought of Daniel dying was like being stabbed with a rusty blade, right in the chest.

What felt like hours later, I was roughly hauled to the ground, feeling like I'd passed through a sauna on my way down. Warm and damp air surrounded me, dampening my skin. As I landed, my already sore head slammed into a hard object, and everything went really fuzzy and dark around the edges.

I must have lay there for some time, until eventually cold seeped into my skin, which had my body violently shaking. With this came a sliver of clarity. My eyes flicked open, and my sight adjusted faster than I expected. I was in a gray room; it looked like a cross between a jail cell and a room in a mental hospital, minus the padded walls. Rolling over, I got to my feet, surprised by how steady I was. My energy felt like it was kicking back in as well. I was somewhere in Imperial.

That had been way too close. I would take Daniel's warnings a lot more seriously from now on. A soul-bond was not something to mess around with.

Moving freely took me a few moments, but once my body was functioning again, I examined the full scope of my surroundings: four gray walls, a hard, dirt-like floor, and a small square glass window on the wall in front of me. No door.

I dragged myself across the room to stare out of the square, but there was nothing except darkness outside. Either it was night or I was in a place devoid of all light. My cell was lit, though, the brightness at the point of hurting my eyes.

The room held no bed. Or toilet. Nothing which would improve my situation. I didn't need to pee right this second, but eventually I would. Slumping against the wall, I tried not to think about Daniel. My yearning for him did not need to gather any speed. We were a team, that was true, but I was also going to hold on to as much of my independence as I could. No waiting for my knight in shining armor to arrive. I had to save myself.

Lifting myself off the floor, I did another sweep around the room, eyeing off each corner and seam of the walls, looking for a weakness, trying to figure out an escape route. When I reached the glass partition, I tapped it a few times, hoping for a flimsy sort of material. The sound had a high pitch ... maybe there was a chance I could break it. Pulling off my sweater, I wrapped my hand and gave the panel a gentle smack. A low thud, followed by a slight reverberation, but no sign of cracking.

Cocking my arm even further back, I sucked in deeply and slammed my hand into the glass. Pain spiked across my hand and down my forearm and I bit back a cry. I rubbed my free hand across the glass ... not a single blemish on it. It was definitely too thick for me to punch out; I'd only hurt myself if I continued.

But ... maybe I could kick hard enough.

I still wore my school uniform, with the stupid dress shoes, but it was better than bare feet. Taking a step back, I yanked my skirt up and tucked it into the band at my waist. If anyone had been in here, I would have been flashing them a perfect view of the school-issued tights.

Falling into a balanced stance, I started to breathe as I was taught in all of my fight classes. Deep breaths, centering my body and focusing my mind. *A fight is won or lost, most of the time, before the first punch is thrown. Lose your cool, lose the fight. Never let emotions control you. You always control them.*

The mantras ran round and round my head as I took the time to calm down. There had been a lot going on in my life recently, and through it all, I had been running on autopilot. Now, it was time to take back my control.

Standing there, contemplating the right angle to slam my heel into the glass, my mind was finally quiet for the first time in days. I released another deep breath and swung my leg into a high kick. I channeled every ounce of power I had into the connection, satisfied with the solid thud. I could always tell if I'd landed a good shot by the sound of my hit.

The panel shuddered strongly; there was a creak as I connected, but no cracks yet. I tried again. And again. Not ready to give up. With each unsuccessful hit, my thoughts got darker. I blamed the moroseness on many things. The fact I was being held prisoner in a doorless room, that my mom was dead, that Daniel had made me reliant on him and now he wasn't here. Which was completely unfair.

Slam. Slam. Slam.

I kicked that panel until my legs felt like they were about to collapse under me, but giving up was not in my vocabulary.

Slam. Slam. Slam.

My muscles burned, my eyes burned, my soul burned as screams racked me internally, begging to be let free. Finally, when I couldn't contain my fury any longer, I dropped my leg, and reaching forward slammed both fists into the glass and screamed. The agonized sound came from my gut, deep and rasping.

My face and body were on fire, tears running down my

cheeks as I screamed. The salty tears started to sizzle off my face, turning into streams of steam.

What in the...?

The glass under my hands caught my attention then, because it was now a dark red. I raised my palms up and a long strand of sticky material lifted with them.

What was happening?

The red of the glass started to fade as soon as I wasn't touching it, so I dropped my hands back down, releasing more of my anger as I did. It burned red again, and as I asserted more pressure, my hands moved through the thick material. Almost like they were ... melting it away.

How was this possible? My hands should be charred bones at this point – I was melting glass, which if I remembered correctly had to be done at some stupidly high temperature.

Logically, I wanted to stop, to wrench myself back, but since it didn't seem to be hurting me, I continued channeling my fury, pushing through. It was soon obvious why my kicking had done nothing. This window had to be ten inches thick. No human could kick through that. Not even my idol, Bruce Lee.

And I was pretty sure he could do almost everything.

I was elbow deep when I finally busted out the other side, the resistance giving out, almost causing me to faceplant into the wall. The sparks of heat in my body started to fade away, so I quickly pulled my hands back through. Glass remained attached to me, but it still wasn't hurting, and by the time I was free and my skin was cool, the long strings of glass had dropped off.

There wasn't a big enough hole in the panel for me to crawl through; I'd only gotten two hands in, but hopefully it would be more brittle now. My kick might actually work. As my anger vanished, so did the last of the heat in my body. My brain was already trying to work out how I'd done that, and the only logical explanation I had was Daniel. He could turn into a flaming fireball. I was sharing some of his abilities.

Whatever it was, I'd just be grateful I at least had a chance to escape now.

As soon as the red faded from the partially-destroyed panel, I kicked it with all of my strength. This time it shattered, glass tinkling out into the dark world beyond my prison. The hole, which I was pretty sure I could squeeze through, was now completely clear. Well, there were a couple of little ragged edges, but I didn't care. I was getting out of here.

It was not easy to leverage myself up and through the window. The only reason I somewhat managed was from years of being forced to climb that damn rope in the gym. Ignoring the cuts in my palms, I wiggled my top half through the opening. The fit was tight, and I didn't like the sensation of being wedged in, especially with so much darkness on the other side. I couldn't see a thing out there, no noises...

But the dark had to be better than waiting to starve in this prison. Twisting and squirming through as far as I could, eventually I let gravity do its job. My arms went out to prevent my head from smashing into the ground, and I managed to half roll, so landing wasn't quite as painful as I'd anticipated. When I was standing in the darkness, my heart pounding rapidly, I waited for my eyes to adjust. Because despite my words about taking my chances, randomly walking in this level of darkness seemed kind of stupid.

I waited and waited, but that unnatural blanket of black remained. Dropping down, I ran my hands across the ground. It felt slightly textured, like a compacted dirt. Probably the same as my jail. I couldn't see my hands to know if there was any sort of residue on them, but my fingers felt dusty as I rubbed them together.

My fear was getting harder to control. I'd never hated the dark, but I also wasn't overly fond of it. And this was no ordinary night, this was magical in nature, and that was messing with my nerves. With no other choice, I started to walk away from the box with its small window of light, my movements slow, cautious, both hands out in front of me as my only option of stopping an obstacle from smashing me in the face. The entire time I walked my eyes strained to see anything. This darkness ... I'd never experienced anything like it before.

This world was making me really nervous.

After walking for what felt like a few hours, I decided to sit for a moment. I hadn't run into one thing, hadn't seen another speck of light or felt any energy from a living creature. Where the hell had Laous dumped me? Would I ever find my way out of here?

Sitting got me nowhere, so I started to walk again. After some time, all I had as company was the stomping of my feet and the harsh intake of breath. Two things reminding me that I was alive.

I walked until I collapsed. Closing my eyes, my mind filled with as much darkness as the outside. After seeing nothing for so long, it appeared that's all I would see ever again. I either slept or drifted in a daze, and when clarity returned some time later, it was to an aching neck and a dead left side of my body. I waited for hunger and thirst to kick in. I had to be needing sustenance soon. But ... neither did. My mouth wasn't even dry.

As I started to move again, I tried not to think. Protecting the fragile nature of my mind seemed to be the most important thing. So ... denial it was. Denial wasn't keeping my anger at bay though; it returned with a vengeance as I walked in darkness. My life had not been much to talk about for the first eighteen years, and Laous just had to go and one-up that by doing ... whatever this was ...to me.

Fucker.

I felt the burn inside of me again and I welcomed it, hoping like hell that my hands would light up and show me whatever was out there. I just couldn't do this darkness for one more moment. "Come on!" I screamed, holding my hands out. "Burn, baby, burn."

Nothing.

I thought I heard my name then, like a whisper on the nonexistent breeze of this place, but even when I stilled and held my breath, I didn't hear it again. With no other choice, I walked until I fell again, and then I slept.

This routine continued on for countless days ... nights ... whatever time existed here. My mind was frazzled, my thoughts confused. I still did not hunger or have any thirst. I had no need for a bathroom. It was almost as if time stood still, and all I could do was run.

12

The longer I was trapped in the darkness, the more confused my thoughts got. I kept forgetting who I was and why I was here. I couldn't remember my mom's face, the color of her hair. Even the color of my own hair.

I became nothing more than a mindless machine, walking, resting, walking and resting. When I stumbled for the millionth time, falling to my hands and knees, a spark of red lit up my hands for a split-second. Just a single beat, but with that came a single image. Daniel's face. His beautiful perfect face, bright and strong. I almost sobbed as I realized I had forgotten him until that moment. How could I forget Daniel? We were a team.

Fiery streams of power churned in my center. I was starting to recognize the build of energy, the pulling of power. When Daniel bonded us, he must have shared more than just his life force. He had shared his Imperial powers.

When my hands lit up, burning a bright red, I remembered everything. *I am Callie.* With the whisper of my name, more of my self came back to me; memories returned. Laous must have put me here as a way to break me. He was a clever torturer. I would have preferred he broke every one of my fingers than leave me here in this darkness. Bones could heal. Minds were much harder.

Holding my red hands up, I willed more fire into them, the glow immediately spreading to my wrists and then forearms. Despite the intensity of the heat, my clothes didn't burn. Somehow the magic knew what to burn and what was off limits. I began to walk again, using the light to finally see my surroundings. I really couldn't make out much outside of the grayish ground. I appeared to be moving through a land without a single rock or tree or landmark. Which explained why I hadn't crashed into anything in the dark yet.

I started to run, sobs still racking me, tears dripping along my cheeks, only to sizzle off as the heat dissipated them. I couldn't deny this any longer, I was trapped here, in this eternal darkness.

"Callie!"

This time the call was distinct enough that my feet faltered and I tripped ... again. Fifty million times was the charm, right?

"Keep using the power," the familiar voice said again.

Rolling onto my back, I pushed all of the burning energy out into the world. My fingertips started to tingle, then there was a pop as a small flame shot up into the air. With a low shriek, I rolled to the side, unsure if it was going to fall back down and land on my face. What if I was only safe from the burn when it was attached to me?

"Daniel," I shouted, desperate to see him.

Daniel had owned my freaking soul long before he bound us together. There was no one else in any world who could compare. I had fallen for that huge alien asshole in five damned minutes and there was no taking it back. My brain could deny it all it wanted, but my heart knew the truth.

It had chosen.

My fire was running out, and as the energy died away so did my specks of hope. "Daniel," I cried, frustration and pain my only companion. "Dan ... please."

"Callie! Open your damn eyes."

What was he talking about ... my eyes were open.

"We're losing her," a female cried. "What did Laous do?"

I tried to tell them, explain where I had been, but there was no way to open my mouth. I was just too tired.

"Fight, sweetheart. Please, fight for me. Don't let that bastard take one more person I care about."

There was true agony in Daniel's voice and it strummed within my chest. I wanted to comfort him, wanted that so badly, and as I stood in the darkness, I held on to that dying ember of his voice.

Then I threw myself toward it. And...

Brightness burned into me. I cried out and tried to lift my hands, but I couldn't move them. Someone placed a soft cloth over my face, and I had immediate relief. It took me a few minutes to adjust to the light. When I could finally see, I gaped at the three people who stood around me. Daniel, Emma, and Lexen.

My mouth opened and closed, and turning my head, I saw that I was not on the ground in a land of darkness, but instead floating in a tank of thick liquid.

"Wha...?" I tried to talk, but my voice rasped out like it hadn't been used in days.

Daniel reached in and cradled my head in his hands, holding me slightly out of the goo. "Callie? Do you remember me?"

I nodded, tears burning my throat. "I would never forget you, Daniel."

I almost had, but Laous was not strong enough.

He closed his eyes briefly, and I immediately wished he would open them. I didn't like being cut off from him this way. When he did meet my gaze again, gold blazed at me. "We've been trying to get through to you for hours. Laous has your energy tied to the legreto in this rebirth tank. You had to break free on your own. We couldn't do anything, or it might have destroyed your mind completely."

With a cough, I tried to sit up. Daniel slid one of his hands down, so it was under my back, gently drawing me up and into his body. The liquid clung to me for as long as it could, before finally releasing me from its deadly embrace. Bits of goo were still attached, but Daniel didn't seem to care as he pulled me to his chest.

"What happened?" I coughed, looking around.

If I could have screamed at that point, I would have. The room – which was filled with tanks like the one I'd just been pulled from – had a creepy alien-abduction-probing setup going on. "What in the actual hell is this place?"

Daniel, still holding me, started walking, moving with ease through the small spaces between the tanks. "This is an old underground facility in Overworld," he said, and I realized in that moment how flat his voice was. "It was used for mass experimentation when our four houses warred with each other. This is Imperial territory, right on the edge of our land."

Emma's worried face popped into view. She reached out and took my hand, and my heart ached at the sight of tears tracking down her cheeks. "It strips you of everything," she said, sounding like she was repeating what she had been told. "Takes away who you are and leaves a blank canvas. The boys explained it all while we tried to wake you up. They told me to expect you might be gone by the time they freed you."

I didn't understand what they were saying. "You all need to go back and explain from the start," I got out somewhat coherently.

Lexen answered: "The liquid you were floating in is called *concrestia* ... also known as the Soulstealer, a weapon developed by a House of Imperial overlord, the one before Daniel's father. He wanted to go to war when no one else would. He was going to try and create an army of Daelighters to fight for him. Basically, when you go into the water, your mind becomes open to suggestion. You can be brainwashed, and if you're left submerged in it for long enough, eventually your mind will be wiped clean, to be manipulated as needed."

That's why, when I had been running in the darkness, my mind had been slipping away from me. "It almost got me," I told them, swallowing the rough lump in my throat, glad at least that my voice had returned. "For days I have been running through the darkness, and I kept forgetting every-thing. It was only when I used ... a fire power ... that some clarity returned."

I tilted my head back to gauge Daniel's reaction; he was looking straight at me, his expression unreadable.

"I'd never been so lost and alone," I confessed to him. "My mind would drift away. I thought I was going to disappear forever." My voice broke and I choked on the words, small sobs escaping in between each one. "It works, whatever this soul stealer stuff is. It does what it was supposed to."

"How are you still here with us?" Emma sobbed with me, our hands still clinging together.

"Daniel," I breathed, still looking at him.

His steps didn't falter, but there was a twitching on the

corner of his jaw, like he was fighting against saying something.

"When I started to use the fire power, I felt him again. I remembered him. The only thing in the darkness was him, and the energy we shared."

He pulled me closer, jolting my hand out of Emma's.

"That's when I felt your consciousness," he growled. "When I knew we were finally getting through to you."

Since we were nearing the end of this massive, freaky capsule room, I tapped him on the arm. "Put me down, please."

He just growled again.

"Daniel..." I made my voice as stern as I could. "Put me down. I can walk."

Probably a lie, but I needed to stand on my own two feet. I didn't like this distance he was keeping between us. Not physically – he hadn't let me go, not for a second – but he was holding back emotionally. And that both confused and upset me. I was new to this emotions thing, and no doubt missed a lot of things that others would recognize.

And right now, I just wanted to know what to do to fix us.

I thought he was going to ignore my request, but with a huff he finally slowed, and then my shoes hit the ground. My knees faltered for a second, but before I could be swept up again, I managed to gain my footing.

"I should have gotten to you sooner." The self-loathing in his voice made my heart feel like it was being crushed. "You trusted me to keep you safe, to follow you, and I almost lost you to the darkness."

Needing to touch him, I slowly placed my palms flat against the hard planes of his chest muscles. They lifted as he roughly sucked in air.

"This is not your fault," I told him firmly. "You didn't want me to leave. I knew the risks when I did, and you saved me in the end." Popping up on my tiptoes, I went to press a kiss to his cheek. He let out a low rumble and turned his head so hot lips crashed into mine.

A low moan slipped out as our mouths moved together, his tongue caressing mine. My body went weak again, and it was only Daniel's strength that kept me standing. "You're never leaving my side," he said, pulling back briefly, before pressing his lips to mine again.

Lexen cleared his throat, and I blinked a few times before I remembered that we weren't alone here. Daniel and his best friend exchanged a look, and I recognized the urgency in Lexen's eyes.

When Daniel turned back to me, panic immediately took hold. I held my breath as he said, "I'm going to make a liar of myself, because I actually have to leave you alone for a short time. The council has a lead on Laous. They had certain locations tipped to track him, should he go there, and the land of clouds was one of those. We have no idea why he went there, but he's now on our radar. A small party has been assembled to go after him."

No wonder he was so angry at Rao. This was exactly what Laous had been dreading.

"Where will Emma and I be while you're gone?" I asked. "Laous wants us alive. He told me he was going to keep us prisoner, just in case he needed more blood. These tanks..." I waved my arm across the room, "are kind of the perfect solution. Alive, but completely compliant." Ready to obey his every command. Misogynistic asshole.

Daniel's strong arms wrapped around me, and I sank into him. The relief I felt at being back with him was almost impossible to describe. If I had to try, though, I'd guess it was how it felt to come home after being gone for a long time. For those people who had real homes.

He spoke against my hair. "Laous is not going to touch either of you again. I know I promised once, and my word might not mean as much as it should, but I'll do everything in my power to ensure you're safe."

"Your word means everything," I assured him. "Everything in your power is more than enough."

"Hopefully we take him out today," Lexen added. "The council seems pretty confident." He turned to Emma. "You and Callie will be staying with Chase."

Lifting my head from Daniel's chest, I looked up to meet his eyes. He nodded. "Chase is the only overlord not to be in the search party, and that is solely so he can stay and protect you. Laous is afraid of House of Leights. He will never step foot in the trees. He has hurt too many of them over the years to face their wrath."

A tree's wrath? That sounded pretty cool, and scary.

Part of me wanted to argue. I didn't like us separating. This team thing was really growing on me, along with the concept that we were stronger together, especially when it came to dealing with Laous' psycho ass, but I knew he needed to be there. To protect his friends. To protect the secret keepers. Emma didn't argue either, but it was clear she was no happier than me.

We moved toward the door again. My heart fluttered as Daniel made a point to stay by my side. We walked like a couple, like Lexen and Emma, so close that our arms brushed against each other, which sent shivers down my spine and through my stomach. The distance that had been there when I first awoke in the gel was gone, disappearing with his confession of guilt. He had been beating himself up for letting me leave the school, and for not finding me right away. I could already tell he was the sort of guy who took his responsibilities seriously.

We stepped outside – it was nightfall wherever we were. The dark made me shiver, but it wasn't all-encompassing like the world in my head, so I pushed through it without too much distress. I was not alone. That made all the difference.

"How did you find me? How long was I missing?" I asked. It felt like days when I was in the dark, but maybe it hadn't been that long at all.

"Laous thought he was safe, bringing you down here," Daniel replied. "This entire bunker, plus the land around it, is off the grid, so to speak. The network is weaker here. He made a mistake, though, by not bringing you directly here."

"The cloud land," I breathed. "The place he picked up the tracker."

"Why did he take you there?" Emma asked. "That land has nothing in it to help him contain or hide you. It's just a place the council uses for the bigger meetings."

I shook my head. "It wasn't Laous that took me there ... it was Rao. He—"

"What did you just say?" Daniel interrupted, sounding like I'd completely taken him by surprise.

"Uh..." I faltered for a second. "When Laous first tried to take me, I fought him off. Knocked him out, too. I should have run, but I decided to try and find Emma's necklace first. Which would stop Laous from finding any more of the secret keepers." I winced thinking about what had happened next. "I missed Rao stepping out of a transporter. He hit me hard enough to disorient me, and then took Laous and me to the cloud land."

Daniel's voice was glacial. "He hit you?"

I nodded, not going to lie to him. His body started to shake, shoulders lifting as he heaved in breaths. I turned panicked eyes on Lexen, who had already stepped in front of Emma and me.

"Daniel does not take kindly to men hitting women. Especially not his woman," he explained, and I tried not to act stupid about being called "Daniel's." "And Rao is the name of Daniel and Fraizer's older brother – the one that's missing, presumed dead. The story was that he fell into the justices and no one knew. Trapped in the Flames of Ether, where the fire can even burn an Imperial."

Everything stilled in me, the badly scarred and disfigured guy was ... Daniel's brother. He must have fallen into the flames, as they'd thought, but he didn't die. Laous saved him, but also kept him hidden away. *But why?*

The heat around Daniel increased; he was not dealing well. My insides and instincts were screaming at me to get my ass over there and comfort him, but Lexen kept pushing me back, sidling left and right as I tried to step around him.

"I need to go to him," I finally demanded, having enough of this game we were playing.

Lexen just shook his head, crossing huge arms over his chest. He was doing a very good impression of a warrior statue. "Nope. Not happening. Dan is not in control of himself right now, and he would kill me if I let you get hurt. Or attempt to kill me anyway. I'm pretty much unkillable."

On anyone else that would have sounded like the worst kind of arrogance, but for Lexen it seemed to be fact. Still, he was underestimating me and my need to get to Daniel, whom I didn't believe for one second would hurt me. I trusted him.

Hoping to throw Lexen off, I relaxed my stance, taking a

casual step closer to Emma. She caught my eye and I saw her grin. She already knew what I was planning. In an unexpected show of solidarity, she reached forward and wrapped her arm across Lexen's bicep, distracting him. Before he realized what was happening, I dive-rolled right by the side of his leg, popping up behind him. I pushed off toward Daniel, determined to reach his side.

Before I could get close though, Lexen zipped forward and scooped me up, holding my struggling body against his.

"Stop it," he demanded. "I'm trying to save your life."

Flames burst to life across from us; the night air lit up, showcasing the rocky, cave-like structures around us.

Emma sounded a little nervous now. "Lex ... babe, I think you should let her go now. Remember how you reacted when someone was holding me back from you."

Daniel's face was completely covered in flames, eyes glowing as they locked ominously on Lexen. I had stopped fighting, because I really didn't want to get anyone burned, but it didn't seem to matter to the Imperial overlord. With almost comical slowness, Lexen lowered me back to the ground and stepped away. He never took his eyes off Daniel, and I swore I saw something bubble under Lexen's skin, but then it was gone. I didn't even want to know what Lexen and the Draygo people did, because that bubble had not been human. Or Daelighter. It had been very animal-like.

No time to focus on that. I had a soulmate, or whatever the hell label we were putting on it, to talk off a proverbial ledge. "Dan, look at me." I kept my voice low. "You need to calm down and talk to me, because I can't stand not being able to touch you." I was going to risk the fire in about five seconds. "I need you."

I took another step closer, and as his intense heat washed

over me I almost closed my eyes at the comforting sensation. It reminded me of the burning I had done in the dark lands. As I reached for him, Daniel sucked his power back in, the fire disappearing before I could make contact. But it didn't matter. My fire was burning now too, whooshing up from my center, filling the world with warmth, life, and death. I lifted my arms, letting the red lick down my skin and light up the world, just as Daniel had done.

"Callie, are you okay?" His concern broke through my euphoria, and I couldn't stop the brilliant grin.

"Better than okay, I'm a goddamn weapon."

He had no qualms about touching me like this, and as soon as I was in his arms his body responded to my fire with some of its own.

"Well, I thought I'd seen everything, but this is new." Emma's drawled statement would have been hilarious if I wasn't totally distracted by Daniel.

As our eyes locked, I was astonished to see that his were now a rich, molten red. Swirling. Mesmerizing. "What is happening to me?" I asked him, my voice a deeper resonance than I had ever heard before. "The fire ... it fills me with life."

Daniel shifted one hand underneath me, using his strength to hold me up against him. "You're tied to the land of Imperial now. Fire is our specialty. We burn the dead and renew the souls." As his voice vibrated with power, it sent my flames even higher. Along with the emotions in my heart.

I love him.

I might be a clueless, sheltered, naïve human, but there was no way I could deny the truth any longer. Daniel and me, we were a team. We had a bond that could not be broken. And I truly believed this had been decided on the day I was born in House of Imperial and assigned to be a secret keeper. I didn't say those three words out loud, because it was too fast. We hadn't known each other long, and I seriously didn't want to freak him out.

But I could admit it to myself. Finally.

"We really have to go. Do you think you two could maybe quench that fire and pick this up later?" Lexen's question sounded slightly amused and slightly intrigued. But it was enough to snap us out of our fire bubble.

The moment we separated, I managed to contain the energy back to my center, where it simmered away happily. What a relief to know I could access the fire outside of the dark world in my head. To test myself, I brought it forth again, directing it to burn in my right hand. Five flames sprung up on the end of my fingertips, nothing else on my body alight.

My wide eyes lifted to Daniel's and a grin quirked up one corner of his mouth. "You learn quickly," he said, dropping a kiss onto my forehead.

A breathy sigh escaped me, and I knew I was turning into one of those girls. But seriously ... love was the best feeling in the world. And also the scariest.

My feelings gave him so much power over me and it was kind of terrifying.

Before I could dwell on it too much and freak myself out even more, we were moving again, this time with urgency.

13

The trip out of the secret brainwashing facility took a few hours. I asked them lots of questions, learning about how they'd tracked me down. Laous had been easy to follow, apparently, until they reached the part of Imperial where the network cut off. After this, they'd searched the old-fashioned way.

By the time they found me I had been in that tank for three days, the liquid keeping me alive, which was why I didn't thirst or hunger. I was extremely lucky they got to me when they did; my mind had been so fragile. Even now I still felt a little strung out, thoughts wispier than usual.

When we finally reached the spot Daniel could call a transporter down to, I asked, "This tracker on Laous ... is it a permanent thing?"

Lexen shook his head. "No, it was designed similarly to those computer viruses you get on Earth. It lay in wait, and when triggered silently, attached itself to Laous' energy, leaving behind a trail. We'll only get one shot. The moment he knows someone is tracking him, he'll be able to find and destroy the trace."

I didn't pretend to understand how their network worked, but I liked that it was making it hard for Laous to stay under the radar.

To call the transporter, Daniel planted his boots into the ground and I felt the buzz of fire power start to spread under his skin. There was a tingling in my feet, even through the soles of my shoes. Lights slowly appeared, one by one, intertwining with each other to form the familiar ball of a transporter. Daniel took my hand, Lexen took Emma's, and then we stepped through, reappearing on the metal platform between the three lands.

A group was already waiting there for us, gathered near the section with all the trees. I recognized a few of the Daelighters: Chase and Xander, along with Star, who was with two tall, dark-haired men who looked a lot like Lexen. Those five broke away from the main group and hurried toward us.

Star threw her arms around me, letting out a happy cry. "They found you! Oh, my Heralda, I was so worried." I returned her hug, allowing myself a moment to rejoice in the fact that there were people in my life to care about now.

When we pulled away, a beautiful guy with crystalline blue eyes, dark hair streaked with gold, and a scar on his face – which only made him more devilishly handsome – stepped in front of me. He wore a perfectly-fitted dark blue suit, open-collar shirt, and shiny dress shoes. He looked like a billionaire playboy, which was only cemented when he opened his mouth.

"Well, hello there, cupcake. Who do we have here?"

Emma snorted. "Her name is Callie, not that I expect you will use it."

He winked at her before turning his attention back to me. He took my hand, holding it almost intimately. "Jero Darken at your service. I heard Daniel had tied himself to a delectable human, but I have to say, you should leave him immediately and join your soul to mine."

With a chuckle and shake of my head, I removed my hand from his. "Perfectly happy being an Imperial. Thanks for the offer though, Darken." Then I mimicked the wink he'd given Emma.

Jero threw his head back and laughed, before he straightened. "I really need to find a human of my own. You're delightful."

If Emma rolled her eyes any harder, they'd literally be in the back of her head. "How about step one: remember their names. Step two: stop flirting with everything that breathes. Time to stop hiding the worthy Daelighter you are."

He just laughed again, crossing his arms. "I'm never changing for any woman, you know that." He then spread his arms wide open. "Besides, the ladies love me just as I am."

Emma and I exchanged a look, but before we could laugh in his face, the other guy stepped forward. He was a little shorter than Jero but still taller than me. His face was very masculine, not pretty like his brothers, but there was no denying their similarities. Lexen was a brooding prince, Jero was refined and suave, and this new guy was ruggedly handsome.

"I'm Marsil. It's really nice to meet you, Callie."

We shook hands and I marveled at how calm he was. His tone, stance, and manner of speaking was miles from the uber-confident Jero.

"They're Lexen and Star's brothers," Emma explained, even though I'd already figured that out.

"You're all going in this hunting party?" I asked, looking between them.

Everyone nodded, except Chase.

"You as well?" I said to Star.

She squared her shoulders. "Of course, I'm not letting my brothers go out there without me."

"Actually..." Marsil interrupted her, "I was thinking that maybe you and I could stay here and help guard the secret keepers. It's just as important a job, maybe more important. We know Laous has multiple Daelighters working for him, so it's critical we don't let him get his hands on the girls again."

That reminded me of the skin-wearing weirdness, which I'd filled Lexen, Daniel, and Emma in on during our walk here. Who knew how many "suits" Laous had been growing. We'd all have to be careful of strangers.

Star let out a sigh. "I know you're guilting me into staying."

Marsil's full lips twitched, but he shook his head. "I'm Lexen's admiral major and should be protecting his back, but Father is going ... along with all the other overlords. They'll have plenty of power. It makes more sense for me to stay."

"I second this notion," Lexen boomed from his spot, worried gaze locked on his sister.

Star closed her eyes and scrunched her mouth up as she breathed in deeply. "Fine!" she snapped. "I know you're over-protecting me again, but I do agree it's important to keep the girls safe, so I'll stay."

She stormed away then, stopping to speak with another tall, dark-haired man, who was clearly the daddy of the Darken clan. He looked just like his sons. They all had that same handsome, scary vibe. I wondered what Daniel's parents had looked like, if he took after his mom or dad.

I felt eyes on me and I twisted my head to the side. My

heart jumped at the intensity on Daniel's face, the sort of look he'd been shooting my way ever since he pulled me out of the tank. His eyes, which had always been sad, broken, and lost, seemed a little different now.

"You won't lose me," I murmured, leaning closer to him.

Daniel's hands tangled in my messy hair, his thumbs caressing up and down my cheeks as we stared at each other. "Don't get hurt or kidnapped again," he finally said. "I won't be able to control myself if you do. And I have a lot of power now that I am the overlord."

"I'll keep her safe," Marsil told him.

Daniel briefly took his eyes off me to give Marsil a nod. "Thank you. If I'm not back soon, you'll need to return Callie to House of Imperial. Her energy has to be recharged. Right now she's fine, because we just came from there, and she has been with me, but I'm taking no chances with her."

"It will be done. Don't worry about it," Marsil said.

I made a low, devastated sound. It slipped out before I could stop it. Daniel's attention immediately returned to me. "You better come back to me," I murmured fiercely.

"I love you" died on the tip of my tongue again, but I hoped he could see it in my eyes. I'd never said those three words to anyone before, so it felt huge to say them now. And also ... it wasn't the right time. He'd think I was saying it because we were all about to be torn apart again and put in a dangerous situation. Which was definitely not the truth. For now, I'd just have to hope my eyes were telling him how strong my feelings were.

"Come back to me," I whispered again, and then there was a brief pause before he freed his fingers from my hair to cup my face. This time his kiss was gentle, and a burning started low in my body, but it was soon blazing like a thousand suns inside of me. We both kept it contained, not letting it creep onto our skin. When we pulled apart, my breathing was embarrassingly heavy.

"I have to go," he said, sounding more than a little annoyed. Next to us, Lexen and Emma were saying their good-byes, while Jero hugged his sister.

I didn't like this. It reminded me of the old movies where the women and children sent their men off to war, movies where many of those men never returned. Sobs were building in my chest, but I would not fall apart. I knew Daniel was not doing this just for me – if that was the case, I would be hand-cuffing myself to him and probably hanging off his leg to make it extra difficult. But this was the same as when I had to walk out of the school ... bigger than just one life. It was about saving the treaty that kept two worlds from being destroyed.

I grabbed onto his shirt, tightening my fingers in the soft material so I could pull him closer to me. "Be careful," I said, wishing that the million other things in my head could be said as easily.

"I will." He nodded to back up that statement. "If I get a chance, I'll send a message to Marsil or Chase, but it's quite hard to connect to Overworld from Earth. So don't panic if you don't hear from me."

Yeah, right. The chances of me not panicking while he was gone were pretty much zero.

With a final brush against my cheek, Daniel turned to join Lexen and Jero. The three crossed to the main group going after Laous. Then they were gone in the transporter.

I almost lost control of my fire power as my worry immedi-ately went into overdrive, but the thought of possibly hurting one of the people around me was enough to halt my flames and give me a sliver of control. I could be strong while Daniel was gone. I would be strong.

Chase stepped closer to us; I had to crane my neck to see his face clearly. He was at least as tall as Daniel, his face billboard advertisement material: perfect bone structure, dark exotic slant to his eyes – which were the color of shimmery green glass, flawless skin in a mix of dark and light ... brown, with a slight shimmer.

I thought he was the most "otherworldly" of the four overlord best friends ... too beautifully exotic to be real.

"Are you ready to explore the land of Leights?" he asked, a smooth, accented lilt to his words. Holy gods, if I didn't have Daniel to compare him to, I'd think Chase was the sexiest guy I'd ever seen. Okay, Lexen as well. There was no denying the four overlord best friends were total heartbreakers, but I preferred the one my soul was tied to. The darkness he carried didn't bother me – it matched my own. The rugged beauty he wore so effortlessly had my body craving him. And more importantly, his care and consideration toward me ... from pretty much the first moment we met ... was why I considered myself truly blessed.

Come back to me, Daniel.

I was distracted from the heavy thoughts as Chase swung his head toward the land of trees, braids clinking together. I liked the way most of his hair was shorn except for those few longer pieces. It really suited him. His symbols were darker than his skin, but still in the same tone. And they glowed much more brightly.

"Welcome to the House of Leights," he said, and I focused on the land of trees that spanned out into the distance. I couldn't see the end. I couldn't even make out one other landmark, just a single canopy of huge green and gold-tipped leaves. As we took a few more steps closer, I noticed the trunks were not brown but a solid gold. Flaky bark and gnarled whorls gave them a similar appearance to trees from home, but as we stopped right before a massive one – its trunk the width of a truck – I felt the unnatural energy.

I'd always been vitalized by nature, water especially, which was probably why I loved the ocean so much. House of Leights took the normal buzz of nature, multiplied it by a million ... and then threw in a few cans of energy drink.

We were on the edge of the platform, huge trees in front of us towering way above our heads, so tall I had to lean right back to see the top. Star and Marsil remained a little behind, allowing Emma and I the first look. We were the newbies here.

Emma's eyes were wide and filled with wonder and awe. I often forgot that she was an Earthling too. I wasn't alone with these new experiences.

"I've never seen anything like this," she murmured. "I never even realized they were so huge. I wish I'd walked over here sooner."

Chase flashed almost perfect white teeth. Two on the bottom were slightly crooked, but it wasn't even remotely a flaw. I was just being a picky bitch because he was too much of everything. Dude needed a flaw.

"You'll have plenty of time now to become acquainted with my land, and if you treat her with respect, she will return the favor."

This reminded me of what Daniel had said about the trees and Laous. I wanted to know what that meant, so I asked, hoping like heck I wasn't stepping over the line. Thankfully, Chase didn't seem offended. He smiled at me, while placing his hand firmly against the golden trunk closest to him. Almost immediately, a literal glow washed over his skin. I thought I saw his body shimmer and grow larger, but when I blinked again he looked like normal-sized Chase.

"They're called *Galinta*," he answered. "An ancient breed of tree folk. Here, the trees are not inanimate beings like yours on Earth. This is their land. We're just lucky enough that they allow us to share it with them."

Not inanimate? "They walk?" I asked slowly.

Chase nodded. "Yes, if they want to, they can walk and communicate. They're ancient creatures, living here long before Daelighters existed on this world. Most of the time they rest, but ... not always."

Emma had a hand over her mouth. Then removed it to say: "This is why your power is connected to nature." She turned to me. "Leights shift their shape, turning into beings that are very much like the trees here."

Chase shrugged. "We're nothing like the Galinta. They are so much more than we could ever hope to be."

The respect and reverence in his voice, the glow the Galinta still shared with him, it was all very mystical and incredibly emotional to experience. Something inside my tight chest, where the darkness was hovering, waiting to pounce, eased. We were insignificant to these beings, but at the same time, being near them made me feel like I was more, that I could strive further and reach new heights.

Marsil and Star moved forward. "We need to cross into your land now," Marsil told Chase. "It's not safe for us to linger out in the open like this."

Chase turned to the tree and placed his other hand onto it. "We ask for safe passage to the village of *Charwin*."

There was a moment's pause, then a rumble jolted me. At first I thought the platform was shaking, but it turned out to be the trees – Galinta – in front of us. They vibrated hard and fast, leaves drifting down. I fought against the urge to pick one up and see how it felt. Magic trees might possibly be the coolest thing I had seen in Overworld to date.

When I finally lowered my head from watching the leaves fall from above, I choked on my next breath. *What in the...?* Right in front of me was a large rounded pathway through the canopy.

The branches and boughs had shifted and bent themselves to form the path, which was level with the platform we were on. It was like those wooden bridges that hang over gorges, the ones with the planks and small gaps between each board. The boards in this case were tree branches, so we'd have to watch our steps, but it looked relatively safe.

"Well," I said with a breathy gasp, "no wonder they think we'll be safe from Laous here. No one gets in without the blessing of the trees."

"Exactly." Star clapped her hands. "I love this land. We only ever came here a few times when I was a child. But it was so much fun. Their houses are built—"

"No spoilers," Marsil cut her off. "Let them discover it."

She shut her mouth, a chuckle escaping from between her tightly-pressed lips. Emma and I exchanged a look, and I wondered if I looked as excited as she did. I certainly felt an unusual level of anticipation. I wondered if this was what it was like to be a kid at Christmas. You know, for people who didn't have a mother like mine. She had refused to celebrate the holiday, calling it a waste of time and money.

"You okay?" Emma asked.

She must have caught my scowl. "Just thinking about my mom," I admitted. "She's been on my mind a lot."

"Do you think she's actually dead?" Emma's voice was

laced with new pain, and I knew this would be reminding her of the death of her own family.

I kind of nodded and shook my head, before letting it fall to rest on my chest. "Honestly, I don't know. The part that worries me the most is that I'm upset, but ... also okay. I think there might be something wrong with me."

Like I was a sociopath masquerading as a normal person.

Emma grabbed my hand. Star, who had been listening in from the side, took my other hand. "From the little I know, your mom treated you terribly," Emma said fiercely. "You might think you have to grieve just because she was your mom, but the truth is, she doesn't deserve your sorrow."

"You didn't want anything bad to happen to her." Star sounded so sure of this and it made me want to hug her. She thought I was a better person than I actually was.

"No, I didn't want her to die," I agreed. "But I did want to be away from her. I dreamed about escaping all the time. And ... now I'm free, and it's ... great."

Besides the almost dying and having my mind wiped part, I'd never actually been happier. Emotions were no longer a thing I would hide from. Numbness was safe, that was for sure, but it was not living.

"You're a good person, Callie," Emma said with real emotion. "Don't take this guilt on. It's not yours to own."

Before I could reply with the heartfelt thanks she deserved, Chase stepped into the first part of the trees, startling the three of us. Both girls gave my hands a last squeeze, then released me so we could follow his path. There was enough space for us to walk side by side, but it seemed safer to go one at a time. I decided not to think about my mom anymore, focusing instead on where I was stepping.

There was a thick canopy above us, which made it really

dark. As this darkness grew, my nerves kicked in hard. Reaching out, I gently rubbed my hand across a nearby golden trunk. I was seeking something, reassurance, comfort, the knowledge that I was no longer stuck in my own head.

"Thank you for helping us," I whispered randomly.

A low thrumming noise echoed through my mind and I almost fell over. I was pretty sure the sounds were words, in another language. The noise had the cadence and tempo of speech, each word filled with wind and melody and multiple voices. I must have squeaked, because Chase was at my side in a moment. He moved amongst these trees with more grace than I'd ever shown just walking on flat ground.

"Is everything okay, Callie?" he asked, green eyes darting around me, searching for a threat.

I patted his arm, my heart rate starting to slow after the shock of the trees talking to me. "Yes, everything is great. I just … I touched the tree and then there were words in my head. Not in English, though, so I guess it could have just been noise."

"The Galinta spoke to you?" He sounded surprised.

I shrugged. "I … think so." When he didn't reply right away, I started to get worried. "Is that bad? Are they going to kill me now?"

Chase shook his head, no hesitation. "Definitely not, it's a great honor actually. They used to greet all who walked through our land, but the last few decades this occurrence has grown rarer."

Star nodded. "Yes, they did when I was a child. They sound so beautiful. Like a collective of wind and song."

"Yes, that's exactly what it was like."

I felt calmer now, my fear of the darkness fading away under the knowledge that I had friends around me. And the

Galinta. We started to walk again. Chase spent most of his time keeping Emma from falling to her death. That girl was seriously uncoordinated, and she complained the entire time about forced exercise and how it was the bane of her existence. I laughed more than once at her.

"I'm serious," she told me, trying to stomp her foot, before twisting her ankle and almost dying again. "Gym class in school should be banned. Running for fun should be banned. Squats should be banned."

Everyone laughed then. "So what do you like to do?" I teased.

Before she answered, there was a loud rustling from behind us, and I momentarily freaked until I realized that the trees were just closing the path, making it inaccessible again.

"Don't stress," Chase told us. "They're making sure no one follows us. We're not about to be crushed by tree branches."

The Galinta were already on the short list of beings I trusted, so I was not stressed.

"My number one love is reading," Emma said, picking up the previous conversation. "I used to live my life through books. Fantasy especially. Now I get to live out real life fantasy, and it feels like I have been preparing for this my entire life. I also love cooking, eating, knitting, and cats. Totally not a dog person."

"What about dragons?" Star winked at her.

Pink tinged Emma's cheeks, and she narrowed her eyes playfully at her friend. "I can't lie. Dragons might just be my favorite now."

She tripped, and Chase caught her again. With a sigh, she called over her shoulder: "What about you, Callie? What do you like to do for fun?"

I had to think about it for a moment, because she'd had this entire list. I'd never done much in my life I considered fun. "I guess ... I like to fight – or train to fight anyway. The human body is an incredible thing. It can be honed and focused into a weapon. I can scale rock walls and climb ropes, flip and contort myself into a million positions. I like the power and control of that."

I heard Emma's groan. "Always ruining our friendship by liking exercise."

"I can't lie," I said, mimicking her. "I love it. Even running. My mind calms when I am warming up. I usually run five miles before we start training."

Emma sounded like she was choking. "Five. Miles! Are you freaking kidding me?"

She started muttering then about how I wasn't human and the only time humans should run was to get away from angry dogs. "Don't forget I am going to teach you how to fight," I told her.

Her rambling cut off, and she sounded less annoyed when she replied with, "I'm actually not dreading that as much as I thought I would."

I had no idea if I was going to be able to teach another person. I knew how to train and fight, but translating that into teaching a newbie was not easy. I had seen a lot of amazing fighters be really terrible teachers. But I would try.

"I also love cats, Converse shoes, jeans with rips in them, and casual shirts." Because that all had to count for something. "Oh ... and romantic movies."

Her eyes lit up, and she almost died again trying to turn to me. "Hallmark, right? I basically live for the new Christmas movies."

"Same!" I said, showing more enthusiasm than she'd probably seen from me before.

Then both of us laughed, and I once again thanked the fates for this new family I'd found.

We walked for a long time. The scenery didn't change much, different variations of the same trees. "Do you walk like this all the time to get everywhere?" Emma asked Chase, sounding mildly fatigued.

"Yes." His voice was calming. "Walking is the best way to get around. We do not allow transporters in Leights. We also don't connect to the network except in an emergency. The Galinta are all we need."

"Great," Emma groaned. "How much further until we reach your town?"

"We're walking above Fronza Canyon right now, so it should be another mile or so."

I stumbled a little, my eyes drawn down to the gap between the branches. I wasn't sure what a canyon was here, but if it was like Earth, then that meant...

"Holy shit," Emma gasped, her eyes drawn down as well. "There's a thousand foot drop below us."

Chase looked confused, his eyes shifting between me and Emma. "There is no need to worry. We're safe in the trees."

"What if the trees decide to release us?" Emma whisper-shrieked, panic filling her voice.

Chase placed a hand on her shoulder, and ... she visibly calmed. Whoa. He definitely had a magic just like the Galinta. "They will never let you fall." She let out a relieved sigh, until he added. "Not unless you wrong them." Then he winked, and I relaxed somewhat.

Marsil, moving forward, wrapped an arm around Emma,

offering comfort. She leaned into him and I heard her murmur, "I miss Lexen."

"He'll be fine," Marsil reassured her. "He's a Draygo and an overlord minor. That's a tough combination to hurt."

This seemed to mollify her, because she straightened, prepared to continue on. But my worry was back at the forefront of my mind. *Daniel better be okay.*

By the time we finally reached our destination, Emma looked more than a little frazzled. Her long auburn curls were frizzing; strain was evident around her mouth and eyes, and she had somehow managed to tear the sleeve of her white shirt. I, of course, looked fifty times worse than that. I was still wearing my school uniform covered in dried gunk from the tank.

Lately I'd been dirty more than I was clean, which made me uncomfortable because I generally showered twice a day. It would be great if there was some form of indoor plumbing in this village, along with food. Since we were up in the trees, though, that was probably a stretch.

The path ended with a series of step-like branches that deposited us to a lower level of the forest. We weren't on the ground, and I was starting to wonder if there was a ground here. It appeared the trees just went down forever. This lower level had a "floor" of leaves, thick like a canopy, but apparently fine to walk on. Chase stepped right out onto it.

The area was huge, with lots of trunks dotted throughout, spiking up through the leafy floor. "Each one is a home," Star whispered as we followed Chase.

I had no idea what she was talking about until I noticed the rounded door of the trunk nearest us. That's what Marsil had stopped her from telling us before: Leights lived inside the trunks of trees. *Amazing.* They'd taken the concept of a "tree house" to an entirely new level.

Chase led us past dozens of dwellings like this, and the further we got from the stairs, the more villagers and huts emerged. Children ran by us, using branches to swing themselves around, playing and laughing. They all had long hair, mostly to their mid-back, but some even to their waist. Their skin colors ranged from the lightest tan to the darkest of ebony, all beautiful and exotic. The bone structure here alone would keep the modeling industry going for a thousand years.

They also appeared friendly and calm. Even the children. They played, but it was all smooth motions and graceful leaps through the trees. No screams or shrieks, just gentle laughter. Everything had a peaceful feel to it, and I just wanted to sit for a while and take it all in.

"I figure first you might like to wash up, and then food," Chase said when we reached his side. "I'll take you to the bathing areas."

Bathing areas sounded a little too communal for me, but I was past the point of being picky. I needed to be clean. We passed another round area, which had stones and branches scattered about.

"We all eat together here, unless you prefer your own company," Chase explained. "There are multiple villages like this spread out across the land of Leights. I visit between all of them with my parents. The overlord's family is nomadic so that no village is lost or forgotten."

"Do you have any brothers or sisters?" I asked him.

Chase shook his head. "No, my mother was lucky to be able to carry me to full term. We have long gestations, almost fifteen months, and it's hard on a woman's body. My mother was already weakened from a sickness that ravaged her in her youth, so it was very worrying."

"So sorry to hear that. I bet she's glad to have had her one child, though."

Marsil chuckled. "I always thought my mother doted on me until I met Chase's. He's her golden child and can do no wrong."

Chase shrugged, not looking at all embarrassed to be called out on his close relationship to his parents. He loved his family, that much was clear. He owned it with pride.

Beyond the eating area, we came across another set of stairs. These led down to a large platform beside a round pool. *A pool in the trees?* What sort of crazy was this?

The water was so clear that I could see the bottom. It looked like a smooth wooden bowl, made up from half a huge tree trunk. "This is provided by the Galinta," Chase told us. "They form the pool, and the water which falls in to it."

It was about the size of an Olympic pool, but round. "Not much privacy," Emma said with a dry laugh. "I personally keep my lady parts out of the public eye, for multiple reasons."

"Yes, let's not forget that her mate turns into a dragon," Star said with a choked laugh-grimace.

I chuckled at the mental images of Lexen sprouting claws and shooting flames at any dudes caught staring at naked-Emma. It felt good to laugh. I'd been doing a lot of crying lately, so some happy relief was exactly what I needed. I did sober up when I remembered that Daniel was out doing God knows what, going up against Laous. He'd better be okay. I refused to consider any other possibility.

I took a step closer to the water while Chase attempted to explain how this bathing thing worked. "The legreto here has extra-special properties. It will hide whatever you want hidden. You'll see once you go in. Use those trunks there to remove your clothes and then once you're in, you'll understand."

He pointed toward a row of six trunks, which had a veil of leaves across the front of them. I stepped over with Emma; she kept her eyes narrowed suspiciously on the water behind us.

The leafy part of the tree moved as soon as we were in front of the trunk. Behind it was a hollow space, about the size of a decent dressing room in a department store. When I stepped inside, the leaves closed off behind me. There was a bench running the full length of the trunk, so I quickly pulled off my clothes, grimacing as they stuck to me where I was still caked in goo. Dropping them in a pile, I turned around, prepared to step out in all of my naked glory. Chase might think the water was going to hide me, but we still had to walk from this trunk to get into the legreto. Just as I took a step forward, the floor groaned under me, then it opened right up. With a shriek, I dropped down.

14

———

As my feet hit the water, I managed to suck in one lungful of air before I went under. I wasn't a strong swimmer. We'd never lived anywhere with a pool, and my mom didn't care enough about me drowning to get lessons, so the most I got to do was splash at the beach when we lived near it.

It took me a beat, but I finally figured out that I was in some sort of tube ... a slide maybe. Super cool except I couldn't breathe under water, so it was going to get a lot less fun in a few seconds. My feet hit a flimsy barrier, pushing it to the side, and then with a whoosh I was out in the open water. I landed against the smooth wooden base. Pushing hard off the bottom, I broke the top of the water, gasping in air.

Blinking and wiping away the water from my eyes, I was distracted by how weird it was to be completely immersed in the legreto. Its increased denseness turned it almost into a suction as it clung to my body. I wish I knew more science to understand why that might be, but for now it was just a new fun thing to play with.

"I did not see that coming," Emma spluttered behind me, sounding like she was choking.

Turning, I was mostly submerged, but she was standing up and I could see everything. Only, I also couldn't. The water was draped across her breasts like an opaque swim suit. I stood as tall as I could then, glancing down to find I had the same thing happening on my body.

"Okay, that's pretty freaking cool," I said, running my hand across my chest. The water swished with my fingers. I could feel my skin, but I remained covered.

Emma flopped back then, her long hair trailing out behind her. "Some days it feels like I could live in Overworld forever," she said wistfully. "Being born here, I believe there is a special connection between us and this world. That's why it feels so much like home."

I rubbed my arms, making sure all of the goo was gone. "Imperial feels like that for me, too," I admitted. "But I wonder if it's because its energy keeps me alive ... it helped tether my soul to Daniel." As soon as I mentioned his name, I felt a pang of worry. "Do you think they're okay?"

"I'm sure they're fine," Marsil said, from where he was gliding around the large bathing bowl. "Laous is no match for all of the overlords."

Nodding a few times, I put on a brave face before ducking under the water and scrubbing vigorously at my hair. Worrying like this was a new concept to me. I wasn't sure what to do to stop my mind from dwelling on it.

As I popped my head up, it was just Emma and me again, the others having drifted off. Her expression was somber. "He was in a bad way when we found you."

I stilled, taking a step toward her. "When you found me in that memory-wiping liquid?"

She nodded. "Daniel saved my life not long ago, and I have grown to care a lot for him. Lexen considers him a brother, and I'm starting to feel the same way. It was damn hard seeing him like that." She looked like she was searching for the right words. "His eyes, Cal, they're so sad. Every time I look into them, I want to hug the crap out of him."

I chuckled, my heavy emotions giving it a strangled sound. She'd given me a nickname. I'd never had one of those. "I love his eyes," I admitted. "I've never seen a color so rich and deep. And the gold through them ... amazing."

She was right, though. Daniel had sad eyes, and I understood why. He'd lost so much in his life. His older brother, mother, father, younger brother. On top of that, he had Laous constantly trying to kill him in those days before he became overlord. If anyone needed love and a safe haven, it was my Daniel. I wasn't sure fate had chosen the best candidate for him. I was almost as damaged as he was, but maybe together we could be each other's salvation.

"When we arrived at that warehouse, he took off," Emma continued. "He knew which tank you were in, even though it was nowhere near the door. When we finally reached him, he was just standing ... staring at you." Her voice broke and I also had a huge lump in my throat, trying to claw its way out. "I've never seen someone so broken. I'm not sure he would have survived losing you."

The tears were coming now, no stopping them. "How do you do it?" I asked her, sucking down the sobs. "I keep alternating between never wanting to leave Daniel's side and wanting to run as far and fast as I can. Because I understand how he felt when he found me like that – losing him is not something I would recover from. I've had so little in my life, nothing really. To now finally have so much ... I'm petrified to lose it all."

I sensed she wanted to hug me, but since we were actually naked – although disguised as such – she just reached out and took my hand. "I understand better than you'd think. When the fire killed my parents, I lost a huge part of my heart and soul. I was devastated to the point I wasn't sure I would ever be happy again." Her focus shifted out into the trees surrounding us. "Then Lexen came along," she whispered. "He made me feel so much, and at first it was angry emotions – I mostly wanted to throat-punch him – but once we got over our animosity, we realized there was a bond between us. A true bond." She met my gaze again. "Am I afraid now that I might lose the best thing to ever happen to me...?" She nodded. "Hells yes ... freaking terrified. But even if he died tomorrow, I would never give up the time I've had with him. Never. It's worth every ounce of future heartache."

I got that. I truly understood what she was saying. But I wondered if she would say the same thing if Lexen were gone. Maybe she just didn't know how bad the heartache would be because it hadn't happened yet.

She shrugged, a wiry smile crossing her face. "At least they are really hard to kill," she joked. "Unlike Earth men, our guys are made extra tough."

That definitely was a huge bonus. "I wish you didn't have to lose your parents." My heart ached for her. "It's not fair."

Her throat worked as she swallowed, opening and closing her mouth. Finally, she rasped, "Life is a bitch at times, but I know they want me to be happy, so I'm going to do my very best."

Fuck it. I reached out and hugged her. It was just boobs, we both had them, no big deal. Emma gave me an extra tight squeeze and then we pulled away. Things got lighter after that. Chase, Marsil, and Star eventually made their way over to us and we talked and relaxed in the water. The pool constantly rose and fell as the trees took and filtered the water, returning it to the pool. Children, and even a few adult Leights, joined us, but for the most part, we were alone.

When we were clean and ready to get out, the tube slid us back up into the change sections. New clothing was waiting inside, neatly folded in a small pile. My uniform was gone, taken away to hopefully be burned. Dressed, I stepped out with wet hair and a lighter heart. The shirt and shorts I wore were simple, a lightweight material, the same shade as sand. The underwear was built in, which was surprisingly comfortable.

When we were all dressed, it was time for food, my stomach doing flip flops in delight. I was ready to eat all the things. Chase was at my side as we crossed the wooden path again, back to that huge round area designated for food and gatherings. "It's really peaceful here," I found myself saying.

"I couldn't imagine living anywhere else." His voice had this amazing ability to paint pictures just with the beautiful cadence of his tone. "I'm really happy that Daniel found you," he said, changing the subject. "For too long he has been alone."

I forced myself not to think about Daniel, because there was no way I could shed more tears. It was turning into a joke. "You seem to be very ... alone, in a way. People have waved and bowed and acknowledged you. I can see they respect and care for you as their leader, but they are distant." I had no real excuse for being so blunt and forward. In my need to not think about Daniel, I also forgot to think about Chase's feelings. "I'm sor—" I started, but he cut me off with a wave of his hand.

"You're right," he acknowledged. "The Leights are very big on respect, and the overlord and his family always stand slightly apart from the rest of the villagers."

"Probably doesn't help that you move constantly, never settling in one place, never having a true sense of community."

He nodded, his long, thick lashes framing his eyes as he blinked. "I'm used to it by now." I heard the resignation in his voice. He might be used to it, but he didn't particularly like it.

"You, Lexen, Xander, and Daniel ... that makes sense to me now."

He stilled. "What do you mean?"

I shrugged. "I understand how you all came to be so close, to mean so much to each other. You understand the others, because you each bear the burden of being a leader in your world. It's a lonely job at the top. No one else could truly understand."

Chase sighed, rubbing a hand across the shorter parts of his hair, moving the braids around so they clinked together. "I would have been lost without them. There is no denying it. I just wish we saw each other more."

No doubt running different sections of Overworld kept them all busy. "At least you can sit together at school now."

His smile was breathtaking. I had to blink a few times to clear my head. He was lethal to women everywhere, that was for sure. I also admired his strength and tranquil demeanor. But my heart was already spoken for, so he only rocked me a little. Whatever woman fell in love with him, she would probably forget her own name whenever he spoke.

With a bit of luck, I'd be around to see that.

A lot of Leights from this village were already seated. Apparently, it was food time for everyone. Just when we were about to drop into a spare corner of the rock area, a Leights ran up to Chase. He looked young, with very dark eyes and hair. He held out a hand and in it was a yellowed piece of parchment.

Chase took a moment to read it. My gaze immediately went to Emma. She was so still, staring at him, no doubt mentally urging him to hurry up. I switched my focus back to the Leights overlord, holding my breath as I waited to hear the news. Was this about Daniel and the others? Or completely unrelated news?

"Come on," Star said with urgency. "Tell us, are they okay?"

Chase waited a few more beats, before he snapped to attention. "The network is hard to connect with here, but they got a message through. We need to head back to the central transporter. Lexen wants us to return there immediately."

Emma leapt forward, clutching his arm tightly. "He's okay, right? Tell me that he's not hurt."

Chase patted her shoulder and she shuddered like she was trying to keep herself together. "He seems fine. It sounds urgent, but not life-threatening."

Emma sagged forward, and he caught her. I heard her murmuring *Thank God* over and over. I was just opening my mouth to ask about Daniel when Chase caught my eye. "According to this message, everyone appears to be okay at the moment, but we should move now."

He straightened, wearing his calm warrior face. There was something so reassuring about him, just like Daniel. The four overlord minors were so confident that it felt like they could handle anything that was thrown at them.

"Are you sure?" Marsil didn't seem quite as sure. "What if it's a trap?"

Chase nodded. "We have to consider the possibility that it might be. We'll be cautious. No one will leave the protective embrace of the Galinta until we know for sure this is a true message."

We all agreed to this plan, and as excitement bubbled up inside of me, I had to acknowledge that it was seeing Daniel again that had me in this state.

"You're a goner," Emma said with a laugh. "I recognize that expression. And literally, the only reason you could get me to walk through the trees again today was if Lexen was waiting for me at the end. That's love, my friend."

We fist bumped it out, because the girl was so right. We were goners.

THE JOURNEY BACK SEEMED FASTER. I got a good rhythm going with the branches, although I still had nothing on Chase. He was a ninja, silently moving through the trees. Star was fine; she didn't even seem remotely tired. Marsil was practically carrying Emma by the time we reached the end, which was barred off by a bunch of leaves and branches. Through a few gaps I caught sight of the metal platform and the glowing transporter, but it was hard to see much else through the tiny spaces of the Galinta. It was getting late in the night as well, so it was only the light of the transporter illuminating the area.

Chase and Marsil were tall enough to see over the top of Emma and me, so we were all huddled closer together. Star stood back.

"I can't see anyone," I whispered, tilting my head to a new angle to see near the Royale area. Nothing there either.

Marsil shifted around. "I can connect better to the network here. Leights have very limited access. Let me see if there is anything obvious happening."

He didn't close his eyes, or touch anything, he just went

very still and I could see that he was far away. His gaze unfo-cused ... shifting off to the side of my head. After about two minutes of tense silence, he jolted minutely and then blinked. "I can't see anything amiss. There are no signs of unauthorized travel. No other messages waiting for me."

Chase squared his broad shoulders. "I'm going out to check the area. You all wait here."

Marsil raised one eyebrow. "Yeah, that's not going to happen," he said. "We can go together."

Chase shrugged. "Suit yourself." He turned to us. "Are you okay with staying here? I don't mean to treat you as weak or less. Women are warriors as well, but in this case Emma and Callie are very important, so more caution must be taken."

I hugged him; he was good people. He returned my hug, a burst of warmth branding me before I pulled away.

"Thank you," I said. "I can only speak for myself, but I'm okay with this. You know this world better than me."

I might have powers now, but I was still a newbie in Overworld.

"Cool with me, too," Emma said with a smile. "I'm deathly afraid of dying a gruesome death."

Star laughed. "What an odd fear to have."

Emma shrugged. "That's me, irrationally afraid of things. Gruesome deaths, clowns, jogging, centipedes, and whatever the hell a mothball is."

My face actually hurt I was smiling so hard. "I hate dolls," I admitted. "Those creepy eyes always feel like they're watching me."

"Yes!" Emma cried. "Holy shit, yes, dolls are creepy as freak."

We stopped joking around when Chase reached out and

touched the branches – they parted for him. "We'll be right back," he said, stepping forward.

Star and Emma hugged Marsil, but I didn't feel comfortable enough with him to do that. Chase – and Lexen – felt like the next best thing to Daniel. As Emma said, they were brother figures ... family. Marsil was different, but I did pat his arm.

"Good luck. Don't die."

Chase winked, and Marsil just shook his head. As they stepped out, I scanned across the metal area again; there was absolutely nothing out of place. Not a single Daelighter in sight. Once the guys were out of the trees, the leaves closed back across in front of us. The three of us pushed forward, all trying to find a gap to see through.

"I have a bad feeling," Star whispered. "It's too quiet out there. I mean, someone is always coming and going through the transporter, but..."

"Should we call them back?" I asked with urgency. *Daniel, where are you?* He had to be okay. He had to be.

"Just keep an eye out," Emma said. "If they need our help, we're going to have to figure out how to get out of these trees."

I had a feeling they wouldn't let us go easily, and none of us had any idea how to speak with them. For some time, we kept a vigilant watch on Chase and Marsil. They walked the perimeter of the large area. I lost sight of them once or twice when they moved out of the range of my peephole and the light, but they appeared again quickly enough and nothing attacked them.

Eventually they made their way back to where we were waiting. The branches parted under Chase's command and Emma stepped out first. Star and I followed.

"Do you think the message was wrong?" I asked Chase.

His brow furrowed as he answered. "It's possible. I didn't recognize the Leights who handed it to me, but that doesn't mean anything. One of the very outer villages is visiting for a festival, so there are a lot of different Daelighters about."

Or it could have been Laous. What if he'd somehow figured out a way to take people from all four houses and turn them to his cause? That way he could access all four lands easily without having to go there himself. Just as I had that thought, a series of clicks and cracks rang through the air. Chase cursed and threw himself protectively over Emma and me as a blast shattered the air around us.

15

Chase was a big guy. He knocked us down so fast that I didn't get a chance to even throw an arm out to take some of the impact. My head slammed into the ground. My ears rang, and I couldn't focus my eyes – they watered every time I tried. Whatever they'd hit us with continued on for many minutes, ringing and shaking the ground.

Once it stopped, it took me at least fifty rapid blinks to be able to see, only to realize there was a shoulder in front of me. I tried to shift the Daelighter off me, but he was immovable.

"What's going on?" I screamed, my ears still not recovered.

Chase's mouth was opening and closing, but I couldn't get much of what he said. I did manage to lip read the word "attack." He repeated it at least three times.

"Laous?" I guessed.

He pulled his focus from me to look around and I checked on Emma. Her eyes were closed and my heart immediately stopped beating. Jiggling my arm until I managed to get it free, I reached out and shook her shoulder. "Emma," I shouted. "Em!"

No movement or sign of consciousness. I was at an awkward angle to feel for a pulse, but I managed to contort myself into some stupid pose to reach her neck, and almost cried when there was a fluttering under my fingertips. She was alive, that was the most important thing. Hopefully she'd just been knocked unconscious in the blast. I still didn't know what sort of bomb or attack it had even been. There had been a loud bang, shaking ground, and a burst of energy, but no heat or fire.

"We need to move," Chase said. He was on his feet in a heartbeat; I was yanked up in the same instant. Emma was still completely out. Gently, he lifted her into his arms, cradling her body with great care.

Marsil and Star joined us. They had been thrown a few feet away, but both seemed to be okay. "What happened to Emma?" Star asked, her voice high and reedy. My hearing was finally coming back online.

"I think she must have been knocked out when that blast hit," I said. "Her pulse felt fine to me, but I'm not a doctor."

Star didn't look relieved. If anything, her expression grew more strained. "We need to get her to a healer, immediately. Nothing can happen to her."

Chase handed her to the slender woman. "Take her. Take her and go immediately to Darken. And trust no one. We were betrayed here."

Star took Emma's weight like it was nothing, hugging her close before immediately sprinting toward the transporter.

"You should go with her," Chase told me. "That blast was meant to disorientate and injure us but not kill. There's a reason they're trying to keep us in one piece, and I think that reason might be you and Emma."

I agreed with that, but before I could follow Star,

Daelighters were suddenly everywhere on the platform, climbing over the edge of the three lands that surrounded us and appearing through the transporter. Star, who was right at the ball of light now, managed to snag a glowing strand before anyone could touch her. But Chase, Marsil, and I were too far away to use the same escape.

"They're coming in from all territories," Marsil said, his voice a low grumble of anger.

"Who are they?" I asked.

"We're part of the resistance," a man standing in front of House of Darken answered.

He had the Darken "dark" hair going on. "Laous will free us from the control of humans. We're the superior beings and will not bow down to grubbers."

There was a beat of silence. Was he waiting for me to applaud or something? Considering I was mostly "grubber," that was not likely to happen anytime soon.

"What do you want?" Chase looked very unhappy. His eyes locked on the section of the platform which held about half a dozen of his people. The Leights were all male, wearing tan color leather pants, and no shirts. Their ages ranged from very young – maybe twelve – to a few who looked older than us.

"We need to collect the two secret keepers," another one of the resistance members said. "Laous wants them kept safe. They may be important for the final step in freeing the starslight from the Earth."

There was no one here this time for them to threaten and gain my compliance. I trusted that Marsil and Chase could look after themselves. So this time I was going to fight, even if it meant I died here today.

"Come quietly with us and no one will get hurt." Royale this time, the blond group standing close by, their skin still wet. The women wore bikinis and the men boxer briefs, all made from a wetsuit sort of material. Flashes of scales appeared and disappeared in irregular intervals across their bodies, and I would have been much more intrigued by this "almost mermaid" thing, except they were trying to kid-freak-ing-nap me again.

"Is it still called kidnap when I'm an adult?" I fumed, the random question snapping out.

Chase flashed me an amused grin. "Adult-nap?"

I shrugged, narrowing my eyes on some of the resistance closest to me. "That's more like an afternoon nap."

Marsil chimed in: "Maybe abduct?"

I nodded a few times, like I was seriously considering it. "Abduct would work, especially since you're aliens. Yes ... I feel like that's the correct wording."

Our glib conversation died off as the three of us fell in back to back, so we could see the threats coming.

"You need to shut the hell up, grubber," an Imperial told me, creeping closer with other Daelighters at his side. "We warned Daniel not to mess with your kind. He didn't listen."

He sneered at me, and I recognized him then. It was the guy from the hallway at school, the one who'd fought with Daniel.

"He's going to kill you," I said sweetly, smiling as broadly as I could. "I hope you've said all your goodbyes."

I got another sneer. "Some of us are willing to die for our cause."

I chuckled, sucking in a deep breath and willing the energy inside of me to rise again. "Yes," I agreed. "Some of us are."

I leapt forward, flames rising across my body in an instant, waves of heat visible in the air around me. I smashed into the group of Imperials, who had been only a few feet away, preparing to snatch me up.

I knew my power wouldn't do that much to them; they all had this same power from their land. Hopefully mine was stronger because of Daniel. I just needed to buy us enough time that we'd have a chance to run for it, back to the land of Leights.

Screams echoed, and I also heard skin sizzling. I rolled off fast, not wanting to inflict too much damage. It took me longer than it should have to focus on the scene, on the bodies ... which were now nothing more than ash. *No, oh my God, no.* A scream ripped from me in one long sound, my chest heaving in and out.

My flames disappeared as I wrapped my arms around myself, pulling the energy back inside. "I killed them," I whimpered over and over. I couldn't seem to take my eyes from the scene. The piles of ash that reminded me of old-school vampire television shows, like I'd staked them all in the chest.

"Callie, we need to get to the trees. Can you make it?"

I jumped as Chase put a hand on my shoulder. "Don't touch me," I shrieked, eyes still locked on the ash.

The Leights overlord followed my line of sight, and before I could jump away again he wrapped an arm around me and hauled me closer. "You did what you had to, to protect yourself," he said firmly. "They were going to steal you away. This is not your fault."

"What if I hurt you?" I said, breath heaving in and out. "I didn't realize it would do that – just completely ash them."

He shook his head. "You won't hurt me, I've been with you for hours and you have not lost control once. Did you call up this power?" I nodded, and he shrugged. "See, you already have great control. You'll have gotten that from Daniel. He has better control than almost anyone. The only time I've ever seen him lose it, in the last many years, is when they took you from the school."

The truth of what he was saying penetrated. Yes, I was now a deadly weapon, but a weapon did not kill on its own. I would just have to work extra hard to always control myself. To always keep the people I cared about safe.

"Can you move now?" he asked me, and I nodded, able to step back from him and stand straight. My breathing and heartrate slowly returned to normal, but I still couldn't look at the piles of ash. Chase nudged me forward, toward the other side of the platform.

"Where is Marsil?" I asked as we turned to run toward the land of Leights. I had killed the Imperials, but there were still three other houses which should be attacking. So where were they?

I got my answer when we stepped past the bright lights of the transporter and I saw the single Daelighter going up against a large group. Marsil was fighting fiercely, sending out bursts of power that looked like lightning and wind, just managing to hold them off.

When we were a few steps away, someone hit Marsil in the side of the head and he went down. I swung my leg out and cracked that Daelighter across the face, knocking him off Marsil. Chase let out a low vibration of anger; I felt a crackle of energy, and heard ... splintering wood, maybe ... and when I looked at Chase again, he was gone.

In his place stood a ... creature – ten feet tall, four feet wide, with roughly-textured skin that was brown and barky. *Hybrid*. Okay, now I knew what they meant by hybrid.

I stared and stared as his arms whipped out, turning into a long vine that cracked into nearby Daelighters, knocking them down. His legs did the same, shifting into ropey roots that tripped and tied up the resistance members.

"Leave now," he roared, nothing like the calm warrior he had been five minutes earlier, his voice deep and sinister, echoing through my body and into the metal sheet I stood upon. It was scary. I found myself staring into his tree face, which no longer resembled anything human. It was golden brown; his eyes were the same color. A barky nose, slash of mouth, and terrifying eyes. It was singularly the coolest, and also scariest, thing I had ever seen.

Marsil joined him again. I hovered near the back, kicking out and hitting anyone who got too close. I knew I had my fire power to draw on, if needed, but I wasn't sure I could handle more deaths on my conscience. Not unless there was absolutely no other option.

"Why would Laous send you all here?" Marsil was trying to shake answers out of a Darken member. "None of you are of overlord blood. Your energy is nothing to ours. What was the purpose?"

I caught a glimpse then of a familiar face, but before I could see if it was who I thought, the figure disappeared off the side of the platform. In my distraction, I missed the next attack, turning back in time to see one of the Royales flinging something at Marsil. The object moved faster than I could track, like a bullet. One minute it was in the blond female's hand, the next it was in Marsil's chest.

A scream ripped from my throat as I dived forward and caught Marsil just before he hit the ground. He was too heavy for me to hold up, but I managed to keep his head from smashing into the metal. Chase went crazy behind me, his vine-arms and root-like legs snapping back and forth in a rapid succession.

Resistance members tumbled down across the platform, and I saw more weapons appear in their hands. "Chase!" My voice was hoarse from shouting, but I tried again. "They have more weapons," I told him, my hand on Marsil's chest as I tried to stop the bleeding.

Just as I turned away, I saw Chase sweep out with his vines, and throw the remaining resistance members into the trees of house of Leights. The Galinta wrapped their branches around them, holding them in place.

Focusing on Marsil, I tried to figure out how to save the Daelighter bleeding to death right in front of me. My hand dropped to the long cylindrical, silver object that had pierced deep into his chest. I wrapped my fingers around the part still sticking out of him, but it felt so fragile as I tried to tug it out that I had to stop, afraid I would break it off.

"Legreto ..." Marsil choked out.

I flung my head up from the object to meet his eyes. "Water? How will water help?" I asked frantically. I didn't understand what he was saying.

A body dropped down at my side and I swung a fist without thought, cracking it into the side of his face. "Ommph," Chase growled, knocked back onto his butt.

He rubbed his face and worked his jaw for a minute, while I profusely apologized. "I'm so sorry, I didn't realize it was you."

He just shook his head, already at my side again, his eyes on Marsil. There was so much more blood now, it seeped out of the wound, pooling around his body. I reached out to grasp the weapon again, but it was now no more than a small nub above his shirt. "What's happening?" I cried, my voice breaking as more color faded from Marsil's cheeks.

He was still conscious, but there was a glassiness to his eyes that worried me.

"Do you know how to save him?" I asked Chase, who had both hands clenched at his sides, gaze locked on the man before him. "He said 'legreto,'" I tried again. "Help him!"

Chase shook his head. "I can't..." He sounded devastated. "This is a weapon we have no defense against. It's water weaponized using starslight stone. It forms a crystal, and if you don't remove it immediately, it burrows into the chest and shatters, sending shards throughout your entire body, tearing you to pieces internally. It's a practice that has been outlawed for hundreds of years. The knowledge of how to make this was lost. I don't understand how..."

Emma's necklace. That one piece of stone was giving Laous an entirely new arsenal to attack us with – the very reason I'd taken the risk to try and get it off him when he lured me from the school.

It was too late now, though. Too late for Marsil. The need to scream and cry rose in my chest. Pain was building within me, choking me. I reached forward to take Marsil's hand. "It's going to be okay," I whispered to him, holding on as tight as I could.

I felt him squeeze one last time, and then his body bucked, straining as he opened his mouth and bellowed. My hand was being crushed, but I didn't care. I held on, sending whatever comfort into him that I could. Marsil's struggles and suffering lasted for far too long, until eventually his eyes closed, and he went limp. Blood slowly leaked from his nose and the corner of his mouth, and I cried out, my chest feeling like it had been crushed as tears tracked down my cheeks.

Chase let out a roar. Animals rose from the trees in the Leights' land, looking like a mix of bird and fluffy bunnies.

Whatever they were, they responded to his pain, and I started to cry harder, snot and tears running down my face, choking me. I didn't care, though.

This couldn't be happening.

He couldn't be dead.

Needing to confirm it, I placed two fingers against his neck. The second person I'd had to feel for a pulse in the last twenty minutes. *Nothing.* I pressed harder, moving my hand around. *Still nothing.*

"Do you have a pulse like humans?" I choked out to Chase, who had finally fallen silent, his head lowered.

"Yes..." His tone was flat. "We are compatible with your species. We don't have the exact same internal structure, but it is similar."

The slightest vibration of fury shook in those last words.

"Can you get a message to Daniel and the others?" I asked, not ready to give up yet.

Chase's chest heaved as he stood, lifting his face, which was back to its normal model-beauty. He stared out toward the glowing light ball. "As soon as I realized this was an ambush, I sent word. But they're on Earth and have to get to a trans-porter. I expect they will be back any moment."

A moment too late, were his unspoken words. I knew we were both thinking it. Marsil might not have been as close to Daniel and Chase as Lexen was, but he was still someone they obviously knew and respected. He was the brother of their best friend, and they would grieve for Lexen.

My eyes settled on what was left of the resistance. I hadn't realized that Chase had killed a few; their bodies lay sprawled in tangled limbs and pools of blood, close to where the others were still secured to the trees. Fire rose in my blood and veins;

I only just managed to stop myself from blasting out and incinerating the entire lot.

"We need to interrogate them," Chase said, steel in his voice. "Learn everything we can about Laous, his plan, and who else is in this resistance. We have traitors in our houses, and if we don't ferret them out soon, Marsil's will not be the only death."

His message was clear: *Don't burn them yet.*

I dropped back to my knees and picked up Marsil's hand. I wanted him to know he was not alone, that we were here with him. I had never been religious, but I was spiritual. I believed in fate. I believed there was more to this life than what we could see. So even if his heart was no longer beating, his spirit might still be around. And I would be with him. I would not leave him alone.

Closing my eyes, I held on, ignoring every ache and pain in my body. This moment was about a man who had protected me, who had held all of the Daelighters back when I had my little breakdown. He was a true hero, and I would honor him as such.

16

———

The next thing I registered was my name being called by a voice that had my heart twisting and stomach turning. Through my grief, there was a spark of hope, a spark of life again. Sitting with Marsil, my eyes closed as I held his limp hand, I had been in darkness. Not the same as when I was stuck in that tank of goo, but another sort, a sorrow and depression that pressed into my chest and sucked everything good from the world. I couldn't feel hope, I couldn't feel happiness.

If today had taught me anything, it was that true darkness was not the absence of light. It was the absence of hope. Hope that things could get better one day. Hope that the light would return.

I opened my eyes to find Chase across from me, Marsil's other hand in his. He had sat with me the entire time, the two of us staying with Marsil until the very end.

"You honored him well," he told me, voice rough.

With a shake of my head, I turned to where Daniel was storming across the platform toward us.

"We failed him," I murmured.

Before another word could be said, Daniel was standing in front of me. Literal fire burned in his eyes, and the sight of that chased away more of the darkness inside. Sorrow held me still, but I was clawing my way back. Piece by piece.

"Are you okay?" His worry was palpable, slamming into me. He hadn't touched me yet, but his hands were hovering at his sides like he was stopping himself from doing so.

"I'm fine," I said, my voice breaking. "Marsil is the one who has paid the price for everything this day." My heart squeezed, and I willed back the tears.

Daniel lost his battle with his hands, reaching out and sweeping me against his body. His chest shook as he held me, and I realized just how close he was to losing control. "Every time I turn my back," he said, "someone is trying to kill you."

It was true. Daniel had only known me for a short time, and already he'd saved my life, had me abducted out from under him, found me almost without memory in a pool of goo, and now I was sitting next to the corpse of one of his friends. It could have been me, we all knew that. Even if Laous wanted me alive, there were no guarantees in war. Accidents happened.

Lexen's guttural roar ripped through the air and the platform did that shaky thing again. His energy rocked the huge metal disc on its foundation.

"Emma?" He was not looking at me, but I answered.

"She was hurt, but she's okay. Star took her back to House of Darken."

Scales appeared across his forehead and cheeks and everyone took a step back.

Lexen dropped down at his brother's side, absolute devastation creasing his features, a pain so deep there was permanence to it. Lexen would never be the same again. From this day on, his very being would be altered.

He reached out with both hands, pressing them to Marsil's chest.

"What happened?" Daniel asked, voice short and hard. I wondered if this was bringing back memories of losing his own brother.

"They hit him with a legreto weapon," I choked out. "Some water crystal made from starslight stone. It embedded itself deeper and deeper into his chest, before it shattered."

More Daelighters joined us now, lots I didn't recognize, and a few I did. Daddy Darken was there, his face creased in grief as he dropped down next to his son. "Marsil, no ... my son..."

Jero joined them, kneeling at his fallen brother's head. The three of them placed their hands on Marsil and lowered their heads. I couldn't look at them any longer. Tears streamed down my cheeks as I stared out into the distance.

Chase broke the silence: "Callie tried to save him. She held his hand until you arrived. He was never alone."

No one said anything until the overlord major lifted his head. He had the same symbols as Lexen etched into the side of his hair, and his face was a mix of his three sons. "Thank you for honoring Marsil," he told me, voice hoarse. "We will not forget this."

Even more tears streamed down my cheeks. I couldn't speak. I just nodded. Daniel lifted me into his arms, and for once, I didn't fight him. I had no fight left. I was exhausted and in pain and ... my heart was breaking a little.

"I need to take Callie back to Imperial," I heard Daniel say. I couldn't see who he was talking to because my head was buried in his neck. "She's drained and needs the land to recharge her."

There were murmured replies, and I heard something about a farewell ceremony, and then we were moving again. I must have drifted off, because when I woke next I was in Daniel's bed. Memories immediately rushed in and I rubbed a hand across my burning eyes. I hadn't cried for most of my life, but I was certainly making up for that in the last little while.

Sitting up, I stared down at my hands, trying to pull myself together. Thankfully, the darkness that had been tainting my soul, that debilitating depression, was gone again. It was becoming abundantly clear that the dark despair I sometimes felt was a side effect of not renewing my bond to Daniel and this land. When I was away from it for too long, I lost pieces of myself. My hope and happiness were the first to go. Then my mental and physical health followed. It was systematic, one thing after another until eventually it would be my life.

Luckily, I had a wonderful man at my side, one determined not to let me fade out of existence.

There were no windows in his room to determine time of day, but I sensed I had slept for a long time. Flashes of images hit me hard, one after another: the memory wiping, the Daelighters I had incinerated, Marsil dying right before me. How could so much go wrong so quickly?

"You're awake."

My head jerked up to find Daniel perched in the doorway, broad shoulder nudged into the side of the frame, eyes focused on me.

"How's Emma?" I asked quickly.

He crossed his arms. "She's fine physically, but devastated about Marsil. They're hoping to have a farewell for him soon. But that might not be possible until we deal with Laous."

I wasn't sure I could handle a farewell, but at least I didn't have to decide right now. I did want to be there for my new friends. And to honor the man who had fought beside me.

Hopefully I'd find the strength to go.

Rubbing a hand across the ache in my chest, I let my gaze linger on Daniel. I was barely stopping myself from jumping out of bed and into his arms. I could have lost him yesterday. Seeing Marsil die hit me extra hard, and not just because he was a good person and did not deserve his fate, but also because it could have been Daniel. He could have died, and I would have never had the chance to tell him I loved him, never truly showed him how much he meant to me, that despite everything shitty that had happened lately, he was the best thing to walk into my life in eighteen years.

"Do you need anything? Want me to grab you some food?"

I was dying for coffee, but for once I wanted something more. I wanted Daniel.

He moved closer. I still couldn't manage to form words.

"Talk to me, Callie." He sounded worried. "Fuck, I'm so sorry you had to deal with that alone. Again ... I failed you. But I'm here now. I'll help you figure it out."

For some inexplicable reason, anger licked across my emotions. "I don't want to talk about it. Talking won't bring Marsil back. Talking won't reverse time so I don't accidentally kill a bunch of those resistance assholes. Talking won't bring my mom back or stop Laous from everything he has done. Talking is useless."

I was standing on the bed. I didn't even remember jumping up. As I stepped forward to the edge, he caught my hand, gently encasing it with his own. He leaned himself forward so both of our hands were pressed to his chest. My anger died as quickly as it had arrived, and as I stared down into his face, all I felt was my soaring love for him.

"I'm sorry, Cal. I wish I could take this pain from you." His eyes shut briefly as if he was fighting his own emotions. "And I should be sorry that I took your free will away, tying you to me. I did it at the time because it was the right thing to do, but now I'm starting to think it was the only thing I could do. Because without you, I have nothing."

I blinked once slowly, and then again, my breathing ragged and short.

"I love you," I said, without reserve. "I have never said that to anyone, but I'm saying it to you. The only person to own my soul ... and my heart."

I could never regret him. Even with all the pain I was experiencing, love made it all worth it. I finally understood what Emma meant when she said she would not change the now, no matter the future heartache. Daniel let my hand go, cupping my face and pressing his lips to mine. With a sigh, I sank into the kiss. He pulled back far too quickly, but at least he remained close enough for our lips to brush.

"I love you, Callie." Those murmured words set me off again, more tears sprinkling my eyes.

Over the years, I had tried to imagine someone saying those words to me, but just like sitting in the fancy car, I had to experience it myself to truly understand.

"We share a heart and soul," Daniel said, pressing kisses to my lips as he spoke. "I promise, you will never be alone."

We kissed again, deeper, and I could no longer fight my need to be closer to him. My arms went around his neck and I pressed my body firmly to his. His hands dropped from my face, sliding underneath me to bring my body flush against his. I was on fire, liquid heat licking across my insides. Everything inside of me craved him.

"Not close enough," I muttered, leaning back to try to rip his shirt off. My legs were wrapped around his waist though, holding it down.

Daniel's eyes shifted to a burning gold and I had to shut mine to try and find some composure. He was literally the only one who could destroy me with one look. If someone could bottle the emotion and energy of love, they would make a fortune. When I lifted my lashes again, we were moving. He placed me back on the bed, crawling up to hover over me on hands and knees.

"I need to feel you," I told him, ready to combust. Before he could answer, I had his shirt up and over his head.

Greedily, I drank in the sight of his broad, tanned shoulders, following the lines down over defined pectorals, and those abs ... if someone carved a statue of the perfect male physique, they could use Daniel for inspiration. The deep maroon marks, which matched those on his head, filled the skin of his chest and arm. I wanted to trace each and every one. It would take me days. And I would love every single second of it.

"I'm a fan," I said with a grin, running my hands across his abs. They tightened under my touch. I liked to see the way I affected him.

He caught my hand before it went lower. "Callie, love, it kills me to say this, but there's no rush. The last few days have been crazy. A lot has happened. I can wait as long as you want."

I wiggled further under him, my hands back to exploring his delicious body. "Are you even listening to me?" He sounded amused, before he leaned down, his lips pressing to my neck.

I gasped, choking out, "What if I don't want you to wait at all?"

My hands moved toward his belt and he caught them. I paused to try to get my hormones under control.

"You've been through a lot," he repeated, holding himself above me, our gazes locked. "If you need time to adjust to everything, including the fact that we are soul-bonded and soulmates, then you should take the time. There's no rush. If I get my way – and I usually do – you will be here forever. Home. With me."

Home. It was my dream. Daniel was my dream. I reached out for him, wrapping my hand around his jaw, and pulled him down to me. I took control of the kiss, letting him know exactly how I felt about waiting.

I was no virgin, and I was keeping my promise of being with someone I loved. I was done waiting. Pulling myself up, I pushed Daniel back, straddling his body and settling against him. I was pretty bold in the bedroom, always had been. I liked to take control and right now Daniel was trying too hard to be a good guy. He didn't have to try, though. I already knew he was.

"This has nothing to do with grief," I said, pressing my lips to his, over and over. Then moving lower, I kissed across his jaw and down his neck. "This is about our love, this is about life being short ... able to be taken from us at any moment. This is about me wanting you right now more than I've ever wanted anything in my life."

"This is about our forever," Daniel finished, and I nodded.

"You're my forever," I confirmed. I'd never been one for random fleeting loves, so I knew this was it for me. Soul mate and soul bound, I was okay with that.

He took control back then, his kiss hot and deep, our lips

moving with desperation and emotion like nothing I'd ever experienced. His arms wrapped tightly around me, and I rocked against him, needing relief. I managed to get his pants off, leaving him in just a pair of boxer briefs. They were black, fitted to the hard lines of his impressive body. The tatted marks extended down past the waistband, following his perfect vee.

Holy fuck ... someone give me a freaking fan.

I needed to cool down. Looking at Daniel had me burning up. The fire inside of him was igniting the fire inside of me. He removed my shirt in one smooth movement. I was wearing nothing below, because I'd still been in the clothes from Leights.

He touched my bare skin gently, fingertips rubbing across the sensitive peaks until I was a writhing, groaning mess.

"You're beyond beautiful," he said.

I wanted to say the same thing back, but his lips were on me again and I couldn't speak. My shorts were gone soon after, and there were no more words as we loved each other. In that moment with Daniel, it was abundantly clear that while I was not a virgin, I had truly never understood the actual beauty in lovemaking. Sex I'd had, but this was so much more. Every caress brushed more than just my skin. I felt it all the way through my body.

To be this close with a person you cared so deeply for ... it was everything.

FOR THE FIRST time in my life, I didn't wake alone. Warmth surrounded me, and I was so comfortable that it felt like I could doze here for the rest of my life. I wiggled myself back on Daniel, needing more of his touch. A low growl in my ear had a grin stretching across my face. I liked this little power I had over him. A large hand snaked over my stomach and pulled me back into his hardness. I wiggled again, tormenting him the way he was tormenting me.

"Waking with you in my arms," he murmured. "Sign me up for a lifetime?"

A low moan slipped out from between my lips and I pretty much jumped him. A girl only had so much control. If the last few days had taught me anything, it was that every second was precious, and I was not wasting another moment not loving Daniel.

MUCH LATER, I got to experience my second new intimacy. Naked, we sat on the floor of his huge shower and we talked. About everything and nothing. After some time, it grew more serious.

"The lead you had on Laous was completely dead?" I asked, sadness creeping into my heart again. I was hurting for Lexen and Jero and Emma. Also, Marsil's parents, who would have to bury – *farewell* – their son. Life really wasn't fair.

Daniel leaned back. "He had definitely been there but was clearly tipped off before we arrived. We just missed him."

"What about Rao?" I said, a part of me worried for the big scarred dude. "He protected me, Daniel. There's something good in him still, if we can just get him away from Laous."

Daniel reached out and took my hand, our arms forming a bridge between us. I liked being able to watch him like this, water slicking across his face, looking so damn beautiful.

"Rao was gone, also." He paused, and my heart hurt at the grief in his eyes. "I honestly can't believe he's still alive. I thought I lost him. I've mourned him for years. I should have known ... there was no record of his soul through the justices. Every soul that dies is recorded in this large tome. I always assumed my father couldn't bear to see Rao's name, so he wiped the ledger."

I understood a parent doing that. Losing a child was a pain worse than any other, in my opinion.

Speaking of his brother reminded me of something else: "Dan, I think I saw Fraizer on the platform. He was part of the resistance." As he sat straighter, I quickly added: "I don't know for sure. He jumped off the side before I could confirm it. But it definitely looked a lot like him."

"Fraizer is missing." Daniel sounded resigned. "He hasn't been in House of Imperial for two days. And there is no record of him through the network. He's off the grid."

"The council is looking for him?"

Daniel nodded. "He'd better hope they find him before I do."

My voice grew hard. "I guess we know where these leaks and betrayals are coming from. The resistance had members of all four houses."

He cursed. "I've never been so pissed off with my own people. We have to assume there are more than just the ones who attacked you." Flames flickered in his eyes. "The council have those betrayers Chase captured. They will be interrogated, and hopefully we'll find out who the ones still in hiding are. Then they will be punished."

Judging by his expression, this punishment was not going to be pleasant. Since they killed Marsil, I was okay with that.

I straightened then as I realized something. "We're in House of Imperial," I said slowly. Daniel nodded. "Marsil's soul ... is it here?" He nodded again, and my heart raced and ached at the same time. "Well..." I pushed. "Tell me what is happening with him?"

Sorrow carved very fine lines around Daniel's eyes and mouth. "When a Daelighter dies a true death, it's different to what happened with you, or even with Emma when she was thrown into the justices. Marsil has no body left now, it's only his essence. Energy. At the moment it is in the incubation zone, where those domed structures are."

"The egg room..." I pushed.

"Yes, the egg room. He will be there for a few days while his energy deals with the trauma of dying. Then he will be weighed, judged, and make his choices."

"What do you think he will choose?" I whispered, still not fully understanding how their afterlife worked.

Daniel's hand tightened over mine. "I'm not sure. I didn't know Marsil that well, but something tells me he has unfinished business, so he may choose rebirth."

"And we'll never know which child he becomes?"

He gave a simple head shake. "That's a power beyond Imperial."

I still wasn't sure exactly how to wrap my head around my new world.

"So what do we do about Laous now?"

Using just his impressive abdominal muscles, Daniel stood, pulling me with him. "Right now, there's nothing we can do. He's cut off all avenues of tracking. We had the one shot and we blew it. We didn't know about this resistance, but now we will be more aware. Our next step is to find the third family of secret keepers before he does."

"And ferret out all the resistance."

Daniel brushed some water from my cheeks. "Fraizer isn't the only one to disappear. I've already had fifty or more Imperials fall off the radar in the past two days. It's definitely time now for me to get my house in order. I have let them drift along for too long without a solid leader. It ends now."

Determination straightened my spine. I was no doubt channeling that from Daniel, from the sense of team and kinship I felt. "I will support whatever needs to happen," I told him.

He lifted my hand and pressed his lips to it. "You will be at my side. We lead together."

I had no idea if I was even remotely capable of such a feat, but somehow, staring into my love's determined features, I kind of felt like we could do anything. Together.

EPILOGUE
CHASE

*P*lanting my feet, I let the haze of power wash over me. As my mind switched to the other sight, the one that connected to the network, I focused on the criss-crossing streams of power. They were pretty far away, because I was in House of Leights, but I could still connect. I could still fill my body with strength.

Drawing the inner power, my limbs lengthened; my body grew wide and sturdier. The world looked different through the eyes of my other form, hybrid of the Galinta and Daelighter.

"Chase, please, we don't know anything more."

I ignored the pleas of those secured to the wise old Galinta across from me. These were betrayers of Leights. Of my House. Usually I was slow to anger, but when it grew and grew, like it had the last few days, I ended up in a state all should fear. Like nature in itself, I could be calm, or I could bring the wrath of the world down.

"For your sins, you will all die," I told them, my voice much deeper than it was usually.

"What if we told you where the next secret keeper was?"

I paused, my roped hands whipping out to capture the female's head. The council had dropped my defectors off, telling us they got very little information from them. It was up to their overlord on how they would be punished. Father let me deal with them. I was the one they tried to kill. I was there when they killed Marsil.

This was my battle to wage.

"Speak now, or you will not speak again," I said, the branch I was on vibrating as my anger flared once more.

Her long auburn hair was matted and filled with tangles, her face smeared with dirt and blood from whatever the council had done. She was terrified, but her voice did not waver.

"Laous mentioned this just very briefly, but he said he was heading to Washington to find her. Apparently her parents are important diplomats. They actually work for the coalition which handles Daelighter and human relations ... the secret government branch that initiated the entire treaty."

"Does the council know this?" I asked, trying to keep my dread from showing. This was so much worse than we'd originally thought. Kidnappi ... abducting – as Callie would say – the daughter of two treaty diplomats. Laous was going to send us to war before he even found the stone.

The female shook her head. "No. I tell you only so that you might consider some leniency for us. You have the final punishment rights."

She flinched as my ropelike arms tightened across her face.

"Is there anything else you'd like to tell me?" My whisper sounded menacing even to me.

Her throat worked as she swallowed, opening and closing her mouth. "I ... um ... he said she had a stupid grubber name." She paused, swallowed again, and then said, "Maya Anne Lewis."

Maya. I rolled the name over in my mind – the secret keeper from house of Leights.

A sense of purpose started to build within me. I withdrew my vines from her. "Thank you. I wish I could save you from your fate," I told each of them, because it was true. They were my people, which made the betrayal so much harder to bear. "But you made your decision and now you must live with the consequences."

I turned away, not watching what the Galinta did with those they held in their embrace. It was time for me to go to Washington. I was going to save Maya before Laous got to her.

He had hurt his last secret keeper.

ACKNOWLEDGMENTS

For my review team. Thank you for being part of my book family. For being part of my worlds. One day I'm going to figure out how to have a huge party that we can all be at. #bookfamily

ABOUT THE AUTHOR

Jaymin Eve is the USA Today Bestselling author of 25+ YA and NA fantasy/romance novels. She lives in Australia with her husband, two beautiful daughters, and a couple of crazy pets. Since 2013 she has sold over a million ebooks, and has no plans to stop writing anytime in the next 30-50 years.

facebook.com/JayminEve.Author

twitter.com/jaymineve1

instagram.com/jaymineve

ALSO BY JAYMIN EVE

Secret Keepers Series

Book One: House of Darken

Book Two: House of Imperial (1st July 2018)

Book Three: House of Leights (1st August 2018)

Book Four: House of Royale (1st September 2018)

Storm Princess Saga

Book One: The Princess Must Die (September 2018)

Book Two: The Princess Must Strike (October 2018)

Book Three: The Princess Must Reign (November 2018)

Curse of the Gods Series (Reverse Harem Fantasy)

Book One: Trickery

Book Two: Persuasion

Book Three: Seduction

Book Four: Strength (2018)

NYC Mecca Series (Complete - UF series)

Book One: Queen Heir

Book Two: Queen Alpha

Book Three: Queen Fae

Book Four: Queen Mecca

A Walker Saga (Complete - YA Fantasy)

Book One: First World

Book Two: Spurn

Book Three: Crais

Book Four: Regali

Book Five: Nephilius

Book Six: Dronish

Book Seven: Earth

Supernatural Prison Trilogy (Complete - UF series)

Book One: Dragon Marked

Book Two: Dragon Mystics

Book Three: Dragon Mated

Supernatural Prison Stories

Broken Compass

Magical Compass

Louis (late 2018)

Hive Trilogy (Complete UF/PNR series)

Book One: Ash

Book Two: Anarchy

Book Three: Annihilate

Sinclair Stories (Standalone Contemporary Romance)

Songbird